THE
BLACK SEAL
AND OTHER STORIES

THE BLACK SEAL

AND OTHER STORIES

ARTHUR MACHEN

This edition published in 2021 by Arcturus Publishing Limited 26/27 Bickels Yard, 151–153 Bermondsey Street, London SE1 3HA

Cover design: Peter Ridley
Cover illustration: Peter Gray

AD008445US

Printed in the UK

CONTENTS

INTRODUCTION

Arthur Machen (1863-1947) was named by H. P. Lovecraft as one of the four "modern masters" of horror. Born in Monmouthshire in Wales, his interest in the occult began when he discovered an article on alchemy in a copy of *Household Words* in his father's library.

The clergy was the family business. Machen's father was a vicar, just like his father had been before him. Arthur, though, decided to take his life in a different direction. He received a classical education at the Herefordshire Cathedral School, but the family's poverty made university a distant dream. He moved to London, hoping to attend medical school, but the exams proved a stumbling block. Nonetheless, around this time he discovered that he had a talent for writing. His first poem, "Elusinia" was published in 1881.

In his first few years in London, Machen made his living by working as a journalist, a tutor, and as a publisher's clerk. He soon began attracting translation jobs, including the *Memoirs of Casanova*, and the *Heptameron of Marguerite de Navarre*. In 1887 he married a music teacher, Amelia Hogg and, with the help of his wife, he made the acquaintance of a number of literary figures in the capital, including M. P. Shiel and A. E. Waite.

Machen's great breakthrough came in 1894 when he published *The Great God Pan*. The work was considered scandalous at the time for its descriptions of perverse sexual acts and pagan rituals, but found a willing audience in the reading public and proved to be a great commercial success.

A year later, he released the composite novel *The Three Impostors* (1895). It consisted of several loosely related weird tales, linked by the search for a missing Roman coin. "The Black Seal" is the first story from this book. An eccentric academic follows the trail of the coin until he encounters a mysterious artifact which unleashes the wrath of a dangerous supernatural power. The dangers of unbridled curiosity and the results of academic hubris were a theme that inspired writers as different as the master of the modern ghost story, M. R. James, and the founder of cosmic horror, H. P. Lovecraft.

A long period followed in which little of Machen's work saw print, though through no fault of his own. The Oscar Wilde trial of 1895 for gross indecency turned publishers away from Machen's controversial writing and that was soon followed by a personal tragedy—the death of his wife in 1899. Many of his works drew on the landscape of the Welsh countryside and his next major work, *The Hill of Dreams,* written between 1895 and 1897 but not published until 1907, was no exception. In the early 1900s he also wrote a number of short stories, including the acclaimed "The White People."

Arthur Machen was also a deeply religious figure, though not in the conventional manner of his peers. He harked back to a Celtic Christianity and he savored its rituals and symbolism— though throughout his life he remained a committed Anglican. He was also very interested in the myths surrounding King Arthur and the Holy Grail. He took his interest in the occult further than his writing, briefly joining a secret society called the Hermetic Order of the Golden Dawn.

As World War I engulfed Europe, Machen's reputation was briefly restored to the heights it had reached in the 1890s as he wrote mystical-tinged war stories such as "The Bowmen" (1914), which was credited with creating the legend of the Angel of Mons. He wrote little after the war and lived out the rest of his years quietly until his death in 1947.

THE BLACK SEAL

Prologue

"I see you are a determined rationalist," said the lady. "Did you not hear me say that I have had experiences even more terrible? I too was once a skeptic, but after what I have known I can no longer affect to doubt."

"Madam," replied Mr. Phillipps, "no one shall make me deny my faith. I will never believe, nor will I pretend to believe, that two and two make five, nor will I on any pretences admit the existence of two-sided triangles."

"You are a little hasty," rejoined the lady. "But may I ask you if you ever heard the name of Professor Gregg, the authority on ethnology and kindred subjects?"

"I have done much more than merely hear of Professor Gregg," said Phillipps. "I always regarded him as one of our most acute and clear-headed observers; and his last publication, the *Textbook of Ethnology*, struck me as being quite admirable in its kind. Indeed, the book had but come into my hands when I heard of the terrible accident which cut short Gregg's career. He had, I think, taken a country house in the west of England for the summer, and is supposed to have fallen into a river. So far as I remember, his body was never recovered."

"Sir, I am sure that you are discreet. Your conversation seems to declare as much, and the very title of that little work of yours which you mentioned assures me that you are no empty trifler. In a word, I feel that I may depend on you. You appear to be under the impression that Professor Gregg is dead; I have no reason to believe that that is the case."

"What?" cried Phillipps, astonished and perturbed. "You do not hint that there was anything disgraceful? I cannot believe it.

Gregg was a man of clearest character; his private life was one of great benevolence; and though I myself am free from delusions, I believe him to have been a sincere and devout Christian. Surely you cannot mean to insinuate that some disreputable history forced him to flee the country?"

"Again you are in a hurry," replied the lady. "I said nothing of all this. Briefly, then, I must tell you that Professor Gregg left this house one morning in full health both in mind and body. He never returned, but his watch and chain, a purse containing three sovereigns in gold, and some loose silver, with a ring that he wore habitually, were found three days later on a wild and savage hillside, many miles from the river. These articles were placed beside a limestone rock of fantastic form; they had been wrapped into a parcel with a kind of rough parchment which was secured with gut. The parcel was opened, and the inner side of the parchment bore an inscription done with some red substance; the characters were undecipherable, but seemed to be a corrupt cuneiform."

"You interest me intensely," said Phillipps. "Would you mind continuing your story? The circumstance you have mentioned seems to me of the most inexplicable character, and I thirst for an elucidation."

The young lady seemed to meditate for a moment, and she then proceeded to relate the

NOVEL OF THE BLACK SEAL

I must now give you some fuller particulars of my history. I am the daughter of a civil engineer, Steven Lally by name, who was so unfortunate as to die suddenly at the outset of his career, and before he had accumulated sufficient means to support his wife and her two children.

My mother contrived to keep the small household going on resources which must have been incredibly small; we lived in a remote country village, because most of the necessaries of life were cheaper than in a town, but even so we were brought up with the severest economy. My father was a clever and well-read man, and left behind him a small but select collection of books, containing the best Greek, Latin, and English classics, and these books were the only amusement we possessed. My brother, I remember, learnt Latin out of Descartes' *Meditationes*, and I, in place of the little tales which children are usually told to read, had nothing more charming than a translation of the *Gesta Romanorum*. We grew up thus, quiet and studious children, and in course of time my brother provided for himself in the manner I have mentioned. I continued to live at home: my poor mother had become an invalid, and demanded my continual care, and about two years ago she died after many months of painful illness. My situation was a terrible one; the shabby furniture barely sufficed to pay the debts I had been forced to contract, and the books I dispatched to my brother, knowing how he would value them. I was absolutely alone; I was aware how poorly my brother was paid; and though I came up to London in the hope of finding employment, with the understanding that he would defray my expenses, I swore it should only be for a month, and that if I could not in that time find some work I would starve rather than deprive him of the few miserable pounds he had laid by for his day of trouble. I took a little room in a distant suburb; the cheapest that I could find; I lived on bread and tea, and I spent my time in vain answering of advertisements, and vainer walks to addresses I had noted. Day followed on day, and week on week, and still I was unsuccessful, till at last the term I had appointed drew to a close, and I saw before me the grim prospect of slowly dying of starvation. My landlady was good-natured in her way; she knew the slenderness of my means, and I am sure that she would not have turned me out of doors; it remained for me then to go away, and to try to die in some quiet place. It was winter then, and a thick white fog gathered in the early part of the afternoon, becoming more dense as the day wore on; it was a Sunday, I remember, and the people of the house were at chapel. At about three o'clock I crept out and walked away as quickly as I could, for I was weak from abstinence. The white mist wrapped all the streets in silence, a hard frost had gathered thick upon the bare branches of the trees, and frost crystals glittered on the wooden fences, and on the cold, cruel ground beneath my feet. I walked on, turning to right and left in utter haphazard, without caring to look up at the names of the streets, and all that I remember of my walk on that Sunday afternoon seems but the broken fragments of an evil dream. In a confused vision I stumbled on, through roads half town and half country, gray fields melting into the cloudy world of mist on one side of me, and on the other comfortable villas with a glow of fire-light flickering on the walls, but all unreal; red brick walls and lighted windows, vague trees, and glimmering country, gas-lamps beginning to star the white shadows, the vanishing perspectives of the railway line beneath high embankments, the green and red of the signal lamps—all these were but momentary pictures flashed on my tired brain and senses numbed by hunger. Now and then I would hear a quick step ringing on the iron road, and men would pass me well wrapped up, walking fast for the sake of warmth, and no doubt eagerly foretasting the pleasures of a glowing hearth, with curtains tightly drawn about the frosted panes, and the welcomes of their friends, but as the early evening darkened and night approached, foot-passengers got fewer and fewer, and I passed through street after street alone. In the white silence I stumbled on, as desolate as if I trod the streets of a buried city; and as I grew more weak and exhausted, something of the horror of death was folding thickly round my heart. Suddenly, as I turned a corner, some one accosted me courteously beneath the lamp-post, and I heard a voice asking if I could kindly point the way to Avon Road. At the sudden shock of human accents I was prostrated, and my strength gave way; I fell all huddled on the sidewalk, and wept and sobbed and laughed in violent hysteria. I had gone out prepared to die, and as I stepped across the threshold that had sheltered me, I consciously bade adieu to all hopes and all remembrances; the door clanged behind me with the noise of thunder, and I felt that an iron curtain had fallen on the brief passage of my life, that henceforth I was to walk a little way in a world of gloom and shadow; I entered on the stage of the first act of death. Then came my wandering in the mist, the whiteness wrapping all things, the void streets, and muffled silence, till when that voice spoke to me it was as if I had died and life returned to me. In a few minutes I was able to compose my feelings, and as I rose I saw that I was confronted by a middle-aged gentleman of pleasing appearance, neatly and correctly dressed. He looked at me with an expression of great pity, but before I could stammer out my ignorance of the neighborhood, for indeed I had not the slightest notion of where I had wandered, he spoke.

"My dear madam," he said, "you seem in some terrible distress. You cannot think how you alarmed me. But may I inquire the nature of your trouble? I assure you that you can safely confide in me."

"You are very kind," I replied. "But I fear there is nothing to be done. My condition seems a hopeless one."

"Oh, nonsense, nonsense! You are too young to talk like that. Come, let us walk down here and you must tell me your difficulty. Perhaps I may be able to help you."

There was something very soothing and persuasive in his manner, and as we walked together I gave him an outline of my story, and told of the despair that had oppressed me almost to death.

"You were wrong to give in so completely," he said, when I was silent. "A month is too short a time in which to feel one's way in London. London, let me tell you, Miss Lally, does not lie open and undefended; it is a fortified place, fossed and double-moated with curious intricacies. As must always happen in large towns, the conditions of life have become hugely artificial, no mere simple palisade is run up to oppose the man or woman who would take the place by storm, but serried lines of subtle contrivances, mines, and pitfalls which it needs a strange skill to overcome. You, in your simplicity, fancied you had only to shout for these walls to sink into nothingness, but the time is gone for such startling victories as these. Take courage; you will learn the secret of success before very long."

"Alas! sir," I replied, "I have no doubt your conclusions are correct, but at the present moment I seem to be in a fair way to die of starvation. You spoke of a secret; for Heaven's sake tell it me, if you have any pity for my distress."

He laughed genially. "There lies the strangeness of it all. Those who know the secret cannot tell it if they would; it is positively as ineffable as the central doctrine of freemasonry. But I may say this, that you yourself have penetrated at least the outer husk of the mystery," and he laughed again.

"Pray do not jest with me," I said. "What have I done, *que sçais-je?* I am so far ignorant that I have not the slightest idea of how my next meal is to be provided."

"Excuse me. You ask what you have done. You have met me. Come, we will fence no longer. I see you have self-education, the only education which is not infinitely pernicious, and I am in want of a governess for my two children. I have been a widower for some years; my name is Gregg. I offer you the post I have named, and shall we say a salary of a hundred a year?"

I could only stutter out my thanks, and slipping a card with his address, and a banknote by way of earnest, into my hand, Mr. Gregg bade me good-bye, asking me to call in a day or two.

Such was my introduction to Professor Gregg, and can you wonder that the remembrance of despair and the cold blast that had blown from the gates of death upon me made me regard him as a second father?

Before the close of the week I was installed in my new duties. The Professor had leased an old brick manor-house in a western suburb of London, and here, surrounded by pleasant lawns and orchards, and soothed with the murmur of ancient elms that rocked their boughs above the roof, the new chapter of my life began. Knowing as you do the nature of the professor's occupation, you will not be surprised to hear that the house teemed with books, and cabinets full of strange, and even hideous, objects filled every available nook in the vast low rooms. Gregg was a man whose one thought was for knowledge, and I too before long caught something of his enthusiasm, and strove to enter into his passion of research. In a few months I was perhaps more his secretary than the governess of the two children, and many a night I have sat at the desk in the glow of the shaded lamp while he, pacing up and down in the rich gloom of the firelight, dictated to me the substance of his *Textbook of Ethnology*. But amidst these more sober and accurate studies I always detected a something hidden, a longing and desire for some object to which he did not allude; and now and then he would break short in what he was saying and lapse into reverie, entranced, as it seemed to me, by some distant prospect of adventurous discovery. The textbook was at last finished, and we began to receive proofs from the printers, which were entrusted to me for a first reading, and then underwent the final revision of the professor. All the while his weariness of the actual business he was engaged on increased, and it was with the joyous laugh of a schoolboy when term is over that he one day handed me a copy of the book. "There," he said, "I have kept my word; I promised to write it, and it is done with. Now I shall be free to live for stranger things; I confess it, Miss Lally, I covet the renown of Columbus; you will, I hope, see me play the part of an explorer."

"Surely," I said, "there is little left to explore. You have been born a few hundred years too late for that."

"I think you are wrong," he replied; "there are still, depend upon it, quaint, undiscovered countries and continents of strange extent. Ah, Miss Lally! believe me, we stand amidst sacraments and mysteries full of awe, and it doth not yet appear what we shall be. Life, believe me, is no simple thing, no mass of gray matter and congeries of veins and muscles to be laid naked by the surgeon's knife; man is the secret which I am about to explore, and before I can discover him I must cross over weltering seas indeed, and oceans and the mists of many thousand years. You know the myth of the lost Atlantis; what if it be true, and I am destined to be called the discoverer of that wonderful land?"

I could see excitement boiling beneath his words, and in his face was the heat of the hunter; before me stood a man who believed himself summoned to tourney with the unknown. A pang of joy possessed me when I reflected that I was to be in a way associated with him in the adventure, and I, too, burned with the lust of the chase, not pausing to consider that I knew not what we were to unshadow.

The next morning Professor Gregg took me into his inner study, where, ranged against the wall, stood a nest of pigeonholes, every drawer neatly labeled, and the results of years of toil classified in a few feet of space.

"Here," he said, "is my life; here are all the facts which I have gathered together with so much pains, and yet it is all nothing. No, nothing to what I am about to attempt. Look at this"; and he took me to an old bureau, a piece fantastic and faded, which stood in a corner of the room. He unlocked the front and opened one of the drawers.

"A few scraps of paper," he went on, pointing to the drawer, "and a lump of black stone, rudely annotated with queer marks and scratches—that is all that the drawer holds. Here you see is an old envelope with the dark red stamp of twenty years ago, but I have penciled a few lines at the back; here is a sheet of manuscript, and here some cuttings from obscure local journals. And if you ask me the subject-matter of the collection, it will not seem extraordinary—a servant-girl at a farmhouse, who disappeared from her place and has never been heard of, a child supposed to have slipped down some old working on the mountains, some queer scribbling on a limestone rock, a man murdered with a blow from a strange weapon; such is the scent I have to go upon. Yes, as you say, there is a ready explanation for all this; the girl may have run away to London, or Liverpool, or New York; the child may be at the bottom of the disused shaft; and the letters on the rock may be the idle whims of some vagrant. Yes, yes, I admit all that; but I know I hold the true key. Look!" and he held out a slip of yellow paper.

Characters found inscribed on a limestone rock on the Grey Hills, I read, and then there was a word erased, presumably the name of a county, and a date some fifteen years back. Beneath was traced a number of uncouth characters, shaped somewhat like wedges or daggers, as strange and outlandish as the Hebrew alphabet.

"Now the seal," said Professor Gregg, and he handed me the black stone, a thing about two inches long, and something like an old-fashioned tobacco-stopper, much enlarged.

I held it up to the light, and saw to my surprise the characters on the paper repeated on the seal.

"Yes," said the professor, "they are the same. And the marks on the limestone rock were made fifteen years ago, with some red substance. And the characters on the seal are four thousand years old at least. Perhaps much more."

"Is it a hoax?" I said.

"No, I anticipated that. I was not to be led to give my life to a practical joke. I have tested the matter very carefully. Only one person besides myself knows of the mere existence of that black seal. Besides, there are other reasons which I cannot enter into now."

"But what does it all mean?" I said. "I cannot understand to what conclusion all this leads."

"My dear Miss Lally, that is a question that I would rather leave unanswered for some little time. Perhaps I shall never be able to say what secrets are held here in solution; a few vague hints, the outlines of village tragedies, a few marks done with red earth upon a rock, and an ancient seal. A queer set of data to go upon? Half a dozen pieces of evidence, and twenty years before even so much could be got together; and who knows what mirage or *terra incognita* may be beyond all this? I look across deep waters, Miss Lally, and the land beyond may be but a haze after all. But still I believe it is not so, and a few months will show whether I am right or wrong."

He left me, and alone I endeavored to fathom the mystery, wondering to what goal such eccentric odds and ends of evidence could lead. I myself am not wholly devoid of imagination, and I had reason to respect the professor's solidity of intellect; yet I saw in the contents of the drawers but the materials of fantasy, and vainly tried to conceive what theory could be founded on the fragments that had been placed before me. Indeed, I could discover in what I had heard and seen but the first chapter of an extravagant romance; and yet deep in my heart I burned with curiosity, and day after day I looked eagerly in Professor Gregg's face for some hint of what was to happen.

It was one evening after dinner that the word came.

"I hope you can make your preparations without much trouble," he said suddenly to me. "We shall be leaving here in a week's time."

"Really!" I said in astonishment. "Where are we going?"

"I have taken a country house in the west of England, not far from Caermaen, a quiet little town, once a city, and the head-quarters of a Roman legion. It is very dull there, but the country is pretty, and the air is wholesome."

I detected a glint in his eyes, and guessed that this sudden move had some relation to our conversation of a few days before.

"I shall just take a few books with me," said Professor Gregg, "that is all. Everything else will remain here for our return. I have got a holiday," he went on, smiling at me, "and I shan't be sorry to be quit for a time of my old bones and stones and rubbish. Do you know," he went on, "I have been grinding away at facts for thirty years; it is time for fancies."

The days passed quickly; I could see that the professor was all quivering with suppressed excitement, and I could scarce credit the eager appetence of his glance as we left the old manor-house behind us and began our journey. We set out at midday, and it was in the dusk of the evening that we arrived at a little country station. I was tired and excited, and the drive through the lanes seems all a dream. First the deserted streets of a forgotten village, while I heard Professor Gregg's voice talking of the Augustan Legion and the clash of arms, and all the tremendous pomp that followed the eagles; then the broad river swimming to full tide with the last afterglow glimmering duskily in the yellow water, the wide meadows, the cornfields whitening, and the deep lane winding on the slope between the hills and the water. At last we began to ascend, and the air grew rarer. I looked down and saw the pure white mist tracking the outline of the river like a shroud, and a vague and shadowy country; imaginations and fantasy of swelling hills and hanging woods, and half-shaped outlines of hills beyond, and in the distance the glare of the furnace fire on the mountain, glowing by turns a pillar of shining flame and fading to a dull point of red. We were slowly mounting a carriage drive, and then there came to me the cool breath and the secret of the great wood that was above us; I seemed to wander in its deepest depths, and there was the sound of trickling water, the scent of the green leaves, and the breath of the summer night. The carriage stopped at last, and I could scarcely distinguish the form of the house, as I waited a moment at the pillared porch. The rest of the evening seemed a dream of strange things bounded by the great silence of the wood and the valley and the river.

The next morning, when I awoke and looked out of the bow window of the big, old-fashioned bedroom, I saw under a grey sky a country that was still all mystery. The long, lovely valley, with the river winding in and out below, crossed in mid-vision by a mediæval bridge of vaulted and buttressed stone, the clear presence of the rising ground beyond, and the woods that I had only seen in shadow the night before, seemed tinged with enchantment, and the soft breath of air that sighed in at the opened pane was like no other wind. I looked across the valley, and beyond, hill followed on hill as wave on wave, and here a faint blue pillar of smoke rose still in the morning air from the chimney of an ancient grey farmhouse, there was a rugged height crowned with dark firs, and in the distance I saw the white streak of a road that climbed and vanished into some unimagined country. But the boundary of all was a great wall of mountain, vast in the west, and ending like a fortress with a steep ascent and a domed tumulus clear against the sky.

I saw Professor Gregg walking up and down the terrace path below the windows, and it was evident that he was reveling in the sense of liberty, and the thought that he had for a while bidden good-bye to task-work. When I joined him there was exultation in his voice as he pointed out the sweep of valley and the river that wound beneath the lovely hills.

"Yes," he said, "it is a strangely beautiful country; and to me, at least, it seems full of mystery. You have not forgotten the drawer I showed you, Miss Lally? No; and you have guessed that I have come here not merely for the sake of the children and the fresh air?"

"I think I have guessed as much as that," I replied; "but you must remember I do not know the mere nature of your investigations; and as for the connection between the search and this wonderful valley, it is past my guessing."

He smiled queerly at me. "You must not think I am making a mystery for the sake of mystery," he said. "I do not speak out because, so far, there is nothing to be spoken, nothing definite, I mean, nothing that can be set down in hard black and white, as dull and sure and irreproachable as any blue-book. And then I have another reason: Many years ago a chance paragraph in a newspaper caught my attention, and focussed in an instant the vagrant thoughts and half-formed fancies of many idle and speculative hours into a certain hypothesis. I saw at once that I was treading on a thin crust; my theory was wild and fantastic in the extreme, and I would not for any consideration have written a hint of it for publication. But I thought that in the company of scientific men like myself, men who knew the course of discovery, and were aware that the gas that blazes and flares in the gin-palace was once a wild hypothesis—I thought that with such men as these I might hazard my dream—let us say Atlantis, or the philosopher's stone, or what you like—without danger of ridicule. I found I was grossly mistaken; my friends looked blankly at me and at one another, and I could see something of pity, and something also of insolent contempt, in the glances they exchanged. One of them called on me next day, and hinted that I must be suffering from overwork and brain exhaustion. 'In plain terms,' I said, 'you think I am going mad. I think not;' and I showed him out with some little appearance of heat. Since that day I vowed that I would never whisper the nature of my theory to any living soul; to no one but yourself have I ever shown the contents of that drawer. After all, I may be following a rainbow; I may have been misled by the play of coincidence; but as I stand here in this mystic hush and silence, amidst the woods and wild hills, I am more than ever sure that I am hot on the scent. Come, it is time we went in."

To me in all this there was something both of wonder and excitement; I knew how in his ordinary work Professor Gregg moved step by step, testing every inch of the way, and never venturing on assertion without proof that was impregnable. Yet I divined, more from his glance and the vehemence of his tone than from the spoken word, that he had in his every thought the vision of the almost incredible continually with him; and I, who was with some share of imagination no little of a skeptic, offended at a hint of the marvellous, could not help asking myself whether he were cherishing a monomania, and barring out from this one subject all the scientific method of his other life.

Yet, with this image of mystery haunting my thoughts, I surrendered wholly to the charm of the country. Above the faded house on the hillside began the great forest—a long, dark line seen from the opposing hills, stretching above the river for many a mile from north to south, and yielding in the north to even wilder country, barren and savage hills, and ragged commonland, a territory all strange and unvisited, and more unknown to Englishmen than the very heart of Africa. The space of a couple of steep fields alone separated the house from the woods, and the children were delighted to follow me up the long alleys of undergrowth, between smooth pleached walls of shining beech, to the highest point in the wood, whence one looked on one side across the river and the rise and fall of the country to the great western mountain wall, and on the other over the surge and dip of the myriad trees of the forest, over level meadows and the shining yellow sea to the faint coast beyond. I used to sit at this point on the warm sunlit turf which marked the track of the Roman Road, while the two children raced about hunting for the whinberries that grew here and there on the banks. Here, beneath the deep blue sky and the great clouds rolling, like olden galleons with sails full-bellied, from the sea to the hills, as I listened to the whispered charm of the great and ancient wood, I lived solely for delight, and only remembered strange things when we would return to the house and find Professor Gregg either shut up in the little room he had made his study, or else pacing the terrace with the look, patient and enthusiastic, of the determined seeker.

One morning, some eight or nine days after our arrival, I looked out of my window and saw the whole landscape transmuted before me. The clouds had dipped low and hidden the mountain in the west; a southern wind was driving the rain in shifting pillars up the valley, and the little brooklet that burst the hill below the house now raged, a red torrent, down to the river. We were perforce obliged to keep snug within-doors; and when I had attended to my pupils, I sat down in the morning-room, where the ruins of a library still encumbered an old-fashioned bookcase. I had inspected the shelves once or twice, but their contents had failed to attract me; volumes of eighteenth-century sermons, an old book on farriery, a collection of poems by "persons of quality," Prideaus's *Connection*, and an odd volume of Pope, were the boundaries of the library, and there seemed little doubt that everything of interest or value had been removed. Now, however, in desperation, I began to re-examine the musty sheepskin and calf bindings, and found, much to my delight, a fine old quarto printed by the Stephani, containing the three books of Pomponius Mela, *De Situ Orbis*, and other of the ancient geographers. I knew enough of Latin to steer my way through an ordinary sentence, and I soon became absorbed in the odd mixture of fact and fancy—light shining on a little of the space of the world, and beyond, mist and shadow and awful forms. Glancing over the clear-printed pages, my attention was caught by the heading of a chapter in Solinus, and I read the words:

MIRA DE INTIMIS GENTIBUS LIBYAE. DE LAPIDE HEXECONTALITHO,—

"The wonders of the people that inhabit the inner parts of Libya, and of the stone called Sixtystone."

The odd title attracted me, and I read on:

Gens ista avia et secreta habitat, in montibus horrendis foeda mysteria celebrat. De hominibus nihil aliud illi praeferunt quam figuram, ab humano ritu prorsus exulant, oderunt deum lucis.

Stridunt potius quam loquuntur; vox absona nec sine horrore auditur. Lapide quodam gloriantur, quem Hexecontalithon vocant; dicunt enim hunc lapidem sexaginta notas ostendere.

Cujus lapidis nomen secretum ineffabile colunt: quod Ixaxar.

"This folk," I translated to myself, "dwells in remote and secret places, and celebrates foul mysteries on savage hills. Nothing have they in common with men save the face, and the customs of humanity are wholly strange to them; and they hate the sun. They hiss rather than speak; their voices are harsh, and not to be heard without fear. They boast of a certain stone, which they call Sixtystone; for they say that it displays sixty characters. And this stone has a secret unspeakable name; which is Ixaxar."

I laughed at the queer inconsequence of all this, and thought it fit for "Sinbad the Sailor," or other of the supplementary *Nights*. When I saw Professor Gregg in the course of the day, I told him of my find in the bookcase, and the fantastic rubbish I had been reading. To my surprise he looked up at me with an expression of great interest.

"That is really very curious," he said. "I have never thought it worth while to look into the old geographers, and I dare say I have missed a good deal. Ah, that is the passage, is it? It seems a shame to rob you of your entertainment, but I really think I must carry off the book."

The next day the professor called me to come to the study. I found him sitting at a table in the full light of the window, scrutinizing something very attentively with a magnifying glass.

"Ah, Miss Lally," he began, "I want to use your eyes. This glass is pretty good, but not like my old one that I left in town. Would you mind examining the thing yourself, and telling me how many characters are cut on it?"

He handed me the object in his hand. I saw that it was the black seal he had shown me in London, and my heart began to beat with the thought that I was presently to know something. I took the seal, and, holding it up to the light, checked off the grotesque dagger-shaped characters one by one.

"I make sixty-two," I said at last.

"Sixty-two? Nonsense; it's impossible. Ah, I see what you have done, you have counted that and that," and he pointed to two marks which I had certainly taken as letters with the rest.

"Yes, yes," Professor Gregg went on, "but those are obviously scratches, done accidentally; I saw that at once. Yes, then that's quite right. Thank you very much, Miss Lally."

I was going away, rather disappointed at my having been called in merely to count the number of marks on the black seal, when suddenly there flashed into my mind what I had read in the morning.

"But, Professor Gregg," I cried, breathless, "the seal, the seal. Why, it is the stone Hexecontalithos that Solinus writes of; it is Ixaxar."

"Yes," he said, "I suppose it is. Or it may be a mere coincidence. It never does to be too sure, you know, in these matters. Coincidence killed the professor."

I went away puzzled by what I had heard, and as much as ever at a loss to find the ruling clue in this maze of strange evidence. For three days the bad weather lasted, changing from driving rain to a dense mist, fine and dripping, and we seemed to be shut up in a white cloud that veiled all the world away from us. All the while Professor Gregg was darkling in his room, unwilling, it appeared, to dispense confidences or talk of any kind, and I heard him walking to and fro with a quick, impatient step, as if he were in some way wearied of inaction. The fourth morning was fine, and at breakfast the professor said briskly:

"We want some extra help about the house; a boy of fifteen or sixteen, you know. There are a lot of little odd jobs that take up the maids' time which a boy could do much better."

"The girls have not complained to me in any way," I replied. "Indeed, Anne said there was much less work than in London, owing to there being so little dust."

"Ah, yes, they are very good girls. But I think we shall do much better with a boy. In fact, that is what has been bothering me for the last two days."

"Bothering you?" I said in astonishment, for as a matter of fact the professor never took the slightest interest in the affairs of the house.

"Yes," he said, "the weather, you know. I really couldn't go out in that Scotch mist; I don't know the country very well, and I should have lost my way. But I am going to get the boy this morning."

"But how do you know there is such a boy as you want anywhere about?"

"Oh, I have no doubt as to that. I may have to walk a mile or two at the most, but I am sure to find just the boy I require."

I thought the professor was joking, but, though his tone was airy enough, there was something grim and set about his features that puzzled me. He got his stick, and stood at the door looking meditatively before him, and as I passed through the hall he called to me.

"By the way, Miss Lally, there was one thing I wanted to say to you. I dare say you may have heard that some of these country lads are not over-bright; 'idiotic' would be a harsh word to use, and they are usually called 'naturals', or something of the kind. I hope you won't mind if the boy I am after should turn out not too keen-witted; he will be perfectly harmless, of course, and blacking boots doesn't need much mental effort."

With that he was gone, striding up the road that led to the wood, and I remained stupefied; and then for the first time my astonishment was mingled with a sudden note of terror, arising I knew not whence, and all unexplained even to myself, and yet I felt about my heart for an instant something of the chill of death, and that shapeless, formless dread of the unknown that is worse than death itself. I tried to find courage in the sweet air that blew up from the sea, and in the sunlight after rain, but the mystic woods seemed to darken around me; and the vision of the river coiling between the reeds, and the silver grey of the ancient bridge, fashioned in my mind symbols of vague dread, as the mind of a child fashions terror from things harmless and familiar.

Two hours later Professor Gregg returned. I met him as he came down the road, and asked quietly if he had been able to find a boy.

"Oh, yes," he answered; "I found one easily enough. His name is Jervase Cradock, and I expect he will make himself very useful. His father has been dead for many years, and the mother, whom I saw, seemed very glad at the prospect of a few shillings extra coming in on Saturday nights. As I expected, he is not too sharp, has fits at times, the mother said; but as he will not be trusted with the china, that doesn't much matter, does it? And he is not in any way dangerous, you know, merely a little weak."

"When is he coming?"

"Tomorrow morning at eight o'clock. Anne will show him what he has to do, and how to do it. At first he will go home every night, but perhaps it may ultimately turn out more convenient for him to sleep here, and only go home for Sundays."

I found nothing to say to all this; Professor Gregg spoke in a quiet tone of matter-of-fact, as indeed was warranted by the circumstance; and yet I could not quell my sensation of astonishment at the whole affair. I knew that in reality no assistance was wanted in the housework, and the professor's prediction that the boy he was to engage might prove a little "simple," followed by so exact a fulfilment, struck me as bizarre in the extreme. The next morning I heard from the housemaid that the boy Cradock had come at eight, and that she had been trying to make him useful. "He doesn't seem quite all there, I don't think, miss," was her comment, and later in the day I saw him helping the old man who worked in the garden. He was a youth of about fourteen, with black hair and black eyes and an olive skin, and I saw at once from the curious vacancy of his expression that he was mentally weak. He touched his forehead awkwardly as I went by, and I heard him answering the gardener in a queer, harsh voice that caught my attention; it gave me the impression of some one speaking deep below under the earth, and there was a strange sibilance, like the hissing of the phonograph as the pointer travels over the cylinder. I heard that he seemed anxious to do what he could, and was quite docile and obedient, and Morgan the gardener, who knew his mother, assured me he was perfectly harmless. "He's always been a bit queer," he said, "and no wonder, after what his mother went through before he was born. I did know his father, Thomas Cradock, well, and a very fine workman he was too, indeed. He got something wrong with his lungs owing to working in the wet woods, and never got over it, and went off quite sudden like. And they do say as how Mrs. Cradock was quite off her head: anyhow, she was found by Mr. Hillyer, Ty Coch, all crouched up on the Grey Hills, over there, crying and weeping like a lost soul. And Jervase, he was born about eight months afterwards, and, as I was saying, he was a bit queer always; and they do say when he could scarcely walk he would frighten the other children into fits with the noises he would make."

A word in the story had stirred up some remembrance within me, and, vaguely curious, I asked the old man where the Grey Hills were.

"Up there," he said, with the same gesture he had used before; "you go past the 'Fox and Hounds,' and through the forest, by the old ruins. It's a good five mile from here, and a strange sort of a place. The poorest soil between this and Monmouth, they do say, though it's good feed for sheep. Yes, it was a sad thing for poor Mrs. Cradock."

The old man turned to his work, and I strolled on down the path between the espaliers, gnarled and gouty with age, thinking of the story I had heard, and groping for the point in it that had some key to my memory. In an instant it came before me; I had seen the phrase "Grey Hills" on the slip of yellowed paper that Professor Gregg had taken from the drawer in his cabinet. Again I was seized with pangs of mingled curiosity and fear; I remembered the strange characters copied from the limestone rock, and then again their identity with the inscription of the age-old seal, and the fantastic fables of the Latin geographer. I saw beyond doubt that, unless coincidence had set all the scene and disposed all these bizarre events with curious art, I was to be a spectator of things far removed from the usual and customary traffic and jostle of life. Professor Gregg I noted day by day; he was hot on his trail, growing lean with eagerness; and in the evenings, when the sun was swimming on the verge of the mountain, he would pace the terrace to and fro with his eyes on the ground, while the mist grew white in the valley, and the stillness of the evening brought far voices near, and the blue smoke rose a straight column from the diamond-shaped chimney of the grey farmhouse, just as I had seen it on the first morning. I have told you I was of skeptical habit; but though I understood little or nothing, I began to dread, vainly proposing to myself the iterated dogmas of science that all life is material, and that in the system of things there is no undiscovered land, even beyond the remotest stars, where the supernatural can find a footing. Yet there struck in on this the thought that matter is as really awful and unknown as spirit, that science itself but dallies on the threshold, scarcely gaining more than a glimpse of the wonders of the inner place.

There is one day that stands up from amidst the others as a grim red beacon, betokening evil to come. I was sitting on a bench in the garden, watching the boy Cradock weeding, when I was suddenly alarmed by a harsh and choking sound, like the cry of a wild beast in anguish, and I was unspeakably shocked to see the unfortunate lad standing in full view before me, his whole body quivering and shaking at short intervals as though shocks of electricity were passing through him, his teeth grinding, foam gathering on his lips, and his face all swollen and blackened to a hideous mask of humanity. I shrieked with terror, and Professor Gregg came running; and as I pointed to Cradock, the boy with one convulsive shudder fell face forward, and lay on the wet earth, his body writhing like a wounded blind-worm, and an inconceivable babble of sounds bursting and rattling and hissing from his lips. He seemed to pour forth an infamous jargon, with words, or what seemed words, that might have belonged to a tongue dead since untold ages and buried deep beneath Nilotic mud, or in the inmost recesses of the Mexican forest. For a moment the thought passed through my mind, as my ears were still revolted with that infernal clamor, "Surely this is the very speech of hell," and then I cried out again and again, and ran away shuddering to my inmost soul. I had seen Professor Gregg's face as he stooped over the wretched boy and raised him, and I was appalled by the glow of exultation that shone on every lineament and feature. As I sat in my room with drawn blinds, and my eyes hidden in my hands, I heard heavy steps beneath, and I was told afterwards that Professor Gregg had carried Cradock to his study, and had locked the door. I heard voices murmur indistinctly, and I trembled to think of what might be passing within a few feet of where I sat; I longed to escape to the woods and sunshine, and yet I dreaded the sights that might confront me on the way; and at last, as I held the handle of the door nervously, I heard Professor Gregg's voice calling to me with a cheerful ring. "It's all right now, Miss Lally," he said. "The poor fellow has got over it, and I have been arranging for him to sleep here after tomorrow. Perhaps I may be able to do something for him."

"Yes," he said later, "it was a very painful sight, and I don't wonder you were alarmed. We may hope that good food will build him up a little, but I am afraid he will never be really cured," and he affected the dismal and conventional air with which one speaks of hopeless illness; and yet beneath it I detected the delight that leapt up rampant within him, and fought and struggled to find utterance. It was as if one glanced down on the even surface of the sea, clear and immobile, and saw beneath raging depths and a storm of contending billows. It was indeed to me a torturing and offensive problem that this man, who had so bounteously rescued me from the sharpness of death, and showed himself in all the relations of life full of benevolence, and pity, and kindly forethought, should so manifestly be for once on the side of the demons, and take a ghastly pleasure in the torments of an afflicted fellow creature. Apart, I struggled with the horned difficulty, and strove to find the solution; but without the hint of a clue, beset by mystery and contradiction. I saw nothing that might help me, and began to wonder whether, after all, I had not escaped from the white mist of the suburb at too dear a rate. I hinted something of my thought to the professor; I said enough to let him know that I was in the most acute perplexity, but the moment after regretted what I had done when I saw his face contort with a spasm of pain.

"My dear Miss Lally," he said, "you surely do not wish to leave us? No, no, you would not do it. You do not know how I rely on you; how confidently I go forward, assured that you are here to watch over my children. You, Miss Lally, are my rear-guard; for let me tell you the business in which I am engaged is not wholly devoid of peril. You have not forgotten what I said the first morning here; my lips are shut by an old and firm resolve till they can open to utter no ingenious hypothesis or vague surmise, but irrefragable fact, as certain as a demonstration in mathematics. Think over it, Miss Lally; not for a moment would I endeavor to keep you here against your own instincts, and yet I tell you frankly that I am persuaded it is here, here amidst the woods, that your duty lies."

I was touched by the eloquence of his tone, and by the remembrance that the man, after all, had been my salvation, and I gave him my hand on a promise to serve him loyally and without question. A few days later the rector of our church—a little church, grey and severe and quaint, that hovered on the very banks of the river and watched the tides swim and return—came to see us, and Professor Gregg easily persuaded him to stay and share our dinner. Mr. Meyrick was a member of an antique family of squires, whose old manor-house stood amongst the hills some seven miles away, and thus rooted in the soil, the rector was a living store of all the old fading customs and lore of the country. His manner, genial, with a deal of retired oddity, won on Professor Gregg; and towards the cheese, when a curious Burgundy had begun its incantations, the two men glowed like the wine, and talked of philology with the enthusiasm of a burgess over the peerage. The parson was expounding the pronunciation of the Welsh *ll*, and producing sounds like the gurgle of his native brooks, when Professor Gregg struck in.

"By the way," he said, "that was a very odd word I met with the other day. You know my boy, poor Jervase Cradock? Well, he has got the bad habit of talking to himself, and the day before yesterday I was walking in the garden here and heard him; he was evidently quite unconscious of my presence. A lot of what he said I couldn't make out, but one word struck me distinctly. It was such an odd sound, half sibilant, half guttural, and as quaint as those double *l*'s you have been demonstrating. I do not know whether I can give you an idea of the sound; 'Ishakshar' is perhaps as near as I can get. But the *k* ought to be a Greek *chi* or a Spanish *j*. Now what does it mean in Welsh?"

"In Welsh?" said the parson. "There is no such word in Welsh, nor any word remotely resembling it. I know the book-Welsh, as they call it, and the colloquial dialects as well as any man, but there's no word like that from Anglesea to Usk. Besides, none of the Cradocks speak a word of Welsh; it's dying out about here."

"Really. You interest me extremely, Mr. Meyrick. I confess the word didn't strike me as having the Welsh ring. But I thought it might be some local corruption."

"No, I never heard such a word, or anything like it. Indeed," he added, smiling whimsically, "if it belongs to any language, I should say it must be that of the fairies—the Tylwydd Têg, as we call them."

The talk went on to the discovery of a Roman villa in the neighborhood; and soon after I left the room, and sat down apart to wonder at the drawing together of such strange clues of evidence. As the professor had spoken of the curious word, I had caught the glint in his eye upon me; and though the pronunciation he gave was grotesque in the extreme, I recognized the name of the stone of sixty characters mentioned by Solinus, the black seal shut up in some secret drawer of the study, stamped for ever by a vanished race with signs that no man could read, signs that might, for all I knew, be the veils of awful things done long ago, and forgotten before the hills were moulded into form.

When the next morning I came down, I found Professor Gregg pacing the terrace in his eternal walk.

"Look at that bridge," he said, when he saw me; "observe the quaint and Gothic design, the angles between the arches, and the silvery grey of the stone in the awe of the morning light. I confess it seems to me symbolic; it should illustrate a mystical allegory of the passage from one world to another."

"Professor Gregg," I said quietly, "it is time that I knew something of what has happened, and of what is to happen."

For the moment he put me off, but I returned again with the same question in the evening, and then Professor Gregg flamed with excitement. "Don't you understand yet?" he cried. "But I have told you a good deal; yes, and shown you a good deal; you have heard pretty nearly all that I have heard, and seen what I have seen; or at least," and his voice chilled as he spoke, "enough to make a good deal clear as noonday. The servants told you, I have no doubt, that the wretched boy Cradock had another seizure the night before last; he awoke me with cries in that voice you heard in the garden, and I went to him, and God forbid you should see what I saw that night. But all this is useless; my time here is drawing to a close; I must be back in town in three weeks, as I have a course of lectures to prepare, and need all my books about me. In a very few days it will be all over, and I shall no longer hint, and no longer be liable to ridicule as a madman and a quack. No, I shall speak plainly, and I shall be heard with such emotions as perhaps no other man has ever drawn from the breasts of his fellows."

He paused, and seemed to grow radiant with the joy of great and wonderful discovery.

"But all that is for the future, the near future certainly, but still the future," he went on at length. "There is something to be done yet; you will remember my telling you that my researches were not altogether devoid of peril? Yes, there, is a certain amount

of danger to be faced; I did not know how much when I spoke
on the subject before, and to a certain extent I am still in the
dark. But it will be a strange adventure, the last of all, the last
demonstration in the chain."

He was walking up and down the room as he spoke, and I
could hear in his voice the contending tones of exultation and
despondence, or perhaps I should say awe, the awe of a man
who goes forth on unknown waters, and I thought of his allusion
to Columbus on the night he had laid his book before me. The
evening was a little chilly, and a fire of logs had been lighted in
the study where we were; the remittent flame and the glow on
the walls reminded me of the old days. I was sitting silent in an
armchair by the fire, wondering over all I had heard, and still
vainly speculating as to the secret springs concealed from me
under all the phantasmagoria I had witnessed, when I became
suddenly aware of a sensation that change of some sort had been
at work in the room, and that there was something unfamiliar
in its aspect. For some time I looked about me, trying in vain to
localize the alteration that I knew had been made; the table by
the window, the chairs, the faded settee were all as I had known
them. Suddenly, as a sought-for recollection flashes into the mind,
I knew what was amiss. I was facing the professor's desk, which
stood on the other side of the fire, and above the desk was a
grimy-looking bust of Pitt, that I had never seen there before.
And then I remembered the true position of this work of art; in
the furthest corner by the door was an old cupboard, projecting
into the room, and on the top of the cupboard, fifteen feet from
the floor, the bust had been, and there, no doubt, it had delayed,
accumulating dirt, since the early days of the century.

I was utterly amazed, and sat silent, still in a confusion of
thought. There was, so far as I knew, no such thing as a stepladder
in the house, for I had asked for one to make some alteration
in the curtains of my room, and a tall man standing on a chair
would have found it impossible to take down the bust. It had
been placed, not on the edge of the cupboard, but far back

against the wall; and Professor Gregg was, if anything, under the average height.

"How on earth did you manage to get down Pitt?" I said at last.

The professor looked curiously at me, and seemed to hesitate a little.

"They must have found you a step-ladder, or perhaps the gardener brought in a short ladder from outside?"

"No, I have had no ladder of any kind. Now, Miss Lally," he went on with an awkward simulation of jest, "there is a little puzzle for you; a problem in the manner of the inimitable Holmes; there are the facts, plain and patent: summon your acuteness to the solution of the puzzle. For Heaven's sake," he cried with a breaking voice, "say no more about it! I tell you, I never touched the thing," and he went out of the room with horror manifest on his face, and his hand shook and jarred the door behind him.

I looked round the room in vague surprise, not at all realizing what had happened, making vain and idle surmises by way of explanation, and wondering at the stirring of black waters by an idle word and the trivial change of an ornament. "This is some petty business, some whim on which I have jarred." I reflected; "the professor is perhaps scrupulous and superstitious over trifles, and my question may have outraged unacknowledged fears, as though one killed a spider or spilled the salt before the very eyes of a practical Scotchwoman." I was immersed in these fond suspicions, and began to plume myself a little on my immunity from such empty fears, when the truth fell heavily as lead upon my heart, and I recognized with cold terror that some awful influence had been at work. The bust was simply inaccessible; without a ladder no one could have touched it.

I went out to the kitchen and spoke as quietly as I could to the housemaid.

"Who moved that bust from the top of the cupboard, Anne?" I said to her. "Professor Gregg says he has not touched it. Did you find an old step-ladder in one of the outhouses?"

The girl looked at me blankly.

"I never touched it," she said. "I found it where it is now the other morning when I dusted the room. I remember now, it was Wednesday morning, because it was the morning after Cradock was taken bad in the night. My room is next to his, you know, miss," the girl went on piteously, "and it was awful to hear how he cried and called out names that I couldn't understand. It made me feel all afraid; and then master came, and I heard him speak, and he took down Cradock to the study and gave him something."

"And you found that bust moved the next morning?"

"Yes, miss. There was a queer sort of smell in the study when I came down and opened the windows; a bad smell it was, and I wondered what it could be. Do you know, miss, I went a long time ago to the Zoo in London with my cousin Thomas Barker, one afternoon that I had off, when I was at Mrs. Prince's in Stanhope Gate, and we went into the snake-house to see the snakes, and it was just the same sort of smell; very sick it made me feel, I remember, and I got Barker to take me out. And it was just the same kind of smell in the study, as I was saying, and I was wondering what it could be from, when I see that bust with Pitt cut in it, standing on the master's desk, and I thought to myself, 'Now who has done that, and how have they done it?' And when I came to dust the things, I looked at the bust, and I saw a great mark on it where the dust was gone, for I don't think it can have been touched with a duster for years and years, and it wasn't like finger-marks, but a large patch like, broad and spread out. So I passed my hand over it, without thinking what I was doing, and where that patch was it was all sticky and slimy, as if a snail had crawled over it. Very strange, isn't it, miss? and I wonder who can have done it, and how that mess was made."

The well-meant gabble of the servant touched me to the quick; I lay down upon my bed, and bit my lip that I should not cry out loud in the sharp anguish of my terror and bewilderment. Indeed, I was almost mad with dread; I believe that if it had been daylight I should have fled hot foot, forgetting all courage and all the debt of gratitude that was due to Professor Gregg, not caring whether my fate were that I must starve slowly, so long as I might escape from the net of blind and panic fear that every day seemed to draw a little closer round me. If I knew, I thought, if I knew what there was to dread, I could guard against it; but here, in this lonely house, shut in on all sides by the olden woods and the vaulted hills, terror seems to spring inconsequent from every covert, and the flesh is aghast at the half-hearted murmurs of horrible things. All in vain I strove to summon skepticism to my aid, and endeavored by cool common sense to buttress my belief in a world of natural order, for the air that blew in at the open window was a mystic breath, and in the darkness I felt the silence go heavy and sorrowful as a mass of requiem, and I conjured images of strange shapes gathering fast amidst the reeds, beside the wash of the river.

In the morning from the moment that I set foot in the breakfast-room, I felt that the unknown plot was drawing to a crisis; the professor's face was firm and set, and he seemed hardly to hear our voices when we spoke.

"I am going out for a rather long walk," he said, when the meal was over. "You mustn't be expecting me, now, or thinking anything has happened if I don't turn up to dinner. I have been getting stupid lately, and I dare say a miniature walking tour will do me good. Perhaps I may even spend the night in some little inn, if I find any place that looks clean and comfortable."

I heard this, and knew by my experience of Professor Gregg's manner that it was no ordinary business of pleasure that impelled him. I knew not, nor even remotely guessed, where he was bound, nor had I the vaguest notion of his errand, but all the fear of the night before returned; and as he stood, smiling, on the terrace, ready to set out, I implored him to stay, and to forget all his dreams of the undiscovered continent.

"No, no, Miss Lally," he replied, still smiling, "it's too late now. *Vestigia nulla retrorsum*, you know, is the device of all true explorers, though I hope it won't be literally true in my case. But, indeed, you are wrong to alarm yourself so; I look upon my little expedition as quite commonplace; no more exciting than a day with the geological hammers. There is a risk, of course, but so there is on the commonest excursion. I can afford to be jaunty; I am doing nothing so hazardous as 'Arry does a hundred times over in the course of every Bank Holiday. Well, then, you must look more cheerfully; and so good-bye till tomorrow at latest."

He walked briskly up the road, and I saw him open the gate that marks the entrance of the wood, and then he vanished in the gloom of the trees.

All the day passed heavily with a strange darkness in the air, and again I felt as if imprisoned amidst the ancient woods, shut in an olden land of mystery and dread, and as if all was long ago and forgotten by the living outside. I hoped and dreaded; and when the dinner-hour came I waited, expecting to hear the professor's step in the hall, and his voice exulting at I knew not what triumph. I composed my face to welcome him gladly, but the night descended dark, and he did not come.

In the morning, when the maid knocked at my door, I called out to her, and asked if her master had returned; and when she replied that his bedroom door stood open and empty, I felt the cold clasp of despair. Still, I fancied he might have discovered genial company, and would return for luncheon, or perhaps in the afternoon, and I took the children for a walk in the forest, and tried my best to play and laugh with them, and to shut out the thoughts of mystery and veiled terror.

Hour after hour I waited, and my thoughts grew darker; again the night came and found me watching, and at last, as I was making much ado to finish my dinner, I heard steps outside and the sound of a man's voice.

The maid came in and looked oddly at me. "Please, miss," she began, "Mr. Morgan, the gardener, wants to speak to you for a minute, if you didn't mind."

"Show him in, please," I answered, and set my lips tight.

The old man came slowly into the room, and the servant shut the door behind him.

"Sit down, Mr. Morgan," I said; "what is it that you want to say to me?"

"Well, miss, Mr. Gregg he gave me something for you yesterday morning, just before he went off, and he told me particular not to hand it up before eight o'clock this evening exactly, if so be as he wasn't back again home before, and if he should come home before I was just to return it to him in his own hands. So, you see, as Mr. Gregg isn't here yet, I suppose I'd better give you the parcel directly."

He pulled out something from his pocket, and gave it to me, half rising. I took it silently, and seeing that Morgan seemed doubtful as to what he was to do next. I thanked him and bade him good night, and he went out. I was left alone in the room with the parcel in my hand—a paper parcel, neatly sealed and directed to me, with the instructions Morgan had quoted, all written in the professor's large, loose hand. I broke the seals with a choking at my heart, and found an envelope inside, addressed also, but open, and I took the letter out.

My dear Miss Lally, it began—*To quote the old logic manual, the case of your reading this note is a case of my having made a blunder of some sort, and, I am afraid, a blunder that turns these lines into a farewell. It is practically certain that neither you nor any one else will ever see me again. I have made my will with provision for this eventuality, and I hope you will consent to accept the small remembrance addressed to you, and my sincere thanks for the way in which you joined your fortunes to mine. The fate which has come upon me is desperate and terrible beyond the remotest dreams of man; but this fate you have a right to know—if you please. If you look in the left-hand drawer of my dressing-table, you will find the key of the escritoire, properly labeled. In the well of the escritoire is a large envelope sealed and addressed to your name. I advise you to throw it forthwith into the fire; you will sleep better of nights if you do so. But if you must know the history of what has happened, it is all written down for you to read.*

The signature was firmly written below, and again I turned the page and read out the words one by one, aghast and white to the lips, my hands cold as ice, and sickness choking me. The dead silence of the room, and the thought of the dark woods and hills closing me in on every side, oppressed me, helpless and without capacity, and not knowing where to turn for counsel. At last I resolved that though knowledge should haunt my whole life and all the days to come, I must know the meaning of the strange terrors that had so long tormented me, rising grey, dim, and awful, like the shadows in the wood at dusk. I carefully carried out Professor Gregg's directions, and not without reluctance broke the seal of the envelope, and spread out his manuscript before me. That manuscript I always carry with me, and I see that I cannot deny your unspoken request to read it. This, then, was what I read that night, sitting at the desk, with a shaded lamp beside me.

The young lady who called herself Miss Lally then proceeded to recite

THE STATEMENT OF WILLIAM GREGG. F.R.S., etc.

It is many years since the first glimmer of the theory which is now almost, if not quite, reduced to fact dawned on my mind. A somewhat extensive course of miscellaneous and obsolete reading had done a great deal to prepare the way, and, later, when I became somewhat of a specialist, and immersed myself in the studies known as ethnological, I was now and then startled by facts that would not square with orthodox scientific opinion, and by discoveries that seemed to hint at something still hidden for all our research. More particularly I became convinced that much of the folk-lore of the world is but an exaggerated account of events that really happened, and I was especially drawn to consider the stories of the fairies, the good folk of the Celtic races. Here, I thought I could detect the fringe of embroidery and exaggeration, the fantastic guise, the little people dressed in green and gold sporting in the flowers, and I thought I saw a distinct analogy between the name given to this race (supposed to be imaginary) and the description of their appearance and manners. Just as our remote ancestors called the dreaded beings "fair" and "good" precisely because they dreaded them, so they had dressed them up in charming forms, knowing the truth to be the very reverse. Literature, too, had gone early to work, and had lent a powerful hand in the transformation, so that the playful elves of Shakespeare are already far removed from the true original, and the real horror is disguised in a form of prankish mischief. But in the older tales, the stories that used to make men cross themselves as they sat around the burning logs, we tread a different stage; I saw a widely opposed spirit in certain histories of children and of men and women who vanished strangely from the earth. They would be seen by a peasant in the fields walking towards some green and rounded hillock, and seen no more on earth; and there are stories of mothers who have left a child quietly sleeping, with the cottage door rudely barred with a piece of wood, and have returned, not to find the plump and rosy little Saxon, but a thin and wizened creature, with sallow skin and black, piercing eyes, the child of another race. Then, again, there were myths darker still; the dread of witch and wizard, the lurid evil of the Sabbath, and the hint of demons who mingled with the daughters of men. And just as we have turned the terrible "fair folk" into a company of benignant, if freakish elves, so we have hidden from us the black foulness of the witch and her companions under a popular *diablerie* of

old women and broomsticks, and a comic cat with tail
on end. So the Greeks called the hideous furies benevo-
lent ladies, and thus the northern nations have followed
their example. I pursued my investigations, stealing odd
hours from other and more imperative labors, and I asked
myself the question: Supposing these traditions to be
true, who were the demons who are reported to have
attended the Sabbaths? I need not say that I laid aside
what I may call the supernatural hypothesis of the Middle
Ages, and came to the conclusion that fairies and devils
were of one and the same race and origin; invention, no
doubt, and the Gothic fancy of old days, had done much
in the way of exaggeration and distortion; yet I firmly
believe that beneath all this imagery there was a black
background of truth. As for some of the alleged wonders,
I hesitated. While I should be very loath to receive any
one specific instance of modern spiritualism as containing
even a grain of the genuine, yet I was not wholly prepared
to deny that human flesh may now and then, once
perhaps in ten million cases, be the veil of powers which
seem magical to us—powers which, so far from
proceeding from the heights and leading men thither, are
in reality survivals from the depths of being. The amoeba
and the snail have powers which we do not possess; and
I thought it possible that the theory of reversion might
explain many things which seem wholly inexplicable.
Thus stood my position; I saw good reason to believe
that much of the tradition, a vast deal of the earliest and
uncorrupted tradition of the so-called fairies, represented
solid fact, and I thought that the purely supernatural
element in these traditions was to be accounted for on
the hypothesis that a race which had fallen out of the
grand march of evolution might have retained, as a
survival, certain powers which would be to us wholly
miraculous. Such was my theory as it stood conceived

in my mind; and working with this in view, I seemed to gather confirmation from every side, from the spoils of a tumulus or a barrow, from a local paper reporting an antiquarian meeting in the country, and from general literature of all kinds. Amongst other instances, I remember being struck by the phrase "articulate-speaking men" in Homer, as if the writer knew or had heard of men whose speech was so rude that it could hardly be termed articulate; and on my hypothesis of a race who had lagged far behind the rest, I could easily conceive that such a folk would speak a jargon but little removed from the inarticulate noises of brute beasts.

Thus I stood, satisfied that my conjecture was at all events not far removed from fact, when a chance paragraph in a small country print one day arrested my attention. It was a short account of what was to all appearance the usual sordid tragedy of the village—a young girl unaccountably missing, and evil rumor blatant and busy with her reputation. Yet I could read between the lines that all this scandal was purely hypothetical, and in all probability invented to account for what was in any other manner unaccountable. A flight to London or Liverpool, or an undiscovered body lying with a weight about its neck in the foul depths of a woodland pool, or perhaps murder—such were the theories of the wretched girl's neighbors. But as I idly scanned the paragraph, a flash of thought passed through me with the violence of an electric shock: what if the obscure and horrible race of the hills still survived, still remained haunting wild places and barren hills, and now and then repeating the evil of Gothic legend, unchanged and unchangeable as the Turanian Shelta, or the Basques of Spain? I have said that the thought came with violence; and indeed I drew in my breath sharply, and clung with both hands to my elbow-chair, in a strange confusion of horror and elation. It was as if one

of my *confrères* of physical science, roaming in a quiet
English wood, had been suddenly stricken aghast by the
presence of the slimy and loathsome terror of the
ichthyosaurus, the original of the stories of the awful
worms killed by valorous knights, or had seen the sun
darkened by the pterodactyl, the dragon of tradition. Yet
as a resolute explorer of knowledge, the thought of such
a discovery threw me into a passion of joy, and I cut out
the slip from the paper and put it in a drawer in my old
bureau, resolved that it should be but the first piece in a
collection of the strangest significance. I sat long that
evening dreaming of the conclusions I should establish,
nor did cooler reflection at first dash my confidence. Yet
as I began to put the case fairly, I saw that I might be
building on an unstable foundation; the facts might possibly
be in accordance with local opinion, and I regarded the
affair with a mood of some reserve. Yet I resolved to remain
perched on the look-out, and I hugged to myself the
thought that I alone was watching and wakeful, while the
great crowd of thinkers and searchers stood heedless and
indifferent, perhaps letting the most prerogative facts pass
by unnoticed.

Several years elapsed before I was enabled to add to
the contents of the drawer; and the second find was in
reality not a valuable one, for it was a mere repetition
of the first, with only the variation of another and distant
locality. Yet I gained something; for in the second case,
as in the first, the tragedy took place in a desolate and
lonely country, and so far my theory seemed justified.
But the third piece was to me far more decisive. Again,
amongst outland hills, far even from a main road of traffic,
an old man was found done to death, and the instrument
of execution was left beside him. Here, indeed, there
were rumor and conjecture, for the deadly tool was a
primitive stone axe, bound by gut to the wooden handle,

and surmises the most extravagant and improbable were indulged in. Yet, as I thought with a kind of glee, the wildest conjectures went far astray; and I took the pains to enter into correspondence with the local doctor, who was called at the inquest. He, a man of some acuteness, was dumbfounded. "It will not do to speak of these things in country places," he wrote to me; "but frankly, there is some hideous mystery here. I have obtained possession of the stone axe, and have been so curious as to test its powers. I took it into the back garden of my house one Sunday afternoon when my family and the servants were all out, and there, sheltered by the poplar hedges, I made my experiments. I found the thing utterly unmanageable; whether there is some peculiar balance, some nice adjustment of weights, which require incessant practice, or whether an effectual blow can be struck only by a certain trick of the muscles, I do not know; but I can assure you that I went into the house with but a sorry opinion of my athletic capacities. I was like an inexperienced man trying 'putting the hammer;' the force exerted seemed to return on oneself, and I found myself hurled backwards with violence, while the axe fell harmless to the ground. On another occasion I tried the experiment with a clever woodman of the place; but this man, who had handled his axe for forty years, could do nothing with the stone implement, and missed every stroke most ludicrously. In short, if it were not so supremely absurd, I should say that for four thousand years no one on earth could have struck an effective blow with the tool that undoubtedly was used to murder the old man." This, as may be imagined, was to me rare news; and afterwards, when I heard the whole story, and learned that the unfortunate old man had babbled tales of what might be seen at night on a certain wild hillside, hinting at unheard-of wonders, and that he had been found cold one morning on the very

hill in question, my exultation was extreme, for I felt I
was leaving conjecture far behind me. But the next step
was of still greater importance. I had possessed for many
years an extraordinary stone seal—a piece of dull black
stone, two inches long from the handle to the stamp, and
the stamping end a rough hexagon an inch and a quarter
in diameter. Altogether, it presented the appearance of
an enlarged tobacco stopper of an old-fashioned make.
It had been sent to me by an agent in the East, who
informed me that it had been found near the site of the
ancient Babylon. But the characters engraved on the seal
were to me an intolerable puzzle. Somewhat of the cuneiform pattern, there were yet striking differences, which
I detected at the first glance, and all efforts to read the
inscription on the hypothesis that the rules for deciphering the arrow-headed writing would apply proved
futile. A riddle such as this stung my pride, and at odd
moments I would take the Black Seal out of the cabinet,
and scrutinize it with so much idle perseverance that
every letter was familiar to my mind, and I could have
drawn the inscription from memory without the slightest
error. Judge, then, of my surprise when I one day received
from a correspondent in the west of England a letter and
an enclosure that positively left me thunderstruck. I saw
carefully traced on a large piece of paper the very characters of the Black Seal, without alteration of any kind,
and above the inscription my friend had written:
*Inscription found on a limestone rock on the Grey Hills,
Monmouthshire. Done in some red earth, and quite
recent.* I turned to the letter. My friend wrote: "I send
you the enclosed inscription with all due reserve. A shep-
herd who passed by the stone a week ago swears that
there was then no mark of any kind. The characters, as
I have noted, are formed by drawing some red earth over
the stone, and are of an average height of one inch. They

look to me like a kind of cuneiform character, a good deal altered, but this, of course, is impossible. It may be either a hoax, or more probably some scribble of the gipsies, who are plentiful enough in this wild country. They have, as you are aware, many hieroglyphics which they use in communicating with one another. I happened to visit the stone in question two days ago in connection with a rather painful incident which has occurred here."

As it may be supposed, I wrote immediately to my friend, thanking him for the copy of the inscription, and asking him in a casual manner the history of the incident he mentioned. To be brief, I heard that a woman named Cradock, who had lost her husband a day before, had set out to communicate the sad news to a cousin who lived some five miles away. She took a short cut which led by the Grey Hills. Mrs. Cradock, who was then quite a young woman, never arrived at her relative's house. Late that night a farmer, who had lost a couple of sheep, supposed to have wandered from the flock, was walking over the Grey Hills, with a lantern and his dog. His attention was attracted by a noise, which he described as a kind of wailing, mournful and pitiable to hear; and, guided by the sound, he found the unfortunate Mrs. Cradock crouched on the ground by the limestone rock, swaying her body to and fro, and lamenting and crying in so heart-rending a manner that the farmer was, as he says, at first obliged to stop his ears, or he would have run away. The woman allowed herself to be taken home, and a neighbor came to see to her necessities. All the night she never ceased her crying, mixing her lament with words of some unintelligible jargon, and when the doctor arrived he pronounced her insane. She lay on her bed for a week, now wailing, as people said, like one lost and damned for eternity, and now sunk in a heavy coma; it was thought that grief at the loss of her husband had unsettled her mind, and the medical man did not at one time expect her to live. I need not say that I was deeply interested in this story, and I made my friend write to me at intervals with all the particulars of the case. I heard then that in the course of six weeks the woman gradually recovered the use of her faculties, and some months later she gave birth to a son, christened Jervase, who unhappily proved to be of weak intellect. Such were the facts known to the village; but to me, while I whitened at the suggested thought of the hideous enormities that had doubtless been committed, all this was nothing short of conviction, and I incautiously hazarded a hint of something like the truth to some scientific friends. The moment the words had left my lips I bitterly regretted having spoken, and thus given away the great secret of my life, but with a good deal of relief mixed with indignation I found my fears altogether misplaced, for my friends ridiculed me to my face, and I was regarded as a madman; and beneath a natural anger I chuckled to myself, feeling as secure amidst these blockheads as if I had confided what I knew to the desert sands.

But now, knowing so much, I resolved I would know all, and I concentrated my efforts on the task of deciphering the inscription on the Black Seal. For many years I made this puzzle the sole object of my leisure moments, for the greater portion of my time was, of course, devoted to other duties, and it was only now and then that I could snatch a week of clear research. If I were to tell the full history of this curious investigation, this statement would be wearisome in the extreme, for it would contain simply the account of long and tedious failure. But with what I knew already of ancient scripts I was well equipped for the chase, as I always termed it to myself. I had correspondents amongst all the scientific men in Europe, and, indeed, in the world, and I could not believe that in these days any character, however ancient and however perplexed, could long resist the search-light I should bring to bear upon it. Yet in point of fact, it was fully fourteen years before I succeeded. With every year my professional duties increased and my leisure became smaller. This no doubt retarded me a good deal; and yet, when I look back on those years, I am astonished at the vast scope of my investigation of the Black Seal. I made my bureau a center, and from all the world and from all the ages I gathered transcripts of ancient writing.

Nothing, I resolved, should pass me unawares, and the faintest hint should be welcomed and followed up. But as one covert after another was tried and proved empty of result, I began in the course of years to despair, and to wonder whether the Black Seal were the sole relic of some race that had vanished from the world, and left no other trace of its existence—had perished, in fine, as Atlantis is said to have done, in some great cataclysm, its secrets perhaps drowned beneath the ocean or moulded into the heart of the hills. The thought chilled my warmth a little, and though I still persevered, it was no longer with the same certainty of faith. A chance came to the rescue. I was staying in a considerable town in the north of England, and took the opportunity of going over the very creditable museum that had for some time been established in the place. The curator was one of my correspondents; and, as we were looking through one of the mineral cases, my attention was struck by a specimen, a piece of black stone some four inches square, the appearance of which reminded me in a measure of the Black Seal. I took it up carelessly, and was turning it over in my hand, when I saw, to my astonishment, that the under side was inscribed. I said, quietly enough, to my friend the curator that the specimen interested me, and that I should be much obliged if he would allow me to take it with me to my hotel for a couple of days. He, of course, made no objection, and I hurried to my rooms and found that my first glance had not deceived me. There were two inscriptions; one in the regular cuneiform character, another in the character of the Black Seal, and I realized that my task was accomplished. I made an exact copy of the two inscriptions; and when I got to my London study, and had the seal before me, I was able seriously to grapple with the great problem. The interpreting inscription on the museum specimen, though in itself curious enough, did not bear on my quest, but the transliteration made me master of the secret of the Black Seal. Conjecture, of course, had to enter into my calculations; there was here and there uncertainty about a particular ideograph, and one sign recurring again and again on the seal baffled me for many successive nights. But at last the secret stood open before me in plain English, and I read the key of the awful transmutation of the hills. The last word was hardly written, when with fingers all trembling and unsteady I tore the scrap of paper into the minutest fragments, and saw them flame and blacken in the red hollow of the fire, and then I crushed the grey films that remained into finest powder. Never since then have I written those words; never will I write the phrases which tell how man can be reduced to the slime from which he came, and be forced to put on the flesh of the reptile and the snake.

There was now but one thing remaining. I knew, but I desired to see, and I was after some time able to take a house in the neighborhood of the Grey Hills, and not far from the cottage where Mrs. Cradock and her son Jervase resided. I need not go into a full and detailed account of the apparently inexplicable events which have occurred here, where I am writing this. I knew that I should find in Jervase Cradock something of the blood of the "Little People," and I found later that he had more than once encountered his kinsmen in lonely places in that lonely land. When I was summoned one day to the garden, and found him in a seizure speaking or hissing the ghastly jargon of the Black Seal, I am afraid that exultation prevailed over pity. I heard bursting from his lips the secrets of the underworld, and the word of dread, "Ishakshar," signification of which I must be excused from giving.

But there is one incident I cannot pass over unnoticed. In the waste hollow of the night I awoke at the sound of those hissing syllables I knew so well; and on going to the wretched boy's room, I found him convulsed and foaming at the mouth, struggling on the bed as if he strove to escape the grasp of writhing demons. I took him down to my room and lit the lamp, while he lay twisting on the floor, calling on the power within his flesh to leave him. I saw his body swell and become distended as a bladder, while the face blackened before my eyes; and then at the crisis I did what was necessary according to the directions on the Seal, and putting all scruple on one side, I became a man of science, observant of what was passing. Yet the sight I had to witness was horrible, almost beyond the power of human conception and the most fearful fantasy. Something pushed out from the body there on the floor, and stretched forth a slimy, wavering tentacle, across the room, grasped the bust upon the cupboard, and laid it down on my desk.

When it was over, and I was left to walk up and down all the rest of the night, white and shuddering, with sweat pouring from my flesh, I vainly tried to reason within myself: I said, truly enough, that I had seen nothing really supernatural, that a snail pushing out his horns and drawing them in was but an instance on a smaller scale of what I had witnessed; and yet horror broke through all such reasonings and left me shattered and loathing myself for the share I had taken in the night's work.

There is little more to be said. I am going now to the final trial and encounter; for I have determined that there shall be nothing wanting, and I shall meet the "Little People" face to face. I shall have the Black Seal and the knowledge of its secrets to help me, and if I unhappily do not return from my journey, there is no need to conjure up here a picture of the awfulness of my fate.

Pausing a little at the end of Professor Gregg's statement, Miss Lally continued her tale in the following words:

Such was the almost incredible story that the professor had left behind him. When I had finished reading it, it was late at night, but the next morning I took Morgan with me, and we proceeded to search the Grey Hills for some trace of the lost professor. I will not weary you with a description of the savage desolation of that tract of country, a tract of utterest loneliness, of bare green hills dotted over with grey limestone boulders, worn by the ravages of time into fantastic semblances of men and beast. Finally, after many hours of weary searching, we found what I told you—the watch and chain, and purse, and the ring— wrapped in a piece of coarse parchment. When Morgan cut the gut that bound the parcel together, and I saw the professor's property, I burst into tears, but the sight of the dreaded characters of the Black Seal repeated on the parchment froze me to silent horror, and I think I understood for the first time the awful fate that had come upon my late employer.

I have only to add that Professor Gregg's lawyer treated my account of what had happened as a fairy tale, and refused even to glance at the documents I laid before him. It was he who was responsible for the statement that appeared in the public press, to the effect that Professor Gregg had been drowned, and that his body must have been swept into the open sea.

Miss Lally stopped speaking, and looked at Mr. Phillipps, with a glance of some inquiry. He, for his part, was sunken in a deep reverie of thought; and when he looked up and saw the bustle of the evening gathering in the square, men and women hurrying to partake of dinner, and crowds already besetting the music-halls, all the hum and press of actual life seemed unreal and visionary, a dream in the morning after an awakening.

THE GREAT GOD PAN

I

THE EXPERIMENT

"I am glad you came, Clarke; very glad indeed. I was not sure you could spare the time."

"I was able to make arrangements for a few days; things are not very lively just now. But have you no misgivings, Raymond? Is it absolutely safe?"

The two men were slowly pacing the terrace in front of Dr. Raymond's house. The sun still hung above the western mountain-line, but it shone with a dull red glow that cast no shadows, and all the air was quiet; a sweet breath came from the great wood on the hillside above, and with it, at intervals, the soft murmuring call of the wild doves. Below, in the long lovely valley, the river wound in and out between the lonely hills, and, as the sun hovered and vanished into the west, a faint mist, pure white, began to rise from the hills. Dr. Raymond turned sharply to his friend.

"Safe? Of course it is. In itself the operation is a perfectly simple one; any surgeon could do it."

"And there is no danger at any other stage?"

"None; absolutely no physical danger whatsoever, I give you my word. You are always timid, Clarke, always; but you know my history. I have devoted myself to transcendental medicine for the last twenty years. I have heard myself called quack and charlatan and impostor, but all the while I knew I was on the right path. Five years ago I reached the goal, and since then every day has been a preparation for what we shall do tonight."

"I should like to believe it is all true." Clarke knit his brows, and looked doubtfully at Dr. Raymond. "Are you perfectly sure, Raymond, that your theory is not a phantasmagoria—a splendid vision, certainly, but a mere vision after all?"

Dr. Raymond stopped in his walk and turned sharply. He was a middle-aged man, gaunt and thin, of a pale yellow complexion, but as he answered Clarke and faced him, there was a flush on his cheek.

"Look about you, Clarke. You see the mountain, and hill following after hill, as wave on wave, you see the woods and orchard, the fields of ripe corn, and the meadows reaching to the reed-beds by the river. You see me standing here beside you, and hear my voice; but I tell you that all these things—yes, from that star that has just shone out in the sky to the solid ground beneath our feet—I say that all these are but dreams and shadows; the shadows that hide the real world from our eyes. There is a real world, but it is beyond this glamor and this vision, beyond these 'chases in Arras, dreams in a career,' beyond them all as beyond a veil. I do not know whether any human being has ever lifted that veil; but I do know, Clarke, that you and I shall see it lifted this very night from before another's eyes. You may think this all strange nonsense; it may be strange, but it is true, and the ancients knew what lifting the veil means. They called it seeing the god Pan."

Clarke shivered; the white mist gathering over the river was chilly.

"It is wonderful indeed," he said. "We are standing on the brink of a strange world, Raymond, if what you say is true. I suppose the knife is absolutely necessary?"

"Yes; a slight lesion in the grey matter, that is all; a trifling rearrangement of certain cells, a microscopical alteration that would escape the attention of ninety-nine brain specialists out of a hundred. I don't want to bother you with 'shop,' Clarke; I might give you a mass of technical detail which would sound very imposing, and would leave you as enlightened as you are now. But I suppose you have read, casually, in out-of-the-way corners of your paper, that immense strides have been made recently in the physiology of the brain. I saw a paragraph the other day about Digby's theory, and Browne Faber's discoveries. Theories and discoveries! Where they are standing now, I stood fifteen years ago, and I need not tell you that I have not been standing still for the last fifteen years. It will be enough if I say that five years ago I made the discovery that I alluded to when I said that ten years ago I reached the goal. After years of labor, after years of toiling and groping in the dark, after days and nights of disappointments and sometimes of despair, in which I used now and then to tremble and grow cold with the thought that perhaps there were others seeking for what I sought, at last, after so long, a pang of sudden joy thrilled my soul, and I knew the long journey was at an end. By what seemed then and still seems a chance, the suggestion of a moment's idle thought followed up upon familiar lines and paths that I had tracked a hundred times already, the great truth burst upon me, and I saw, mapped out in lines of sight, a whole world, a sphere unknown; continents and islands, and great oceans in which no ship has sailed (to my belief) since a Man first lifted up his eyes and beheld the sun, and the stars of heaven, and the quiet earth beneath. You will think this all high-flown language, Clarke, but it is hard to be literal. And yet; I do not know whether what I am hinting at cannot be set forth in plain and lonely terms. For instance, this world of ours is pretty well girded now with the telegraph wires and cables; thought, with something less than the speed of thought, flashes from sunrise to sunset, from north to south, across the floods and the desert places. Suppose that an electrician of today were suddenly to perceive that he and his friends have merely been playing with pebbles and mistaking them for the foundations of the world; suppose that such a man saw uttermost space lie open before the current, and words of men flash forth to the sun and beyond the sun into the systems beyond, and the voice of articulate-speaking men echo in the waste void that bounds our thought. As analogies go, that is a pretty good analogy of what I have done; you can understand now a little of what I felt as I stood here one evening; it was a summer evening, and the valley looked much as it does now; I stood here, and saw before me the unutterable, the unthinkable gulf that yawns profound between two worlds, the world of matter and the world of spirit; I saw the great empty deep stretch dim before me, and in that instant a bridge of light leapt from the earth to the unknown shore, and the abyss was spanned. You may look in Browne Faber's book, if you like, and you will find that to the present day men of science are unable to account for the presence, or to specify the functions of a certain group of nerve-cells in the brain. That group is, as it were, land to let, a mere waste place for fanciful theories. I am not in the position of Browne Faber and the specialists, I am perfectly instructed as to the possible functions of those nerve-centers in the scheme of things. With a touch I can bring them into play, with a touch, I say, I can set free the current, with a touch I can complete the communication between this world of sense and—we shall be able to finish the sentence later on. Yes, the knife is necessary; but think what that knife will effect. It will level utterly the solid wall of sense, and probably, for the first time since man was made, a spirit will gaze on a spirit-world. Clarke, Mary will see the god Pan!"

"But you remember what you wrote to me? I thought it would be requisite that she—"

He whispered the rest into the doctor's ear.

"Not at all, not at all. That is nonsense. I assure you. Indeed, it is better as it is; I am quite certain of that."

"Consider the matter well, Raymond. It's a great responsibility. Something might go wrong; you would be a miserable man for the rest of your days."

"No, I think not, even if the worst happened. As you know, I rescued Mary from the gutter, and from almost certain starvation, when she was a child; I think her life is mine, to use as I see fit. Come, it's getting late; we had better go in."

Dr. Raymond led the way into the house, through the hall, and down a long dark passage. He took a key from his pocket and opened a heavy door, and motioned Clarke into his laboratory. It had once been a billiard-room, and was lighted by a glass dome in the center of the ceiling, whence there still shone a sad grey light on the figure of the doctor as he lit a lamp with a heavy shade and placed it on a table in the middle of the room.

Clarke looked about him. Scarcely a foot of wall remained bare; there were shelves all around laden with bottles and phials of all shapes and colors, and at one end stood a little Chippendale book-case. Raymond pointed to this.

"You see that parchment Oswald Crollius? He was one of the first to show me the way, though I don't think he ever found it himself. That is a strange saying of his: 'In every grain of wheat there lies hidden the soul of a star.'"

There was not much furniture in the laboratory. The table in the center, a stone slab with a drain in one corner, the two armchairs on which Raymond and Clarke were sitting; that was all, except an odd-looking chair at the furthest end of the room. Clarke looked at it, and raised his eyebrows.

"Yes, that is the chair," said Raymond. "We may as well place it in position." He got up and wheeled the chair to the light, and began raising and lowering it, letting down the seat, setting the back at various angles, and adjusting the foot-rest. It looked comfortable enough, and Clarke passed his hand over the soft green velvet, as the doctor manipulated the levers.

"Now, Clarke, make yourself quite comfortable. I have a couple hours' work before me; I was obliged to leave certain matters to the last."

Raymond went to the stone slab, and Clarke watched him drearily as he bent over a row of phials and lit the flame under the crucible. The doctor had a small hand-lamp, shaded as the larger one, on a ledge above his apparatus, and Clarke, who sat in the shadows, looked down at the great shadowy room, wondering at the bizarre effects of brilliant light and undefined darkness contrasting with one another. Soon he became conscious of an odd odor, at first the merest suggestion of odor, in the room, and as it grew more decided he felt surprised that he was not reminded of the chemist's shop or the surgery. Clarke found himself idly endeavoring to analyze the sensation, and half conscious, he began to think of a day, fifteen years ago, that he had spent roaming through the woods and meadows near his own home. It was a burning day at the beginning of August, the heat had dimmed the outlines of all things and all distances with a faint mist, and people who observed the thermometer spoke of an abnormal register, of a temperature that was almost tropical. Strangely that wonderful hot day of the fifties rose up again in Clarke's imagination; the sense of dazzling all-pervading sunlight seemed to blot out the shadows and the lights of the laboratory, and he felt again the heated air beating in gusts about his face, saw the shimmer rising from the turf, and heard the myriad murmur of the summer.

"I hope the smell doesn't annoy you, Clarke; there's nothing unwholesome about it. It may make you a bit sleepy, that's all."

Clarke heard the words quite distinctly, and knew that Raymond was speaking to him, but for the life of him he could not rouse himself from his lethargy. He could only think of the lonely walk he had taken fifteen years ago; it was his last look at the fields and woods he had known since he was a child, and now it all stood out in brilliant light, as a picture, before him. Above all there came to his nostrils the scent of summer, the smell of flowers mingled, and the odor of the woods, of cool shaded places, deep in the green depths, drawn forth by the sun's heat; and the scent of the good earth, lying as it were with arms stretched forth, and smiling lips, overpowered all. His fancies made him wander, as he had wandered long ago, from the fields into the wood, tracking a little path between the shining undergrowth of beech-trees; and the trickle of water dropping from the limestone rock sounded as a clear melody in the dream. Thoughts began to go astray and to mingle with other thoughts; the beech alley was transformed to a path between ilex-trees, and here and there a vine climbed from bough to bough, and sent up waving tendrils and drooped with purple grapes, and the sparse grey-green leaves of a wild olive-tree stood out against the dark shadows of the ilex. Clarke, in the deep folds of dream, was conscious that the path from his father's house had led him into an undiscovered country, and he was wondering at the strangeness of it all, when suddenly, in place of the hum and murmur of the summer, an infinite silence seemed to fall on all things, and the wood was hushed, and for a moment in time he stood face to face there with a presence, that was neither man nor beast, neither the living nor the dead, but all things mingled, the form of all things but devoid of all form. And in that moment, the sacrament of body and soul was dissolved, and a voice seemed to cry "Let us go hence," and then the darkness of darkness beyond the stars, the darkness of everlasting.

When Clarke woke up with a start he saw Raymond pouring a few drops of some oily fluid into a green phial, which he stoppered tightly.

"You have been dozing," he said; "the journey must have tired you out. It is done now. I am going to fetch Mary; I shall be back in ten minutes."

Clarke lay back in his chair and wondered. It seemed as if he had but passed from one dream into another. He half expected to see the walls of the laboratory melt and disappear, and to awake in London, shuddering at his own sleeping fancies. But at last the door opened, and the doctor returned, and behind him came a girl of about seventeen, dressed all in white. She was so beautiful that Clarke did not wonder at what the doctor had written to him. She was blushing now over face and neck and arms, but Raymond seemed unmoved.

"Mary," he said, "the time has come. You are quite free. Are you willing to trust yourself to me entirely?"

"Yes, dear."

"Do you hear that, Clarke? You are my witness. Here is the chair, Mary. It is quite easy. Just sit in it and lean back. Are you ready?"

"Yes, dear, quite ready. Give me a kiss before you begin."

The doctor stooped and kissed her mouth, kindly enough. "Now shut your eyes," he said. The girl closed her eyelids, as if she were tired, and longed for sleep, and Raymond placed the green phial to her nostrils. Her face grew white, whiter than her dress; she struggled faintly, and then with the feeling of submission strong within her, crossed her arms upon her breast as a little child about to say her prayers. The bright light of the lamp fell full upon her, and Clarke watched changes fleeting over her face as the changes of the hills when the summer clouds float across the sun. And then she lay all white and still, and the doctor turned up one of her eyelids. She was quite unconscious. Raymond pressed hard on one of the levers and the chair instantly sank back. Clarke saw him cutting away a circle, like a tonsure, from her hair, and the lamp was moved nearer. Raymond took a small glittering instrument from a little case, and Clarke turned away shudderingly. When he looked again the doctor was binding up the wound he had made.

"She will awake in five minutes." Raymond was still perfectly cool. "There is nothing more to be done; we can only wait."

The minutes passed slowly; they could hear a slow, heavy, ticking. There was an old clock in the passage. Clarke felt sick and faint; his knees shook beneath him, he could hardly stand.

Suddenly, as they watched, they heard a long-drawn sigh, and suddenly did the color that had vanished return to the girl's cheeks, and suddenly her eyes opened. Clarke quailed before them. They shone with an awful light, looking far away, and a great wonder fell upon her face, and her hands stretched out as if to touch what was invisible; but in an instant the wonder faded, and gave place to the most awful terror. The muscles of her face were hideously convulsed, she shook from head to foot; the soul seemed struggling and shuddering within the house of flesh. It was a horrible sight, and Clarke rushed forward, as she fell shrieking to the floor.

Three days later Raymond took Clarke to Mary's bedside. She was lying wide-awake, rolling her head from side to side, and grinning vacantly.

"Yes," said the doctor, still quite cool, "it is a great pity; she is a hopeless idiot. However, it could not be helped; and, after all, she has seen the Great God Pan."

II

MR. CLARKE'S MEMOIRS

Mr. Clarke, the gentleman chosen by Dr. Raymond to witness the strange experiment of the god Pan, was a person in whose character caution and curiosity were oddly mingled; in his sober moments he thought of the unusual and eccentric with undisguised aversion, and yet, deep in his heart, there was a wide-eyed inquisitiveness with respect to all the more recondite and esoteric elements in the nature of men. The latter tendency had prevailed when he accepted Raymond's invitation, for though his considered judgment had always repudiated the doctor's theories as the wildest nonsense, yet he secretly hugged a belief in fantasy, and would have rejoiced to see that belief confirmed. The horrors that he witnessed in the dreary laboratory were to a certain extent salutary; he was conscious of being involved in an affair not altogether reputable, and for many years afterwards he clung bravely to the commonplace, and rejected all occasions of occult investigation. Indeed, on some homeopathic principle, he for some time attended the seances of distinguished mediums, hoping that the clumsy tricks of these gentlemen would make him altogether disgusted with mysticism of every kind, but the remedy, though caustic, was not efficacious. Clarke knew that he still pined for the unseen, and little by little, the old passion began to reassert itself, as the face of Mary, shuddering and convulsed with an unknown terror, faded slowly from his memory. Occupied all day in pursuits both serious and lucrative, the temptation to relax in the evening was too great, especially in the winter months, when the fire cast a warm glow over his snug bachelor apartment, and a bottle of some choice claret stood ready by his elbow. His dinner digested, he would make a brief pretence of reading the evening paper, but the mere catalogue of news soon palled upon him, and Clarke would find himself casting glances of warm desire in the direction of an old Japanese bureau, which stood at a pleasant distance from the hearth. Like a boy before a jam-closet, for a few minutes he would hover indecisive, but lust always prevailed, and Clarke ended by drawing up his chair, lighting a candle, and sitting down before the bureau. Its pigeon-holes and drawers teemed with documents on the most morbid subjects, and in the well reposed a large manuscript volume, in which he had painfully entered the gems of his collection. Clarke had a fine contempt for published literature; the most ghostly story ceased to interest him if it happened to be printed; his sole pleasure was in the reading, compiling, and rearranging what he called his "Memoirs to prove the Existence of the Devil," and engaged in this pursuit the evening seemed to fly and the night appeared too short.

On one particular evening, an ugly December night, black with fog, and raw with frost, Clarke hurried over his dinner, and scarcely deigned to observe his customary ritual of taking up the paper and laying it down again. He paced two or three times up and down the room, and opened the bureau, stood still a moment, and sat down. He leant back, absorbed in one of those dreams to which he was subject, and at length drew out his book, and opened it at the last entry. There were three or four pages densely covered with Clarke's round, set penmanship, and at the beginning he had written in a somewhat larger hand:

Singular Narrative told me by my Friend, Dr. Phillips. He assures me that all the facts related therein are strictly and wholly True, but refuses to give either the Surnames of the Persons Concerned, or the Place where these Extraordinary Events occurred.

Mr. Clarke began to read over the account for the tenth time, glancing now and then at the pencil notes he had made when it was told him by his friend. It was one of his humors to pride himself on a certain literary ability; he thought well of his style, and took pains in arranging the circumstances in dramatic order. He read the following story:—

The persons concerned in this statement are Helen V., who, if she is still alive, must now be a woman of twenty-three, Rachel M., since deceased, who was a year younger than the above, and Trevor W., an imbecile, aged eighteen. These persons were at the period of the story inhabitants of a village on the borders of Wales, a place of some importance in the time of the Roman occupation, but now a scattered hamlet, of not more than five hundred souls. It is situated on rising ground, about six miles from the sea, and is sheltered by a large and picturesque forest.

Some eleven years ago, Helen V. came to the village under rather peculiar circumstances. It is understood that she, being an orphan, was adopted in her infancy by a distant relative, who brought her up in his own house until she was twelve years old. Thinking, however, that it would be better for the child to have playmates of her own age, he advertised in several local papers for a good home in a comfortable farmhouse for a girl of twelve, and this advertisement was answered by Mr. R., a well-to-do farmer in the above-mentioned village. His references proving satisfactory, the gentleman sent his adopted daughter to Mr. R., with a letter, in which he stipulated that the girl should have a room to herself, and stated that her guardians need be at no trouble in the matter of education, as she was already sufficiently educated for the position in life which she would occupy. In fact, Mr. R. was given to understand that the girl be allowed to find her own occupations and to spend her time almost as she liked. Mr. R. duly met her at the nearest station, a town seven miles away from his house, and seems to have remarked nothing extraordinary about the child except that she was reticent as to her former life and her adopted father. She was, however, of a very different type from the inhabitants of the village; her skin was a pale, clear olive, and her features were strongly marked, and of a somewhat foreign character. She appears to have settled down easily enough into farmhouse life, and became a favorite with the children, who sometimes went with her on her rambles in the forest, for this was her amusement. Mr. R. states that he has known her to go out by herself directly after their early breakfast, and not return till after dusk, and that, feeling uneasy at a young girl being out alone for so many hours, he communicated with her adopted father, who replied in a brief note that Helen must do as she chose. In the winter, when the forest paths are impassable, she spent most of her time in her bedroom, where she slept alone, according to the instructions of her relative. It was on one of these expeditions to the forest that the first of the singular incidents with which this girl is connected occurred, the date being about a year after her arrival at the village. The preceding winter had been remarkably severe, the snow drifting to a great depth, and the frost continuing for an unexampled period, and the summer following was as noteworthy for its extreme heat. On one of the very hottest days in this summer, Helen V. left the farmhouse for one of her long rambles in the forest, taking with her, as usual, some bread and meat for lunch. She was seen by some men in the fields making for the old Roman Road, a green causeway which traverses the highest part of the wood, and they were astonished to observe that the girl had taken off her hat, though the heat of the sun was already tropical. As it happened, a laborer, Joseph W. by name, was working in the forest near the Roman Road, and at twelve o'clock his little son, Trevor, brought the man his dinner of bread and cheese. After the meal, the boy, who was about seven years old at the time, left his father at work, and, as he said, went to look for flowers in the wood, and the man, who could hear him shouting with delight at his discoveries, felt no uneasiness. Suddenly, however, he was horrified at hearing the most dreadful screams, evidently the result of great terror, proceeding from the direction in which his son had gone, and he hastily threw down his tools and ran to see what had happened. Tracing his path by the sound, he met the little boy, who was running headlong, and was evidently terribly frightened, and on questioning him the man elicited that after picking a posy of flowers he felt tired, and lay down on the grass and fell asleep. He was suddenly awakened, as he stated, by a peculiar noise, a sort of singing he called it, and on peeping through the branches he saw Helen V. playing on the grass with a "strange naked man," who he seemed unable to describe more fully. He said he felt dreadfully frightened and ran away crying for his father. Joseph W. proceeded in the direction indicated by his son, and found Helen V. sitting on the grass in the middle of a glade or open space left by charcoal burners. He angrily charged her with frightening his little boy, but she entirely denied the accusation and laughed at the child's story of a "strange man," to which he himself did not attach much credence. Joseph W. came to the conclusion that the boy had woke up with a sudden fright, as children sometimes do, but Trevor persisted in his story, and continued in such evident distress that at last his father took him home, hoping that his mother would be able to soothe him. For many weeks, however, the boy gave his parents much anxiety; he became nervous and strange in his manner, refusing to leave the cottage by himself, and constantly alarming the household by waking in the night with cries of "The man in the wood! father! father!"

In course of time, however, the impression seemed to have worn off, and about three months later he accompanied his father to the home of a gentleman in the neighborhood, for whom Joseph W. occasionally did work. The man was shown into the study, and the little boy was left sitting in the hall, and a few minutes later, while the gentleman was giving W. his instructions, they were both horrified by a piercing shriek and the sound of a fall, and rushing out they found the child lying senseless on the floor, his face contorted with terror. The doctor was immediately summoned, and after some examination he pronounced the child to be suffering form a kind of fit, apparently produced by a sudden shock. The boy was taken to one of the bedrooms, and after some time recovered consciousness, but only to pass into a condition described by the medical man as one of violent hysteria. The doctor exhibited a strong sedative, and in the course of two hours pronounced him fit to walk home, but in passing through the hall the paroxysms of fright returned and with additional violence. The father perceived that the child was pointing at some object, and heard the old cry, "The man in the wood," and looking in the direction indicated saw a stone head of grotesque appearance, which had been built into the wall above one of the doors. It seems the owner of the house had recently made alterations in his premises, and on digging the foundations for some offices, the men had found a curious head, evidently of the Roman period, which had been placed in the manner described. The head is pronounced by the most experienced archaeologists of the district to be that of a faun or satyr. [Dr. Phillips tells me that he has seen the head in question, and assures me that he has never received such a vivid presentment of intense evil.]

From whatever cause arising, this second shock seemed too severe for the boy Trevor, and at the present date he suffers from a weakness of intellect, which gives but little promise of amending. The matter caused a good deal of sensation at the time, and the girl Helen was closely questioned by Mr. R., but to no purpose, she steadfastly denying that she had frightened or in any way molested Trevor.

The second event with which this girl's name is connected took place about six years ago, and is of a still more extraordinary character.

At the beginning of the summer of 1882, Helen contracted a friendship of a peculiarly intimate character with Rachel M., the daughter of a prosperous farmer in the neighborhood. This girl, who was a year younger than Helen, was considered by most people to be the prettier of the two, though Helen's features had to a great extent softened as she became older. The two girls, who were together on every available opportunity, presented a singular contrast, the one with her clear, olive skin and almost Italian appearance, and the other of the proverbial red and white of our rural districts. It must be stated that the payments made to Mr. R. for the maintenance of Helen were known in the village for their excessive liberality, and the impression was general that she would one day inherit a large sum of money from her relative. The parents of Rachel were therefore not averse from their daughter's friendship with the girl, and even encouraged the intimacy, though they now bitterly regret having done so. Helen still retained her extraordinary fondness for the forest, and on several occasions Rachel accompanied her, the two friends setting out early in the morning, and remaining in the wood until dusk. Once or twice after these excursions Mrs. M. thought her daughter's manner rather peculiar; she seemed languid and dreamy, and as it has been expressed, "different from herself," but these peculiarities seem to have been thought too trifling for remark. One evening, however, after Rachel had come home, her mother heard a noise which sounded like suppressed weeping in the girl's room, and on going in found her lying, half undressed, upon the bed, evidently in the greatest distress. As soon as she saw her mother, she exclaimed, "Ah, mother, mother, why did you let me go to the forest with Helen?" Mrs. M. was astonished at so strange a question, and proceeded to make inquiries. Rachel told her a wild story. She said—

Clarke closed the book with a snap, and turned his chair towards the fire. When his friend sat one evening in that very chair, and told his story, Clarke had interrupted him at a point a little subsequent to this, had cut short his words in a paroxysm of horror. "My God!" he had exclaimed, "think, think what you are saying. It is too incredible, too monstrous; such things can never be in this quiet world, where men and women live and die, and struggle, and conquer, or maybe fail, and fall down under sorrow, and grieve and suffer strange fortunes for many a year; but not this, Phillips, not such things as this. There must be some explanation, some way out of the terror. Why, man, if such a case were possible, our earth would be a nightmare."

But Phillips had told his story to the end, concluding: "Her flight remains a mystery to this day; she vanished in broad sunlight; they saw her walking in a meadow, and a few moments later she was not there."

Clarke tried to conceive the thing again, as he sat by the fire, and again his mind shuddered and shrank back, appalled before the sight of such awful, unspeakable elements enthroned as it were, and triumphant in human flesh. Before him stretched the long dim vista of the green causeway in the forest, as his friend had described it; he saw the swaying leaves and the quivering shadows on the grass, he saw the sunlight and the flowers, and far away, far in the long distance, the two figures moved toward him. One was Rachel, but the other?

Clarke had tried his best to disbelieve it all, but at the end of the account, as he had written it in his book, he had placed the inscription:

ET DIABOLUS INCARNATE EST. ET HOMO FACTUS EST.

III

THE CITY OF RESURRECTIONS

"Herbert! Good God! Is it possible?"

"Yes, my name's Herbert. I think I know your face, too, but I don't remember your name. My memory is very queer."

"Don't you recollect Villiers of Wadham?"

"So it is, so it is. I beg your pardon, Villiers, I didn't think I was begging of an old college friend. Good-night."

"My dear fellow, this haste is unnecessary. My rooms are close by, but we won't go there just yet. Suppose we walk up Shaftesbury Avenue a little way? But how in heaven's name have you come to this pass, Herbert?"

"It's a long story, Villiers, and a strange one too, but you can hear it if you like."

"Come on, then. Take my arm, you don't seem very strong."

The ill-assorted pair moved slowly up Rupert Street; the one in dirty, evil-looking rags, and the other attired in the regulation uniform of a man about town, trim, glossy, and eminently well-to-do. Villiers had emerged from his restaurant after an excellent dinner of many courses, assisted by an ingratiating little flask of Chianti, and, in that frame of mind which was with him almost chronic, had delayed a moment by the door, peering round in the dimly-lighted street in search of those mysterious incidents and persons with which the streets of London teem in every quarter and every hour. Villiers prided himself as a practised explorer of such obscure mazes and byways of London life, and in this unprofitable pursuit he displayed an assiduity which was worthy of more serious employment. Thus he stood by the lamp-post surveying the passers-by with undisguised curiosity, and with that gravity known only to the systematic diner, had just enunciated in his mind the formula: "London has been called the city of encounters; it is more than that, it is the city of Resurrections," when these reflections were suddenly interrupted by a piteous whine at his elbow, and a deplorable appeal for alms. He looked around in some irritation, and with a sudden shock found himself confronted with the embodied proof of his somewhat stilted fancies. There, close beside him, his face altered and disfigured by poverty and disgrace, his body barely covered by greasy ill-fitting rags, stood his old friend Charles Herbert, who had matriculated on the same day as himself, with whom he had been merry and wise for twelve revolving terms. Different occupations and varying interests had interrupted the friendship, and it was six years since Villiers had seen Herbert; and now he looked upon this wreck of a man with grief and dismay, mingled with a certain inquisitiveness as to what dreary chain of circumstances had dragged him down to such a doleful pass. Villiers felt together with compassion all the relish of the amateur in mysteries, and congratulated himself on his leisurely speculations outside the restaurant.

They walked on in silence for some time, and more than one passer-by stared in astonishment at the unaccustomed spectacle of a well-dressed man with an unmistakable beggar hanging on to his arm, and, observing this, Villiers led the way to an obscure street in Soho. Here he repeated his question.

"How on earth has it happened, Herbert? I always understood you would succeed to an excellent position in Dorsetshire. Did your father disinherit you? Surely not?"

"No, Villiers; I came into all the property at my poor father's death; he died a year after I left Oxford. He was a very good father to me, and I mourned his death sincerely enough. But you know what young men are; a few months later I came up to town and went a good deal into society. Of course I had excellent introductions, and I managed to enjoy myself very much in a harmless sort of way. I played a little, certainly, but never for heavy stakes, and the few bets I made on races brought me in money—only a few pounds, you know, but enough to pay for cigars and such petty pleasures. It was in my second season that the tide turned. Of course you have heard of my marriage?"

"No, I never heard anything about it."

"Yes, I married, Villiers. I met a girl, a girl of the most wonderful and most strange beauty, at the house of some people whom I knew. I cannot tell you her age; I never knew it, but, so far as I can guess, I should think she must have been about nineteen when I made her acquaintance. My friends had come to know her at Florence; she told them she was an orphan, the child of an English father and an Italian mother, and she charmed them as she charmed me. The first time I saw her was at an evening party. I was standing by the door talking to a friend, when suddenly above the hum and babble of conversation I heard a voice which seemed to thrill to my heart. She was singing an Italian song. I was introduced to her that evening, and in three months I married Helen. Villiers, that woman, if I can call her woman, corrupted my soul. The night of the wedding I found myself sitting in her bedroom in the hotel, listening to her talk. She was sitting up in bed, and I listened to her as she spoke in her beautiful voice, spoke of things which even now I would not dare whisper in the blackest night, though I stood in the midst of a wilderness. You, Villiers, you may think you know life, and London, and what goes on day and night in this dreadful city; for all I can say you may have heard the talk of the vilest, but I tell you you can have no conception of what I know, not in your most fantastic, hideous dreams can you have imaged forth the faintest shadow of what I have heard—and seen. Yes, seen. I have seen the incredible, such horrors that even I myself sometimes stop in the middle of the street and ask whether it is possible for a man to behold such things and live. In a year, Villiers, I was a ruined man, in body and soul—in body and soul."

"But your property, Herbert? You had land in Dorset."

"I sold it all; the fields and woods, the dear old house—everything."

"And the money?"

"She took it all from me."

"And then left you?"

"Yes; she disappeared one night. I don't know where she went, but I am sure if I saw her again it would kill me. The rest of my story is of no interest; sordid misery, that is all. You may think, Villiers, that I have exaggerated and talked for effect; but I have not told you half. I could tell you certain things which would convince you, but you would never know a happy day again. You would pass the rest of your life, as I pass mine, a haunted man, a man who has seen hell."

Villiers took the unfortunate man to his rooms, and gave him a meal. Herbert could eat little, and scarcely touched the glass of wine set before him. He sat moody and silent by the fire, and seemed relieved when Villiers sent him away with a small present of money.

"By the way, Herbert," said Villiers, as they parted at the door, "what was your wife's name? You said Helen, I think? Helen what?"

"The name she passed under when I met her was Helen Vaughan, but what her real name was I can't say. I don't think she had a name. No, no, not in that sense. Only human beings have names, Villiers; I can't say anymore. Good-bye; yes, I will not fail to call if I see any way in which you can help me. Good-night."

The man went out into the bitter night, and Villiers returned to his fireside. There was something about Herbert which shocked him inexpressibly; not his poor rags nor the marks which poverty had set upon his face, but rather an indefinite terror which hung about him like a mist. He had acknowledged that he himself was not devoid of blame; the woman, he had avowed, had corrupted him body and soul, and Villiers felt that this man, once his friend, had been an actor in scenes evil beyond the power of words. His story needed no confirmation: he himself was the embodied proof of it. Villiers mused curiously over the story he had heard, and wondered whether he had heard both the first and the last of it. "No," he thought, "certainly not the last, probably only the beginning. A case like this is like a nest of Chinese boxes; you open one after the other and find a quainter workmanship in every box. Most likely poor Herbert is merely one of the outside boxes; there are stranger ones to follow."

Villiers could not take his mind away from Herbert and his story, which seemed to grow wilder as the night wore on. The fire seemed to burn low, and the chilly air of the morning crept into the room; Villiers got up with a glance over his shoulder, and, shivering slightly, went to bed.

A few days later he saw at his club a gentleman of his acquaintance, named Austin, who was famous for his intimate knowledge of London life, both in its tenebrous and luminous phases. Villiers, still full of his encounter in Soho and its consequences, thought Austin might possibly be able to shed some light on Herbert's history, and so after some casual talk he suddenly put the question:

"Do you happen to know anything of a man named Herbert— Charles Herbert?"

Austin turned round sharply and stared at Villiers with some astonishment.

"Charles Herbert? Weren't you in town three years ago? No; then you have not heard of the Paul Street case? It caused a good deal of sensation at the time."

"What was the case?"

"Well, a gentleman, a man of very good position, was found dead, stark dead, in the area of a certain house in Paul Street, off Tottenham Court Road. Of course the police did not make the discovery; if you happen to be sitting up all night and have a light in your window, the constable will ring the bell, but if you happen to be lying dead in somebody's area, you will be left alone. In this instance, as in many others, the alarm was raised by some kind of vagabond; I don't mean a common tramp, or a public-house loafer, but a gentleman, whose business or pleasure, or both, made him a spectator of the London streets at five o'clock in the morning. This individual was, as he said, 'going home,' it did not appear whence or whither, and had occasion to pass through Paul Street between four and five a.m. Something or other caught his eye at Number 20; he said, absurdly enough, that the house had the most unpleasant physiognomy he had ever observed, but, at any rate, he glanced down the area and was a good deal astonished to see a man lying on the stones, his limbs all huddled together, and his face turned up. Our gentleman thought his face looked peculiarly ghastly, and so set off at a run in search of the nearest policeman. The constable was at first inclined to treat the matter lightly, suspecting common drunkenness; however, he came, and after looking at the man's face, changed his tone, quickly enough. The early bird, who had picked up this fine worm, was sent off for a doctor, and the policeman rang and knocked at the door till a slatternly servant girl came down looking more than half asleep. The constable pointed out the contents of the area to the maid, who screamed loudly enough to wake up the street, but she knew nothing of the man; had never seen him at the house, and so forth. Meanwhile, the original discoverer had come back with a medical man, and the next thing was to get into the area. The gate was open, so the whole quartet stumped down the steps. The doctor hardly needed a moment's examination; he said the poor fellow had been dead for several hours, and it was then the case began to get interesting. The dead man had not been robbed, and in one of his pockets were papers identifying him as—well, as a man of good family and means, a favorite in society, and nobody's enemy, as far as could be known. I don't give his name, Villiers, because it has nothing to do with the story, and because it's no good raking up these affairs about the dead when there are no relations living. The next curious point was that the medical men couldn't agree as to how he met his death. There were some slight bruises on his shoulders, but they were so slight that it looked as if he had been pushed roughly out of the kitchen door, and not thrown over the railings from the street or even dragged down the steps. But there were positively no other marks of violence about him, certainly none that would account for his death; and when they came to the autopsy there wasn't a trace of poison of any kind. Of course the police wanted to know all about the people at Number 20, and here again, so I have heard from private sources, one or two other very curious points came out. It appears that the occupants of the house were a Mr. and Mrs. Charles Herbert; he was said to be a landed proprietor, though it struck most people that Paul Street was not exactly the place to look for country gentry. As for Mrs. Herbert, nobody seemed to know who or what she was, and, between ourselves, I fancy the divers after her history found themselves in rather strange waters. Of course they both denied knowing anything about the deceased, and in default of any evidence against them they were discharged. But some very odd things came out about them. Though it was between five and six in the morning when the dead man was removed, a large crowd had collected, and several of the neighbors ran to see what was going on. They were pretty free with their comments, by all accounts, and from these it appeared that Number 20 was in very bad odor in Paul Street. The detectives tried to trace down these rumors to some solid foundation of fact, but could not get hold of anything. People shook their heads and raised their eyebrows and thought the Herberts rather 'queer,' 'would rather not be seen going into their house,' and so on, but there was nothing tangible. The authorities were morally certain the man met his death in some way or another in the house and was thrown out by the kitchen door, but they couldn't prove it, and the absence of any indications of violence or poisoning left them helpless. An odd case, wasn't it? But curiously enough, there's something more that I haven't told you. I happened to know one of the doctors who was consulted as to the cause of death, and some time after the inquest I met him, and asked him about it. 'Do you really mean to tell me,' I said, 'that you were baffled by the case, that you actually don't know what the man died of?' 'Pardon me,' he replied, 'I know perfectly well what caused death. Blank died of fright, of sheer, awful terror; I never saw features so hideously contorted in the entire course of my practice, and I have seen the faces of a whole host of dead.' The doctor was usually a cool customer enough, and a certain vehemence in his manner struck me, but I couldn't get anything more out of him. I suppose the Treasury didn't see their way to prosecuting the Herberts for frightening a man to death; at any rate, nothing was done, and the case dropped out of men's minds. Do you happen to know anything of Herbert?"

"Well," replied Villiers, "he was an old college friend of mine."

"You don't say so? Have you ever seen his wife?"

"No, I haven't. I have lost sight of Herbert for many years."

"It's queer, isn't it, parting with a man at the college gate or at Paddington, seeing nothing of him for years, and then finding him pop up his head in such an odd place. But I should like to have seen Mrs. Herbert; people said extraordinary things about her."

"What sort of things?"

"Well, I hardly know how to tell you. Everyone who saw her at the police court said she was at once the most beautiful woman and the most repulsive they had ever set eyes on. I have spoken to a man who saw her, and I assure you he positively shuddered as he tried to describe the woman, but he couldn't tell why. She seems to have been a sort of enigma; and I expect if that one dead man could have told tales, he would have told some uncommonly queer ones. And there you are again in another puzzle; what could a respectable country gentleman like Mr. Blank (we'll call him that if you don't mind) want in such a very queer house as Number 20? It's altogether a very odd case, isn't it?"

"It is indeed, Austin; an extraordinary case. I didn't think, when I asked you about my old friend, I should strike on such strange metal. Well, I must be off; good-day."

Villiers went away, thinking of his own conceit of the Chinese boxes; here was quaint workmanship indeed.

IV

THE DISCOVERY IN PAUL STREET

A few months after Villiers' meeting with Herbert, Mr. Clarke was sitting, as usual, by his after-dinner hearth, resolutely guarding his fancies from wandering in the direction of the bureau. For more than a week he had succeeded in keeping away from the "Memoirs," and he cherished hopes of a complete self-reformation; but, in spite of his endeavors, he could not hush the wonder and the strange curiosity that the last case he had written down had excited within him. He had put the case, or rather the outline of it, conjecturally to a scientific friend, who shook his head, and thought Clarke getting queer, and on this particular evening Clarke was making an effort to rationalize the story, when a sudden knock at the door roused him from his meditations.

"Mr. Villiers to see you sir."

"Dear me, Villiers, it is very kind of you to look me up; I have not seen you for many months; I should think nearly a year. Come in, come in. And how are you, Villiers? Want any advice about investments?"

"No, thanks, I fancy everything I have in that way is pretty safe. No, Clarke, I have really come to consult you about a rather curious matter that has been brought under my notice of late. I am afraid you will think it all rather absurd when I tell my tale. I sometimes think so myself, and that's just what I made up my mind to come to you, as I know you're a practical man."

Mr. Villiers was ignorant of the "Memoirs to prove the Existence of the Devil."

"Well, Villiers, I shall be happy to give you my advice, to the best of my ability. What is the nature of the case?"

"It's an extraordinary thing altogether. You know my ways; I always keep my eyes open in the streets, and in my time I have chanced upon some queer customers, and queer cases too, but this, I think, beats all. I was coming out of a restaurant one nasty winter night about three months ago; I had had a capital dinner and a good bottle of Chianti, and I stood for a moment on the pavement, thinking what a mystery there is about London streets and the companies that pass along them. A bottle of red wine encourages these fancies, Clarke, and I dare say I should have thought a page of small type, but I was cut short by a beggar who had come behind me, and was making the usual appeals. Of course I looked round, and this beggar turned out to be what was left of an old friend of mine, a man named Herbert. I asked him how he had come to such a wretched pass, and he told me. We walked up and down one of those long and dark Soho streets, and there I listened to his story. He said he had married a beautiful girl, some years younger than himself, and, as he put it, she had corrupted him body and soul. He wouldn't go into details; he said he dare not, that what he had seen and heard haunted him by night and day, and when I looked in his face I knew he was speaking the truth. There was something about the man that made me shiver. I don't know why, but it was there. I gave him a little money and sent him away, and I assure you that when he was gone I gasped for breath. His presence seemed to chill one's blood."

"Isn't this all just a little fanciful, Villiers? I suppose the poor fellow had made an imprudent marriage, and, in plain English, gone to the bad."

"Well, listen to this." Villiers told Clarke the story he had heard from Austin.

"You see," he concluded, "there can be but little doubt that this Mr. Blank, whoever he was, died of sheer terror; he saw something so awful, so terrible, that it cut short his life. And what he saw, he most certainly saw in that house, which, somehow or other, had got a bad name in the neighborhood. I had the curiosity to go and look at the place for myself. It's a saddening kind of street; the houses are old enough to be mean and dreary, but not old enough to be quaint. As far as I could see most of them are let in lodgings, furnished and unfurnished, and almost every door has three bells to it. Here and there the ground floors have been made into shops of the commonest kind; it's a dismal street in every way. I found Number 20 was to let, and I went to the agent's and got the key. Of course I should have heard nothing of the Herberts in that quarter, but I asked the man, fair and square, how long they had left the house and whether there had been other tenants in the meanwhile. He looked at me queerly for a minute, and told me the Herberts had left immediately after the unpleasantness, as he called it, and since then the house had been empty."

Mr. Villiers paused for a moment.

"I have always been rather fond of going over empty houses; there's a sort of fascination about the desolate empty rooms, with the nails sticking in the walls, and the dust thick upon the window-sills. But I didn't enjoy going over Number 20, Paul Street. I had hardly put my foot inside the passage when I noticed a queer, heavy feeling about the air of the house. Of course all empty houses are stuffy, and so forth, but this was something quite different; I can't describe it to you, but it seemed to stop the breath. I went into the front room and the back room, and the kitchens downstairs; they were all dirty and dusty enough, as you would expect, but there was something strange about them all. I couldn't define it to you, I only know I felt queer. It was one of the rooms on the first floor, though, that was the worst. It was a largish room, and once on a time the paper must have been cheerful enough, but when I saw it, paint, paper, and everything were most doleful. But the room was full of horror; I felt my teeth grinding as I put my hand on the door, and when I went in, I thought I should have fallen fainting to the floor. However, I pulled myself together, and stood against the end wall, wondering what on earth there could be about the room to make my limbs tremble, and my heart beat as if I were at the hour of death. In one corner there was a pile of newspapers littered on the floor, and I began looking at them; they were papers of three or four years ago, some of them half torn, and some crumpled as if they had been used for packing. I turned the whole pile over, and amongst them I found a curious drawing; I will show it to you presently. But I couldn't stay in the room; I felt it was overpowering me. I was thankful to come out, safe and sound, into the open air. People stared at me as I walked along the street, and one man said I was drunk. I was staggering about from one side of the pavement to the other, and it was as much as I could do to take the key back to the agent and get home. I was in bed for a week, suffering from what my doctor called nervous shock and exhaustion. One of those days I was reading the evening paper, and happened to notice a paragraph headed:'Starved to Death.' It was the usual style of thing; a model lodging-house in Marylebone, a door locked for several days, and a dead man in his chair when they broke in. 'The deceased,' said the paragraph, 'was known as Charles Herbert, and is believed to have been once a prosperous country gentleman. His name was familiar to the public three years ago in connection with the mysterious death in Paul Street, Tottenham Court Road, the deceased being the tenant of the house Number 20, in the area of which a gentleman of good position was found dead under circumstances not devoid of suspicion.' A tragic ending, wasn't it? But after all, if what he told me were true, which I am sure it was, the man's life was all a tragedy, and a tragedy of a stranger sort than they put on the boards."

"And that is the story, is it?" said Clarke musingly.

"Yes, that is the story."

"Well, really, Villiers, I scarcely know what to say about it. There are, no doubt, circumstances in the case which seem peculiar, the finding of the dead man in the area of Herbert's house, for instance, and the extraordinary opinion of the physician as to the cause of death; but, after all, it is conceivable that the facts may be explained in a straightforward manner. As to your own sensations, when you went to see the house, I would suggest that they were due to a vivid imagination; you must have been brooding, in a semi-conscious way, over what you had heard. I don't exactly see what more can be said or done in the matter; you evidently think there is a mystery of some kind, but Herbert is dead; where then do you propose to look?"

"I propose to look for the woman; the woman whom he married. She is the mystery."

The two men sat silent by the fireside; Clarke secretly congratulating himself on having successfully kept up the character of advocate of the commonplace, and Villiers wrapped in his gloomy fancies.

"I think I will have a cigarette," he said at last, and put his hand in his pocket to feel for the cigarette-case.

"Ah!" he said, starting slightly, "I forgot I had something to show you. You remember my saying that I had found a rather curious sketch amongst the pile of old newspapers at the house in Paul Street? Here it is."

Villiers drew out a small thin parcel from his pocket. It was covered with brown paper, and secured with string, and the knots were troublesome. In spite of himself Clarke felt inquisitive; he bent forward on his chair as Villiers painfully undid the string, and unfolded the outer covering. Inside was a second wrapping of tissue, and Villiers took it off and handed the small piece of paper to Clarke without a word.

There was dead silence in the room for five minutes or more; the two men sat so still that they could hear the ticking of the tall old-fashioned clock that stood outside in the hall, and in the mind of one of them the slow monotony of sound woke up a far, far memory. He was looking intently at the small pen-and-ink sketch of the woman's head; it had evidently been drawn with great care, and by a true artist, for the woman's soul looked out of the eyes, and the lips were parted with a strange smile. Clarke gazed still at the face; it brought to his memory one summer evening, long ago; he saw again the long lovely valley, the river winding between the hills, the meadows and the cornfields, the dull red sun, and the cold white mist rising from the water. He heard a voice speaking to him across the waves of many years, and saying "Clarke, Mary will see the god Pan!" and then he was standing in the grim room beside the doctor, listening to the heavy ticking of the clock, waiting and watching, watching the figure lying on the green chair beneath the lamplight. Mary rose up, and he looked into her eyes, and his heart grew cold within him.

"Who is this woman?" he said at last. His voice was dry and hoarse.

"That is the woman who Herbert married."

Clarke looked again at the sketch; it was not Mary after all. There certainly was Mary's face, but there was something else, something he had not seen on Mary's features when the white-clad girl entered the laboratory with the doctor, nor at her terrible awakening, nor when she lay grinning on the bed. Whatever it was, the glance that came from those eyes, the smile on the full lips, or the expression of the whole face, Clarke shuddered before it at his inmost soul, and thought, unconsciously, of Dr. Phillip's words, "the most vivid presentment of evil I have ever seen." He turned the paper over mechanically in his hand and glanced at the back.

"Good God! Clarke, what is the matter? You are as white as death."

Villiers had started wildly from his chair, as Clarke fell back with a groan, and let the paper drop from his hands.

"I don't feel very well, Villiers, I am subject to these attacks. Pour me out a little wine; thanks, that will do. I shall feel better in a few minutes."

Villiers picked up the fallen sketch and turned it over as Clarke had done.

"You saw that?" he said. "That's how I identified it as being a portrait of Herbert's wife, or I should say his widow. How do you feel now?"

"Better, thanks, it was only a passing faintness. I don't think I quite catch your meaning. What did you say enabled you to identify the picture?"

"This word—'Helen'—was written on the back. Didn't I tell you her name was Helen? Yes; Helen Vaughan."

Clarke groaned; there could be no shadow of doubt.

"Now, don't you agree with me," said Villiers, "that in the story I have told you tonight, and in the part this woman plays in it, there are some very strange points?"

"Yes, Villiers," Clarke muttered, "it is a strange story indeed; a strange story indeed. You must give me time to think it over; I may be able to help you or I may not. Must you be going now? Well, good-night, Villiers, good-night. Come and see me in the course of a week."

V

THE LETTER OF ADVICE

"Do you know, Austin," said Villiers, as the two friends were pacing sedately along Piccadilly one pleasant morning in May, "do you know I am convinced that what you told me about Paul Street and the Herberts is a mere episode in an extraordinary history? I may as well confess to you that when I asked you about Herbert a few months ago I had just seen him."

"You had seen him? Where?"

"He begged of me in the street one night. He was in the most pitiable plight, but I recognized the man, and I got him to tell me his history, or at least the outline of it. In brief, it amounted to this—he had been ruined by his wife."

"In what manner?"

"He would not tell me; he would only say that she had destroyed him, body and soul. The man is dead now."

"And what has become of his wife?"

"Ah, that's what I should like to know, and I mean to find her sooner or later. I know a man named Clarke, a dry fellow, in fact a man of business, but shrewd enough. You understand my meaning; not shrewd in the mere business sense of the word, but a man who really knows something about men and life. Well, I laid the case before him, and he was evidently impressed. He said it needed consideration, and asked me to come again in the course of a week. A few days later I received this extraordinary letter."

Austin took the envelope, drew out the letter, and read it curiously. It ran as follows:—

"MY DEAR VILLIERS,—I have thought over the matter on which you consulted me the other night, and my advice to you is this. Throw the portrait into the fire, blot out the story from your mind. Never give it another thought, Villiers, or you will be sorry. You will think, no doubt, that I am in possession of some secret information, and to a certain extent that is the case. But I only know a little; I am like a traveler who has peered over an abyss, and has drawn back in terror. What I know is strange enough and horrible enough, but beyond my knowledge there are depths and horrors more frightful still, more incredible than any tale told of winter nights about the fire. I have resolved, and nothing shall shake that resolve, to explore no whit farther, and if you value your happiness you will make the same determination.

"Come and see me by all means; but we will talk on more cheerful topics than this."

Austin folded the letter methodically, and returned it to Villiers.

"It is certainly an extraordinary letter," he said, "what does he mean by the portrait?"

"Ah! I forgot to tell you I have been to Paul Street and have made a discovery."

Villiers told his story as he had told it to Clarke, and Austin listened in silence. He seemed puzzled.

"How very curious that you should experience such an unpleasant sensation in that room!" he said at length. "I hardly gather that it was a mere matter of the imagination; a feeling of repulsion, in short."

"No, it was more physical than mental. It was as if I were inhaling at every breath some deadly fume, which seemed to penetrate to every nerve and bone and sinew of my body. I felt racked from head to foot, my eyes began to grow dim; it was like the entrance of death."

"Yes, yes, very strange certainly. You see, your friend confesses that there is some very black story connected with this woman. Did you notice any particular emotion in him when you were telling your tale?"

"Yes, I did. He became very faint, but he assured me that it was a mere passing attack to which he was subject."

"Did you believe him?"

"I did at the time, but I don't now. He heard what I had to say with a good deal of indifference, till I showed him the portrait. It was then that he was seized with the attack of which I spoke. He looked ghastly, I assure you."

"Then he must have seen the woman before. But there might be another explanation; it might have been the name, and not the face, which was familiar to him. What do you think?"

"I couldn't say. To the best of my belief it was after turning the portrait in his hands that he nearly dropped from the chair. The name, you know, was written on the back."

"Quite so. After all, it is impossible to come to any resolution in a case like this. I hate melodrama, and nothing strikes me as more commonplace and tedious than the ordinary ghost story of commerce; but really, Villiers, it looks as if there were something very queer at the bottom of all this."

The two men had, without noticing it, turned up Ashley Street, leading northward from Piccadilly. It was a long street, and rather a gloomy one, but here and there a brighter taste had illuminated the dark houses with flowers, and gay curtains, and a cheerful paint on the doors. Villiers glanced up as Austin stopped speaking, and looked at one of these houses; geraniums, red and white, drooped from every sill, and daffodil-colored curtains were draped back from each window.

"It looks cheerful, doesn't it?" he said.

"Yes, and the inside is still more cheery. One of the pleasantest houses of the season, so I have heard. I haven't been there myself, but I've met several men who have, and they tell me it's uncommonly jovial."

"Whose house is it?"

"A Mrs. Beaumont's."

"And who is she?"

"I couldn't tell you. I have heard she comes from South

America, but after all, who she is is of little consequence. She is a very wealthy woman, there's no doubt of that, and some of the best people have taken her up. I hear she has some wonderful claret, really marvellous wine, which must have cost a fabulous sum. Lord Argentine was telling me about it; he was there last Sunday evening. He assures me he has never tasted such a wine, and Argentine, as you know, is an expert. By the way, that reminds me, she must be an oddish sort of woman, this Mrs. Beaumont. Argentine asked her how old the wine was, and what do you think she said? 'About a thousand years, I believe.' Lord Argentine thought she was chaffing him, you know, but when he laughed she said she was speaking quite seriously and offered to show him the jar. Of course, he couldn't say anything more after that; but it seems rather antiquated for a beverage, doesn't it? Why, here we are at my rooms. Come in, won't you?"

"Thanks, I think I will. I haven't seen the curiosity-shop for a while."

It was a room furnished richly, yet oddly, where every jar and bookcase and table, and every rug and jar and ornament seemed to be a thing apart, preserving each its own individuality.

"Anything fresh lately?" said Villiers after a while.

"No; I think not; you saw those queer jugs, didn't you? I thought so. I don't think I have come across anything for the last few weeks."

Austin glanced around the room from cupboard to cupboard, from shelf to shelf, in search of some new oddity. His eyes fell at last on an odd chest, pleasantly and quaintly carved, which stood in a dark corner of the room.

"Ah," he said, "I was forgetting, I have got something to show you." Austin unlocked the chest, drew out a thick quarto volume, laid it on the table, and resumed the cigar he had put down.

"Did you know Arthur Meyrick the painter, Villiers?"

"A little; I met him two or three times at the house of a friend of mine. What has become of him? I haven't heard his name mentioned for some time."

"He's dead."

"You don't say so! Quite young, wasn't he?"

"Yes; only thirty when he died."

"What did he die of?"

"I don't know. He was an intimate friend of mine, and a thoroughly good fellow. He used to come here and talk to me for hours, and he was one of the best talkers I have met. He could even talk about painting, and that's more than can be said of most painters. About eighteen months ago he was feeling rather overworked, and partly at my suggestion he went off on a sort of roving expedition, with no very definite end or aim about it. I believe New York was to be his first port, but I never heard from him. Three months ago I got this book, with a very civil letter from an English doctor practicing at Buenos Ayres, stating that he had attended the late Mr. Meyrick during his illness, and that the deceased had expressed an earnest wish that the enclosed packet should be sent to me after his death. That was all."

"And haven't you written for further particulars?"

"I have been thinking of doing so. You would advise me to write to the doctor?"

"Certainly. And what about the book?"

"It was sealed up when I got it. I don't think the doctor had seen it."

"It is something very rare? Meyrick was a collector, perhaps?"

"No, I think not, hardly a collector. Now, what do you think of these Ainu jugs?"

"They are peculiar, but I like them. But aren't you going to show me poor Meyrick's legacy?"

"Yes, yes, to be sure. The fact is, it's rather a peculiar sort of thing, and I haven't shown it to any one. I wouldn't say anything about it if I were you. There it is."

Villiers took the book, and opened it at haphazard.

"It isn't a printed volume, then?" he said.

"No. It is a collection of drawings in black and white by my poor friend Meyrick."

Villiers turned to the first page, it was blank; the second bore
a brief inscription, which he read:

> *Silet per diem universus, nec sine horrore secretus est;*
> *lucet nocturnis ignibus, chorus Aegipanum undique*
> *personatur: audiuntur et cantus tibiarum, et tinnitus*
> *cymbalorum per oram maritimam.*

On the third page was a design which made Villiers start and
look up at Austin; he was gazing abstractedly out of the window.
Villiers turned page after page, absorbed, in spite of himself, in
the frightful Walpurgis Night of evil, strange monstrous evil, that
the dead artist had set forth in hard black and white. The figures
of Fauns and Satyrs and Aegipans danced before his eyes, the
darkness of the thicket, the dance on the mountain-top, the
scenes by lonely shores, in green vineyards, by rocks and desert
places, passed before him: a world before which the human soul
seemed to shrink back and shudder. Villiers whirled over the
remaining pages; he had seen enough, but the picture on the
last leaf caught his eye, as he almost closed the book.

"Austin!"

"Well, what is it?"

"Do you know who that is?"

It was a woman's face, alone on the white page.

"Know who it is? No, of course not."

"I do."

"Who is it?"

"It is Mrs. Herbert."

"Are you sure?"

"I am perfectly sure of it. Poor Meyrick! He is one more
chapter in her history."

"But what do you think of the designs?"

"They are frightful. Lock the book up again, Austin. If I were
you I would burn it; it must be a terrible companion even though
it be in a chest."

"Yes, they are singular drawings. But I wonder what connection there could be between Meyrick and Mrs. Herbert, or what link between her and these designs?"

"Ah, who can say? It is possible that the matter may end here, and we shall never know, but in my own opinion this Helen Vaughan, or Mrs. Herbert, is only the beginning. She will come back to London, Austin; depend on it, she will come back, and we shall hear more about her then. I doubt it will be very pleasant news."

VI

THE SUICIDES

Lord Argentine was a great favorite in London Society. At twenty he had been a poor man, decked with the surname of an illustrious family, but forced to earn a livelihood as best he could, and the most speculative of money-lenders would not have entrusted him with fifty pounds on the chance of his ever changing his name for a title, and his poverty for a great fortune. His father had been near enough to the fountain of good things to secure one of the family livings, but the son, even if he had taken orders, would scarcely have obtained so much as this, and moreover felt no vocation for the ecclesiastical estate. Thus he fronted the world with no better armor than the bachelor's gown and the wits of a younger son's grandson, with which equipment he contrived in some way to make a very tolerable fight of it. At twenty-five Mr. Charles Aubernon saw himself still a man of struggles and of warfare with the world, but out of the seven who stood before him and the high places of his family three only remained. These three, however, were "good lives," but yet not proof against the Zulu assegais and typhoid fever, and so one morning Aubernon woke up and found himself Lord Argentine, a man of thirty who had faced the difficulties of existence, and had conquered. The situation amused him immensely, and he resolved that riches should be as pleasant to him as poverty had always been. Argentine, after some little consideration, came to the conclusion that dining, regarded as a fine art, was perhaps the most amusing pursuit open to fallen humanity, and thus his dinners became famous in London, and an invitation to his table a thing covetously desired. After ten years of lordship and dinners Argentine still declined to be jaded, still persisted in enjoying life, and by a kind of infection had become recognized as the cause of joy in others, in short, as the best of company. His sudden and tragical death therefore caused a wide and deep sensation. People could scarcely believe it, even though the newspaper was before their eyes, and the cry of "Mysterious Death of a Nobleman" came ringing up from the street. But there stood the brief paragraph: "Lord Argentine was found dead this morning by his valet under distressing circumstances. It is stated that there can be no doubt that his lordship committed suicide, though no motive can be assigned for the act. The deceased nobleman was widely known in society, and much liked for his genial manner and sumptuous hospitality. He is succeeded by," etc., etc.

By slow degrees the details came to light, but the case still remained a mystery. The chief witness at the inquest was the deceased's valet, who said that the night before his death Lord Argentine had dined with a lady of good position, whose name was suppressed in the newspaper reports. At about eleven o'clock Lord Argentine had returned, and informed his man that he should not require his services till the next morning. A little later the valet had occasion to cross the hall and was somewhat astonished to see his master quietly letting himself out at the front door. He had taken off his evening clothes, and was dressed in a Norfolk coat and knickerbockers, and wore a low brown hat. The valet had no reason to suppose that Lord Argentine had seen him, and though his master rarely kept late hours, thought little of the occurrence till the next morning, when he knocked at the bedroom door at a quarter to nine as usual. He received no answer, and, after knocking two or three times, entered the room, and saw Lord Argentine's body leaning forward at an angle from the bottom of the bed. He found that his master had tied a cord securely to one of the short bed-posts, and, after making a running noose and slipping it round his neck, the unfortunate man must have resolutely fallen forward, to die by slow strangulation. He was dressed in the light suit in which the valet had seen him go out, and the doctor who was summoned pronounced that life had been extinct for more than four hours. All papers, letters, and so forth seemed in perfect order, and nothing was discovered which pointed in the most remote way to any scandal either great or small. Here the evidence ended; nothing more could be discovered. Several persons had been present at the dinner-party at which Lord Argentine had assisted, and to all these he seemed in his usual genial spirits. The valet, indeed, said he thought his master appeared a little excited when he came home, but confessed that the alteration in his manner was very slight, hardly noticeable, indeed. It seemed hopeless to seek for any clue, and the suggestion that Lord Argentine had been suddenly attacked by acute suicidal mania was generally accepted.

It was otherwise, however, when within three weeks, three more gentlemen, one of them a nobleman, and the two others men of good position and ample means, perished miserably in almost precisely the same manner. Lord Swanleigh was found one morning in his dressing-room, hanging from a peg affixed to the wall, and Mr. Collier-Stuart and Mr. Herries had chosen to die as Lord Argentine. There was no explanation in either case; a few bald facts; a living man in the evening, and a body with a black swollen face in the morning. The police had been forced to confess themselves powerless to arrest or to explain the sordid murders of Whitechapel; but before the horrible suicides of Piccadilly and Mayfair they were dumbfoundered, for not even the mere ferocity which did duty as an explanation of the crimes of the East End, could be of service in the West. Each of these men who had resolved to die a tortured shameful death was rich, prosperous, and to all appearances in love with the world, and not the acutest research should ferret out any shadow of a lurking motive in either case. There was a horror in the air, and men looked at one another's faces when they met, each wondering whether the other was to be the victim of the fifth nameless tragedy. Journalists sought in vain for their scrapbooks for materials whereof to concoct reminiscent articles; and the morning paper was unfolded in many a house with a feeling of awe; no man knew when or where the next blow would light.

A short while after the last of these terrible events, Austin came to see Mr. Villiers. He was curious to know whether Villiers had succeeded in discovering any fresh traces of Mrs. Herbert, either through Clarke or by other sources, and he asked the question soon after he had sat down.

"No," said Villiers, "I wrote to Clarke, but he remains obdurate, and I have tried other channels, but without any result. I can't find out what became of Helen Vaughan after she left Paul Street, but I think she must have gone abroad. But to tell the truth, Austin, I haven't paid much attention to the matter for the last few weeks; I knew poor Herries intimately, and his terrible death has been a great shock to me, a great shock."

"I can well believe it," answered Austin gravely, "you know Argentine was a friend of mine. If I remember rightly, we were speaking of him that day you came to my rooms."

"Yes; it was in connection with that house in Ashley Street, Mrs. Beaumont's house. You said something about Argentine's dining there."

"Quite so. Of course you know it was there Argentine dined the night before—before his death."

"No, I had not heard that."

"Oh, yes; the name was kept out of the papers to spare Mrs. Beaumont. Argentine was a great favorite of hers, and it is said she was in a terrible state for sometime after."

A curious look came over Villiers' face; he seemed undecided whether to speak or not. Austin began again.

"I never experienced such a feeling of horror as when I read the account of Argentine's death. I didn't understand it at the time, and I don't now. I knew him well, and it completely passes my understanding for what possible cause he—or any of the others for the matter of that—could have resolved in cold blood to die in such an awful manner. You know how men babble away each other's characters in London, you may be sure any buried scandal or hidden skeleton would have been brought to light in such a case as this; but nothing of the sort has taken place. As for the theory of mania, that is very well, of course, for the coroner's jury, but everybody knows that it's all nonsense. Suicidal mania is not small-pox."

Austin relapsed into gloomy silence. Villiers sat silent, also, watching his friend. The expression of indecision still fleeted across his face; he seemed as if weighing his thoughts in the balance, and the considerations he was resolving left him still silent. Austin tried to shake off the remembrance of tragedies as hopeless and perplexed as the labyrinth of Daedalus, and began to talk in an indifferent voice of the more pleasant incidents and adventures of the season.

"That Mrs. Beaumont," he said, "of whom we were speaking, is a great success; she has taken London almost by storm. I met her the other night at Fulham's; she is really a remarkable woman."

"You have met Mrs. Beaumont?"

"Yes; she had quite a court around her. She would be called very handsome, I suppose, and yet there is something about her face which I didn't like. The features are exquisite, but the expression is strange. And all the time I was looking at her, and afterwards, when I was going home, I had a curious feeling that very expression was in some way or another familiar to me."

"You must have seen her in the Row."

"No, I am sure I never set eyes on the woman before; it is that which makes it puzzling. And to the best of my belief I have never seen anyone like her; what I felt was a kind of dim far-off memory, vague but persistent. The only sensation I can compare it to, is that odd feeling one sometimes has in a dream, when fantastic cities and wondrous lands and phantom personages appear familiar and accustomed."

Villiers nodded and glanced aimlessly round the room, possibly in search of something on which to turn the conversation. His eyes fell on an old chest somewhat like that in which the artist's strange legacy lay hid beneath a Gothic scutcheon.

"Have you written to the doctor about poor Meyrick?" he asked.

"Yes; I wrote asking for full particulars as to his illness and death. I don't expect to have an answer for another three weeks or a month. I thought I might as well inquire whether Meyrick knew an Englishwoman named Herbert, and if so, whether the doctor could give me any information about her. But it's very possible that Meyrick fell in with her at New York, or Mexico, or San Francisco; I have no idea as to the extent or direction of his travels."

"Yes, and it's very possible that the woman may have more than one name."

"Exactly. I wish I had thought of asking you to lend me the portrait of her which you possess. I might have enclosed it in my letter to Dr. Matthews."

"So you might; that never occurred to me. We might send it now. Hark! what are those boys calling?"

While the two men had been talking together a confused noise of shouting had been gradually growing louder. The noise rose from the eastward and swelled down Piccadilly, drawing nearer and nearer, a very torrent of sound; surging up streets usually quiet, and making every window a frame for a face, curious or excited. The cries and voices came echoing up the silent street where Villiers lived, growing more distinct as they advanced, and, as Villiers spoke, an answer rang up from the pavement:

"The West End Horrors; Another Awful Suicide; Full Details!"

Austin rushed down the stairs and bought a paper and read out the paragraph to Villiers as the uproar in the street rose and fell. The window was open and the air seemed full of noise and terror.

"Another gentleman has fallen a victim to the terrible epidemic of suicide which for the last month has prevailed in the West End. Mr. Sidney Crashaw, of Stoke House, Fulham, and King's Pomeroy, Devon, was found, after a prolonged search, hanging dead from the branch of a tree in his garden at one o'clock today. The deceased gentleman dined last night at the Carlton Club and seemed in his usual health and spirits. He left the club at about ten o'clock, and was seen walking leisurely up St. James's Street a little later. Subsequent to this his movements cannot be traced. On the discovery of the body medical aid was at once summoned, but life had evidently been long extinct. So far as is known, Mr. Crashaw had no trouble or anxiety of any kind. This painful suicide, it will be remembered, is the fifth of the kind in the last month. The authorities at Scotland Yard are unable to suggest any explanation of these terrible occurrences."

Austin put down the paper in mute horror.

"I shall leave London tomorrow," he said, "it is a city of nightmares. How awful this is, Villiers!"

Mr. Villiers was sitting by the window quietly looking out into the street. He had listened to the newspaper report attentively, and the hint of indecision was no longer on his face.

"Wait a moment, Austin," he replied, "I have made up my mind to mention a little matter that occurred last night. It stated, I think, that Crashaw was last seen alive in St. James's Street shortly after ten?"

"Yes, I think so. I will look again. Yes, you are quite right."

"Quite so. Well, I am in a position to contradict that statement at all events. Crashaw was seen after that; considerably later indeed."

"How do you know?"

"Because I happened to see Crashaw myself at about two o'clock this morning."

"You saw Crashaw? You, Villiers?"

"Yes, I saw him quite distinctly; indeed, there were but a few feet between us."

"Where, in Heaven's name, did you see him?"

"Not far from here. I saw him in Ashley Street. He was just leaving a house."

"Did you notice what house it was?"

"Yes. It was Mrs. Beaumont's."

"Villiers! Think what you are saying; there must be some mistake. How could Crashaw be in Mrs. Beaumont's house at two o'clock in the morning? Surely, surely, you must have been dreaming, Villiers; you were always rather fanciful."

"No; I was wide awake enough. Even if I had been dreaming as you say, what I saw would have roused me effectually."

"What you saw? What did you see? Was there anything strange about Crashaw? But I can't believe it; it is impossible."

"Well, if you like I will tell you what I saw, or if you please, what I think I saw, and you can judge for yourself."

"Very good, Villiers."

The noise and clamor of the street had died away, though now and then the sound of shouting still came from the distance, and the dull, leaden silence seemed like the quiet after an earth-quake or a storm. Villiers turned from the window and began speaking.

"I was at a house near Regent's Park last night, and when I came away the fancy took me to walk home instead of taking a hansom. It was a clear pleasant night enough, and after a few minutes I had the streets pretty much to myself. It's a curious thing, Austin, to be alone in London at night, the gas-lamps stretching away in perspective, and the dead silence, and then perhaps the rush and clatter of a hansom on the stones, and the fire starting up under the horse's hoofs. I walked along pretty briskly, for I was feeling a little tired of being out in the night, and as the clocks were striking two I turned down Ashley Street, which, you know, is on my way. It was quieter than ever there, and the lamps were fewer; altogether, it looked as dark and gloomy as a forest in winter. I had done about half the length of the street when I heard a door closed very softly, and naturally I looked up to see who was abroad like myself at such an hour. As it happens, there is a street lamp close to the house in question, and I saw a man standing on the step. He had just shut the door and his face was towards me, and I recognized Crashaw directly. I never knew him to speak to, but I had often seen him, and I am positive that I was not mistaken in my man. I looked into his face for a moment, and then—I will confess the truth—I set off at a good run, and kept it up till I was within my own door."

"Why?"

"Why? Because it made my blood run cold to see that man's face. I could never have supposed that such an infernal medley of passions could have glared out of any human eyes; I almost fainted as I looked. I knew I had looked into the eyes of a lost soul, Austin, the man's outward form remained, but all hell was within it. Furious lust, and hate that was like fire, and the loss of all hope and horror that seemed to shriek aloud to the night, though his teeth were shut; and the utter blackness of despair. I am sure that he did not see me; he saw nothing that you or I can see, but what he saw I hope we never shall. I do not know when he died; I suppose in an hour, or perhaps two, but when I passed down Ashley Street and heard the closing door, that man no longer belonged to this world; it was a devil's face I looked upon."

There was an interval of silence in the room when Villiers ceased speaking. The light was failing, and all the tumult of an hour ago was quite hushed. Austin had bent his head at the close of the story, and his hand covered his eyes.

"What can it mean?" he said at length.

"Who knows, Austin, who knows? It's a black business, but I think we had better keep it to ourselves, for the present at any rate. I will see if I cannot learn anything about that house through private channels of information, and if I do light upon anything I will let you know."

VII

THE ENCOUNTER IN SOHO

Three weeks later Austin received a note from Villiers, asking him to call either that afternoon or the next. He chose the nearer date, and found Villiers sitting as usual by the window, apparently lost in meditation on the drowsy traffic of the street. There was a bamboo table by his side, a fantastic thing, enriched with gilding and queer painted scenes, and on it lay a little pile of papers arranged and docketed as neatly as anything in Mr. Clarke's office.

"Well, Villiers, have you made any discoveries in the last three weeks?"

"I think so; I have here one or two memoranda which struck me as singular, and there is a statement to which I shall call your attention."

"And these documents relate to Mrs. Beaumont? It was really Crashaw whom you saw that night standing on the doorstep of the house in Ashley Street?"

"As to that matter my belief remains unchanged, but neither my inquiries nor their results have any special relation to Crashaw. But my investigations have had a strange issue. I have found out who Mrs. Beaumont is!"

"Who is she? In what way do you mean?"

"I mean that you and I know her better under another name."

"What name is that?"

"Herbert."

"Herbert!" Austin repeated the word, dazed with astonishment.

"Yes, Mrs. Herbert of Paul Street, Helen Vaughan of earlier adventures unknown to me. You had reason to recognize the expression of her face; when you go home look at the face in Meyrick's book of horrors, and you will know the sources of your recollection."

"And you have proof of this?"

"Yes, the best of proof; I have seen Mrs. Beaumont, or shall we say Mrs. Herbert?"

"Where did you see her?"

"Hardly in a place where you would expect to see a lady who lives in Ashley Street, Piccadilly. I saw her entering a house in one of the meanest and most disreputable streets in Soho. In fact, I had made an appointment, though not with her, and she was precise to both time and place."

"All this seems very wonderful, but I cannot call it incredible. You must remember, Villiers, that I have seen this woman, in the ordinary adventure of London society, talking and laughing, and sipping her coffee in a commonplace drawing-room with commonplace people. But you know what you are saying."

"I do; I have not allowed myself to be led by surmises or fancies. It was with no thought of finding Helen Vaughan that I searched for Mrs. Beaumont in the dark waters of the life of London, but such has been the issue."

"You must have been in strange places, Villiers."

"Yes, I have been in very strange places. It would have been useless, you know, to go to Ashley Street, and ask Mrs. Beaumont to give me a short sketch of her previous history. No; assuming, as I had to assume, that her record was not of the cleanest, it would be pretty certain that at some previous time she must have moved in circles not quite so refined as her present ones. If you see mud at the top of a stream, you may be sure that it was once at the bottom. I went to the bottom. I have always been fond of diving into Queer Street for my amusement, and I found my knowledge of that locality and its inhabitants very useful. It is, perhaps, needless to say that my friends had never heard the name of Beaumont, and as I had never seen the lady, and was quite unable to describe her, I had to set to work in an indirect way. The people there know me; I have been able to do some of them a service now and again, so they made no difficulty about giving their information; they were aware I had no commu- nication direct or indirect with Scotland Yard. I had to cast out a good many lines, though, before I got what I wanted, and when I landed the fish I did not for a moment suppose it was my fish. But I listened to what I was told out of a constitutional liking for useless information, and I found myself in possession of a very curious story, though, as I imagined, not the story I was looking for. It was to this effect. Some five or six years ago, a woman named Raymond suddenly made her appearance in the neighborhood to which I am referring. She was described to me as being quite young, probably not more than seventeen or eighteen, very handsome, and looking as if she came from the country. I should be wrong in saying that she found her level in going to this particular quarter, or associating with these people, for from what I was told, I should think the worst den in London far too good for her. The person from whom I got my information, as you may suppose, no great Puritan, shuddered and grew sick in telling me of the nameless infamies which were laid to her charge. After living there for a year, or perhaps a little more, she disappeared as suddenly as she came, and they saw nothing of her till about the time of the Paul Street case. At first she came to her old haunts only occasionally, then more frequently, and finally took up her abode there as before, and remained for six or eight months. It's of no use my going into details as to the life that woman led; if you want particulars you can look at Meyrick's legacy. Those designs were not drawn from his imag- ination. She again disappeared, and the people of the place saw nothing of her till a few months ago. My informant told me that she had taken some rooms in a house which he pointed out, and these rooms she was in the habit of visiting two or three times a week and always at ten in the morning. I was led to expect that one of these visits would be paid on a certain day about a week ago, and I accordingly managed to be on the look-out in company with my cicerone at a quarter to ten, and the hour and the lady came with equal punctuality. My friend and I were standing under an archway, a little way back from the street, but she saw us, and gave me a glance that I shall be long in forgetting. That look was quite enough for me; I knew Miss Raymond to be Mrs. Herbert; as for Mrs. Beaumont she had quite gone out of my head. She went into the house, and I watched it till four o'clock, when she came out, and then I followed her. It was a long chase, and I had to be very careful to keep a long way in the background, and yet not lose sight of the woman. She took me down to the Strand, and then to Westminster, and then up St. James's Street, and along Piccadilly. I felt queerish when I saw her turn up Ashley Street; the thought that Mrs. Herbert was Mrs. Beaumont came into my mind, but it seemed too impossible to be true. I waited at the corner, keeping my eye on her all the time, and I took particular care to note the house at which she stopped. It was the house with the gay curtains, the home of flowers, the house out of which Crashaw came the night he hanged himself in his garden. I was just going away with my discovery, when I saw an empty carriage come round and draw up in front of the house, and I came to the conclusion that Mrs. Herbert was going out for a drive, and I was right. There, as it happened, I met a man I know, and we stood talking together a little distance from the carriage-way, to which I had my back. We had not been there for ten minutes when my friend took off his hat, and I glanced round and saw the lady I had been following all day. 'Who is that?' I said, and his answer was 'Mrs. Beaumont; lives in Ashley Street.' Of course there could be no doubt after that. I don't know whether she saw me, but I don't think she did. I went home at once, and, on consideration, I thought that I had a sufficiently good case with which to go to Clarke."

"Why to Clarke?"

"Because I am sure that Clarke is in possession of facts about this woman, facts of which I know nothing."

"Well, what then?"

Mr. Villiers leaned back in his chair and looked reflectively at Austin for a moment before he answered:

"My idea was that Clarke and I should call on Mrs. Beaumont."

"You would never go into such a house as that? No, no, Villiers, you cannot do it. Besides, consider; what result..."

"I will tell you soon. But I was going to say that my information does not end here; it has been completed in an extraordinary manner.

"Look at this neat little packet of manuscript; it is paginated, you see, and I have indulged in the civil coquetry of a ribbon of red tape. It has almost a legal air, hasn't it? Run your eye over it, Austin. It is an account of the entertainment Mrs. Beaumont provided for her choicer guests. The man who wrote this escaped with his life, but I do not think he will live many years. The doctors tell him he must have sustained some severe shock to the nerves."

Austin took the manuscript, but never read it. Opening the neat pages at haphazard his eye was caught by a word and a phrase that followed it; and, sick at heart, with white lips and a cold sweat pouring like water from his temples, he flung the paper down.

"Take it away, Villiers, never speak of this again. Are you made of stone, man? Why, the dread and horror of death itself, the thoughts of the man who stands in the keen morning air on the black platform, bound, the bell tolling in his ears, and waits for the harsh rattle of the bolt, are as nothing compared to this. I will not read it; I should never sleep again."

"Very good. I can fancy what you saw. Yes; it is horrible enough; but after all, it is an old story, an old mystery played in our day, and in dim London streets instead of amidst the vineyards and the olive gardens. We know what happened to those who chanced to meet the Great God Pan, and those who are wise know that all symbols are symbols of something, not of nothing. It was, indeed, an exquisite symbol beneath which men long ago veiled their knowledge of the most awful, most secret forces which lie at the heart of all things; forces before which the souls of men must wither and die and blacken, as their bodies blacken under the electric current. Such forces cannot be named, cannot be spoken, cannot be imagined except under a veil and a symbol, a symbol to the most of us appearing a quaint, poetic fancy, to some a foolish tale. But you and I, at all events, have known something of the terror that may dwell in the secret place of life, manifested under human flesh; that which is without form taking to itself a form. Oh, Austin, how can it be? How is it that the very sunlight does not turn to blackness before this thing, the hard earth melt and boil beneath such a burden?"

Villiers was pacing up and down the room, and the beads of sweat stood out on his forehead. Austin sat silent for a while, but Villiers saw him make a sign upon his breast.

"I say again, Villiers, you will surely never enter such a house as that? You would never pass out alive."

"Yes, Austin, I shall go out alive—I, and Clarke with me."

"What do you mean? You cannot, you would not dare..."

"Wait a moment. The air was very pleasant and fresh this morning; there was a breeze blowing, even through this dull street, and I thought I would take a walk. Piccadilly stretched before me a clear, bright vista, and the sun flashed on the carriages and on the quivering leaves in the park. It was a joyous morning, and men and women looked at the sky and smiled as they went about their work or their pleasure, and the wind blew as blithely as upon the meadows and the scented gorse. But somehow or other I got out of the bustle and the gaiety, and found myself walking slowly along a quiet, dull street, where there seemed to be no sunshine and no air, and where the few foot-passengers loitered as they walked, and hung indecisively about corners and archways. I walked along, hardly knowing where I was going or what I did there, but feeling impelled, as one sometimes is, to explore still

further, with a vague idea of reaching some unknown goal. Thus
I forged up the street, noting the small traffic of the milk-shop,
and wondering at the incongruous medley of penny pipes, black
tobacco, sweets, newspapers, and comic songs which here and
there jostled one another in the short compass of a single window.
I think it was a cold shudder that suddenly passed through me
that first told me that I had found what I wanted. I looked up
from the pavement and stopped before a dusty shop, above which
the lettering had faded, where the red bricks of two hundred years
ago had grimed to black; where the windows had gathered to
themselves the dust of winters innumerable. I saw what I required;
but I think it was five minutes before I had steadied myself and
could walk in and ask for it in a cool voice and with a calm face.
I think there must even then have been a tremor in my words,
for the old man who came out of the back parlor, and fumbled
slowly amongst his goods, looked oddly at me as he tied the parcel.
I paid what he asked, and stood leaning by the counter, with a
strange reluctance to take up my goods and go. I asked about the
business, and learnt that trade was bad and the profits cut down
sadly; but then the street was not what it was before traffic had
been diverted, but that was done forty years ago, 'just before my
father died,' he said. I got away at last, and walked along sharply;
it was a dismal street indeed, and I was glad to return to the bustle
and the noise. Would you like to see my purchase?"

Austin said nothing, but nodded his head slightly; he still
looked white and sick. Villiers pulled out a drawer in the bamboo
table, and showed Austin a long coil of cord, hard and new; and
at one end was a running noose.

"It is the best hempen cord," said Villiers, "just as it used to
be made for the old trade, the man told me. Not an inch of jute
from end to end."

Austin set his teeth hard, and stared at Villiers, growing whiter
as he looked.

"You would not do it," he murmured at last. "You would not
have blood on your hands. My God!" he exclaimed, with sudden

vehemence, "you cannot mean this, Villiers, that you will make yourself a hangman?"

"No. I shall offer a choice, and leave Helen Vaughan alone with this cord in a locked room for fifteen minutes. If when we go in it is not done, I shall call the nearest policeman. That is all."

"I must go now. I cannot stay here any longer; I cannot bear this. Good-night."

"Good-night, Austin."

The door shut, but in a moment it was open again, and Austin stood, white and ghastly, in the entrance.

"I was forgetting," he said, "that I too have something to tell. I have received a letter from Dr. Harding of Buenos Ayres. He says that he attended Meyrick for three weeks before his death."

"And does he say what carried him off in the prime of life? It was not fever?"

"No, it was not fever. According to the doctor, it was an utter collapse of the whole system, probably caused by some severe shock. But he states that the patient would tell him nothing, and that he was consequently at some disadvantage in treating the case."

"Is there anything more?"

"Yes. Dr. Harding ends his letter by saying: 'I think this is all the information I can give you about your poor friend. He had not been long in Buenos Ayres, and knew scarcely any one, with the exception of a person who did not bear the best of characters, and has since left—a Mrs. Vaughan.'"

VIII

THE FRAGMENTS

[Amongst the papers of the well-known physician, Dr. Robert Matheson, of Ashley Street, Piccadilly, who died suddenly, of apoplectic seizure, at the beginning of 1892, a leaf of manuscript paper was found, covered with pencil jottings. These notes were in Latin, much abbreviated, and had evidently been made in great haste. The MS. was only deciphered with difficulty, and some words have up to the present time evaded all the efforts of the expert employed. The date, "XXV Jul. 1888," is written on the right-hand corner of the MS. The following is a translation of Dr. Matheson's manuscript.]

"Whether science would benefit by these brief notes if they could be published, I do not know, but rather doubt. But certainly I shall never take the responsibility of publishing or divulging one word of what is here written, not only on account of my oath given freely to those two persons who were present, but also because the details are too abominable. It is probably that, upon mature consideration, and after weighting the good and evil, I shall one day destroy this paper, or at least leave it under seal to my friend D., trusting in his discretion, to use it or to burn it, as he may think fit.

"As was befitting, I did all that my knowledge suggested to make sure that I was suffering under no delusion. At first astounded, I could hardly think, but in a minute's time I was sure that my pulse was steady and regular, and that I was in my real and true senses. I then fixed my eyes quietly on what was before me.

"Though horror and revolting nausea rose up within me, and an odor of corruption choked my breath, I remained firm. I was then privileged or accursed, I dare not say which, to see that which was on the bed, lying there black like ink, transformed before my eyes. The skin, and the flesh, and the muscles, and the bones, and the firm structure of the human body that I had thought to be unchangeable, and permanent as adamant, began to melt and dissolve.

"I know that the body may be separated into its elements by external agencies, but I should have refused to believe what I saw. For here there was some internal force, of which I knew nothing, that caused dissolution and change.

"Here too was all the work by which man had been made repeated before my eyes. I saw the form waver from sex to sex, dividing itself from itself, and then again reunited. Then I saw the body descend to the beasts whence it ascended, and that which was on the heights go down to the depths, even to the abyss of all being. The principle of life, which makes organism, always remained, while the outward form changed.

"The light within the room had turned to blackness, not the darkness of night, in which objects are seen dimly, for I could see clearly and without difficulty. But it was the negation of light; objects were presented to my eyes, if I may say so, without any medium, in such a manner that if there had been a prism in the room I should have seen no colors represented in it.

"I watched, and at last I saw nothing but a substance as jelly. Then the ladder was ascended again... [here the MS. is illegible]...for one instance I saw a Form, shaped in dimness before me, which I will not farther describe. But the symbol of this form may be seen in ancient sculptures, and in paintings which survived beneath the lava, too foul to be spoken of... as a horrible and unspeakable shape, neither man nor beast, was changed into human form, there came finally death.

"I who saw all this, not without great horror and loathing of soul, here write my name, declaring all that I have set on this paper to be true.

"ROBERT MATHESON, Med. Dr."

...Such, Raymond, is the story of what I know and what I have seen. The burden of it was too heavy for me to bear alone, and yet I could tell it to none but you. Villiers, who was with me at the last, knows nothing of that awful secret of the wood, of how what we both saw die, lay upon the smooth, sweet turf amidst the summer flowers, half in sun and half in shadow, and holding the girl Rachel's hand, called and summoned those companions, and shaped in solid form, upon the earth we tread upon, the horror which we can but hint at, which we can only name under a figure. I would not tell Villiers of this, nor of that resemblance, which struck me as with a blow upon my heart, when I saw the portrait, which filled the cup of terror at the end. What this can mean I dare not guess. I know that what I saw perish was not Mary, and yet in the last agony Mary's eyes looked into mine. Whether there can be any one who can show the last link in this chain of awful mystery, I do not know, but if there be any one who can do this, you, Raymond, are the man. And if you know the secret, it rests with you to tell it or not, as you please.

I am writing this letter to you immediately on my getting back to town. I have been in the country for the last few days; perhaps you may be able to guess in which part. While the horror and wonder of London was at its height—for "Mrs. Beaumont," as I have told you, was well known in society—I wrote to my friend Dr. Phillips, giving some brief outline, or rather hint, of what happened, and asking him to tell me the name of the village where the events he had related to me occurred. He gave me the name, as he said with the less hesitation, because Rachel's father and mother were dead, and the rest of the family had gone to a relative in the State of Washington six months before. The parents, he said, had undoubtedly died of grief and horror caused by the terrible death of their daughter, and by what had gone before that death. On the evening of the day which I received Phillips' letter I was at Caermaen, and standing beneath the mouldering Roman walls, white with the winters of seventeen hundred years, I looked over the meadow where once had stood the older temple of the "God of the Deeps," and saw a house gleaming in the sunlight. It was the house where Helen had lived. I stayed at Caermaen for several days. The people of the place, I found, knew little and had guessed less. Those whom I spoke to on the matter seemed surprised that an antiquarian (as I professed myself to be) should trouble about a village tragedy, of which they gave a very commonplace version, and, as you may imagine, I told nothing of what I knew. Most of my time was spent in the great wood that rises just above the village and climbs the hillside, and goes down to the river in the valley; such another long lovely valley, Raymond, as that on which we looked one summer night, walking to and fro before your house. For many an hour I strayed through the maze of the forest, turning now to right and now to left, pacing slowly down long alleys of undergrowth, shadowy and chill, even under the midday sun, and halting beneath great oaks; lying on the short turf of a clearing where the faint sweet scent of wild roses came to me on the wind and mixed with the heavy perfume of the elder, whose mingled odor is like the odor of the room of the dead, a vapor of incense and corruption. I stood at the edges of the wood, gazing at all the pomp and procession of the foxgloves towering amidst the bracken and shining red in the broad sunshine, and beyond them into deep thickets of close under-growth where springs boil up from the rock and nourish the water-weeds, dank and evil. But in all my wanderings I avoided one part of the wood; it was not till yesterday that I climbed to the summit of the hill, and stood upon the ancient Roman road that threads the highest ridge of the wood. Here they had walked, Helen and Rachel, along this quiet causeway, upon the pavement of green turf, shut in on either side by high banks of red earth, and tall hedges of shining beech, and here I followed in their steps, looking out, now and again, through partings in the boughs, and seeing on one side the sweep of the wood stretching far to right and left, and sinking into the broad level, and beyond, the yellow sea, and the land over the sea. On the other side was the valley and the river and hill following hill as wave on wave, and wood and meadow, and cornfield, and white houses gleaming, and a great wall of mountain, and far blue peaks in the north. And so at last I came to the place. The track went up a gentle slope, and widened out into an open space with a wall of thick undergrowth around it, and then, narrowing again, passed on into the distance and the faint blue mist of summer heat. And into this pleasant summer glade Rachel passed a girl, and left it, who shall say what? I did not stay long there.

In a small town near Caermaen there is a museum, containing for the most part Roman remains which have been found in the neighborhood at various times. On the day after my arrival in Caermaen I walked over to the town in question, and took the opportunity of inspecting the museum. After I had seen most of the sculptured stones, the coffins, rings, coins, and fragments of tessellated pavement which the place contains, I was shown a small square pillar of white stone, which had been recently discovered in the wood of which I have been speaking, and, as I found on inquiry, in that open space where the Roman road broadens out. On one side of the pillar was an inscription, of which I took a note. Some of the letters have been defaced, but I do not think there can be any doubt as to those which I supply. The inscription is as follows:

> DEVOMNODENT—i—
> FLA—v—IVSSENILISPOSSV—it—
> PROPTERNVP—tia
> —qua—SVIDITSVBVMB—ra—

"To the great god Nodens (the god of the Great Deep or Abyss) Flavius Senilis has erected this pillar on account of the marriage which he saw beneath the shade."

The custodian of the museum informed me that local antiquaries were much puzzled, not by the inscription, or by any difficulty in translating it, but as to the circumstance or rite to which allusion is made.

...And now, my dear Clarke, as to what you tell me about Helen Vaughan, whom you say you saw die under circumstances of the utmost and almost incredible horror. I was interested in your account, but a good deal, nay all, of what you told me I knew already. I can understand the strange likeness you remarked in both the portrait and in the actual face; you have seen Helen's mother. You remember that still summer night so many years ago, when I talked to you of the world beyond the shadows, and of the god Pan. You remember Mary. She was the mother of Helen Vaughan, who was born nine months after that night.

Mary never recovered her reason. She lay, as you saw her, all the while upon her bed, and a few days after the child was born she died. I fancy that just at the last she knew me; I was standing by the bed, and the old look came into her eyes for a second, and then she shuddered and groaned and died. It was an ill work I did that night when you were present; I broke open the door of the house of life, without knowing or caring what might pass forth or enter in. I recollect your telling me at the time, sharply enough, and rightly too, in one sense, that I had ruined the reason of a human being by a foolish experiment, based on an absurd theory. You did well to blame me, but my theory was not all absurdity. What I said Mary would see she saw, but I forgot that no human eyes can look on such a sight with impunity. And I forgot, as I have just said, that when the house of life is thus thrown open, there may enter in that for which we have no name, and human flesh may become the veil of a horror one dare not express. I played with energies which I did not understand, you have seen the ending of it. Helen Vaughan did well to bind the cord about her neck and die, though the death was horrible. The blackened face, the hideous form upon the bed, changing and melting before your eyes from woman to man, from man to beast, and from beast to worse than beast, all the strange horror that you witness, surprises me but little. What you say the doctor whom you sent for saw and shuddered at I noticed long ago; I knew what I had done the moment the child was born, and when it was scarcely five years old I surprised it, not once or twice but several times with a playmate, you may guess of what kind. It was for me a constant, an incarnate horror, and after a few years I felt I could bear it no more, and I sent Helen Vaughan away. You know now what frightened the boy in the wood. The rest of the strange story, and all else that you tell me, as discovered by your friend, I have contrived to learn from time to time, almost to the last chapter. And now Helen is with her companions...

THE WHITE PEOPLE

Prologue

"Sorcery and sanctity," said Ambrose, "these are the only realities. Each is an ecstasy, a withdrawal from the common life."

Cotgrave listened, interested. He had been brought by a friend to this mouldering house in a northern suburb, through an old garden to the room where Ambrose the recluse dozed and dreamed over his books.

"Yes," he went on, "magic is justified of her children. There are many, I think, who eat dry crusts and drink water, with a joy infinitely sharper than anything within the experience of the 'practical' epicure."

"You are speaking of the saints?"

"Yes, and of the sinners, too. I think you are falling into the very general error of confining the spiritual world to the supremely good; but the supremely wicked, necessarily, have their portion in it. The merely carnal, sensual man can no more be a great sinner than he can be a great saint. Most of us are just indifferent, mixed-up creatures; we muddle through the world without realizing the meaning and the inner sense of things, and, consequently, our wickedness and our goodness are alike second-rate, unimportant."

"And you think the great sinner, then, will be an ascetic, as well as the great saint?"

"Great people of all kinds forsake the imperfect copies and go to the perfect originals. I have no doubt but that many of the very highest among the saints have never done a 'good action' (using the words in their ordinary sense). And, on the other hand, there have been those who have sounded the very depths of sin, who all their lives have never done an 'ill deed.'"

He went out of the room for a moment, and Cotgrave, in high delight, turned to his friend and thanked him for the introduction.

"He's grand," he said. "I never saw that kind of lunatic before."

Ambrose returned with more whisky and helped the two men in a liberal manner. He abused the teetotal sect with ferocity, as he handed the seltzer, and pouring out a glass of water for himself, was about to resume his monologue, when Cotgrave broke in—

"I can't stand it, you know," he said, "your paradoxes are too monstrous. A man may be a great sinner and yet never do anything sinful! Come!"

"You're quite wrong," said Ambrose. "I never make paradoxes; I wish I could. I merely said that a man may have an exquisite taste in Romanée Conti, and yet never have even smelt four ale. That's all, and it's more like a truism than a paradox, isn't it? Your surprise at my remark is due to the fact that you haven't realized what sin is. Oh, yes, there is a sort of connexion between Sin with the capital letter, and actions which are commonly called sinful: with murder, theft, adultery, and so forth. Much the same connexion that there is between the A, B, C and fine literature. But I believe that the misconception—it is all but universal—arises in great measure from our looking at the matter through social spectacles. We think that a man who does evil to us and to his neighbors must be very evil. So he is, from a social standpoint; but can't you realize that Evil in its essence is a lonely thing, a passion of the solitary, individual soul? Really, the average murderer, quâ murderer, is not by any means a sinner in the true sense of the word. He is simply a wild beast that we have to get rid of to save our own necks from his knife. I should class him rather with tigers than with sinners."

"It seems a little strange."

"I think not. The murderer murders not from positive qualities, but from negative ones; he lacks something which non-murderers possess. Evil, of course, is wholly positive—only it is on the wrong side. You may believe me that sin in its proper sense is very rare; it is probable that there have been far fewer sinners than saints. Yes, your standpoint is all very well for practical, social purposes; we are naturally inclined to think that a person who is very disagreeable to us must be a very great sinner! It is very disagreeable to have one's pocket picked, and we pronounce the thief to be a very great sinner. In truth, he is merely an undeveloped man. He cannot be a saint, of course; but he may be, and often is, an infinitely better creature than thousands who have never broken a single commandment. He is a great nuisance to us, I admit, and we very properly lock him up if we catch him; but between his troublesome and unsocial action and evil— Oh, the connexion is of the weakest."

It was getting very late. The man who had brought Cotgrave had probably heard all this before, since he assisted with a bland and judicious smile, but Cotgrave began to think that his "lunatic" was turning into a sage.

"Do you know," he said, "you interest me immensely? You think, then, that we do not understand the real nature of evil?"

"No, I don't think we do. We over-estimate it and we under-estimate it. We take the very numerous infractions of our social 'bye-laws'—the very necessary and very proper regulations which keep the human company together—and we get frightened at the prevalence of 'sin' and 'evil.' But this is really nonsense. Take theft, for example. Have you any horror at the thought of Robin Hood, of the Highland caterans of the seventeenth century, of the moss-troopers, of the company promoters of our day?

"Then, on the other hand, we underrate evil. We attach such an enormous importance to the 'sin' of meddling with our pockets (and our wives) that we have quite forgotten the awfulness of real sin."

"And what is sin?" said Cotgrave.

"I think I must reply to your question by another. What would your feelings be, seriously, if your cat or your dog began to talk to you, and to dispute with you in human accents? You would be overwhelmed with horror. I am sure of it. And if the roses in your garden sang a weird song, you would go mad. And suppose the stones in the road began to swell and grow before your eyes, and if the pebble that you noticed at night had shot out stony blossoms in the morning?

"Well, these examples may give you some notion of what sin really is."

"Look here," said the third man, hitherto placid, "you two seem pretty well wound up. But I'm going home. I've missed my tram, and I shall have to walk."

Ambrose and Cotgrave seemed to settle down more profoundly when the other had gone out into the early misty morning and the pale light of the lamps.

"You astonish me," said Cotgrave. "I had never thought of that. If that is really so, one must turn everything upside down. Then the essence of sin really is—"

"In the taking of heaven by storm, it seems to me," said Ambrose. "It appears to me that it is simply an attempt to penetrate into another and higher sphere in a forbidden manner. You can understand why it is so rare. There are few, indeed, who wish to penetrate into other spheres, higher or lower, in ways allowed or forbidden. Men, in the mass, are amply content with life as they find it. Therefore there are few saints, and sinners (in the proper sense) are fewer still, and men of genius, who partake sometimes of each character, are rare also. Yes; on the whole, it is, perhaps, harder to be a great sinner than a great saint."

"There is something profoundly unnatural about Sin? Is that what you mean?"

"Exactly. Holiness requires as great, or almost as great, an effort; but holiness works on lines that were natural once; it is an effort to recover the ecstasy that was before the Fall. But sin is an effort to gain the ecstasy and the knowledge that pertain alone to angels and in making this effort man becomes a demon. I told you that the mere murderer is not therefore a sinner; that is true, but the sinner is sometimes a murderer. Gilles de Raiz is an instance. So you see that while the good and the evil are unnatural to man as he now is—to man the social, civilized being—evil is unnatural in a much deeper sense than good. The saint endeavors to recover a gift which he has lost; the sinner tries to obtain something which was never his. In brief, he repeats the Fall."

"But are you a Catholic?" said Cotgrave.

"Yes; I am a member of the persecuted Anglican Church."

"Then, how about those texts which seem to reckon as sin that which you would set down as a mere trivial dereliction?"

"Yes; but in one place the word 'sorcerers' comes in the same sentence, doesn't it? That seems to me to give the key-note. Consider: can you imagine for a moment that a false statement which saves an innocent man's life is a sin? No; very good, then, it is not the mere liar who is excluded by those words; it is, above all, the 'sorcerers' who use the material life, who use the failings incidental to material life as instruments to obtain their infinitely wicked ends. And let me tell you this: our higher senses are so blunted, we are so drenched with materialism, that we should probably fail to recognize real wickedness if we encountered it."

"But shouldn't we experience a certain horror—a terror such as you hinted we would experience if a rose tree sang—in the mere presence of an evil man?"

"We should if we were natural: children and women feel this horror you speak of, even animals experience it. But with most of us convention and civilization and education have blinded and deafened and obscured the natural reason. No, sometimes we may recognize evil by its hatred of the good—one doesn't need much penetration to guess at the influence which dictated, quite unconsciously, the 'Blackwood' review of Keats—but this is purely incidental; and, as a rule, I suspect that the Hierarchs of Tophet pass quite unnoticed, or, perhaps, in certain cases, as good but mistaken men."

"But you used the word 'unconscious' just now, of Keats' reviewers. Is wickedness ever unconscious?"

"Always. It must be so. It is like holiness and genius in this as in other points; it is a certain rapture or ecstasy of the soul; a transcendent effort to surpass the ordinary bounds. So, surpassing these, it surpasses also the understanding, the faculty that takes note of that which comes before it. No, a man may be infinitely and horribly wicked and never suspect it. But I tell you, evil in this, its certain and true sense, is rare, and I think it is growing rarer."

"I am trying to get hold of it all," said Cotgrave. "From what you say, I gather that the true evil differs generically from that which we call evil?"

"Quite so. There is, no doubt, an analogy between the two; a resemblance such as enables us to use, quite legitimately, such terms as the 'foot of the mountain' and the 'leg of the table.' And, sometimes, of course, the two speak, as it were, in the same language. The rough miner, or 'puddler,' the untrained, undeveloped 'tiger-man,' heated by a quart or two above his usual measure, comes home and kicks his irritating and injudicious wife to death. He is a murderer. And Gilles de Raiz was a murderer. But you see the gulf that separates the two? The 'word,' if I may so speak, is accidentally the same in each case, but the 'meaning' is utterly different. It is flagrant 'Hobson Jobson' to confuse the two, or rather, it is as if one supposed that Juggernaut and the Argonauts had something to do etymologically with one another. And no doubt the same weak likeness, or analogy, runs between all the 'social' sins and the real spiritual sins, and in some cases, perhaps, the lesser may be 'schoolmasters' to lead one on to the greater— from the shadow to the reality. If you are anything of a Theologian, you will see the importance of all this."

"I am sorry to say," remarked Cotgrave, "that I have devoted very little of my time to theology. Indeed, I have often wondered on what grounds theologians have claimed the title of Science of Sciences for their favorite study; since the 'theological' books I have looked into have always seemed to me to be concerned with feeble and obvious pieties, or with the kings of Israel and Judah. I do not care to hear about those kings."

Ambrose grinned.

"We must try to avoid theological discussion," he said. "I perceive that you would be a bitter disputant. But perhaps the 'dates of the kings' have as much to do with theology as the hobnails of the murderous puddler with evil."

"Then, to return to our main subject, you think that sin is an esoteric, occult thing?"

"Yes. It is the infernal miracle as holiness is the supernal. Now and then it is raised to such a pitch that we entirely fail to suspect its existence; it is like the note of the great pedal pipes of the organ, which is so deep that we cannot hear it. In other cases it may lead to the lunatic asylum, or to still stranger issues. But you must never confuse it with mere social misdoing. Remember how the Apostle, speaking of the 'other side,' distinguishes between 'charitable' actions and charity. And as one may give all one's goods to the poor, and yet lack charity; so, remember, one may avoid every crime and yet be a sinner."

"Your psychology is very strange to me," said Cotgrave, "but I confess I like it, and I suppose that one might fairly deduce from your premisses the conclusion that the real sinner might very possibly strike the observer as a harmless personage enough?"

"Certainly, because the true evil has nothing to do with social life or social laws, or if it has, only incidentally and accidentally. It is a lonely passion of the soul—or a passion of the lonely soul—whichever you like. If, by chance, we understand it, and grasp its full significance, then, indeed, it will fill us with horror and with awe. But this emotion is widely distinguished from the fear and the disgust with which we regard the ordinary criminal, since this latter is largely or entirely founded on the regard which we have for our own skins or purses. We hate a murder, because we know that we should hate to be murdered, or to have any one that we like murdered. So, on the 'other side,' we venerate the saints, but we don't 'like' them as well as our friends. Can you persuade yourself that you would have 'enjoyed' St. Paul's company? Do you think that you and I would have 'got on' with Sir Galahad?

"So with the sinners, as with the saints. If you met a very evil man, and recognized his evil; he would, no doubt, fill you with horror and awe; but there is no reason why you should 'dislike' him. On the contrary, it is quite possible that if you could succeed in putting the sin out of your mind you might find the sinner capital company, and in a little while you might have to reason yourself back into horror. Still, how awful it is. If the roses and the lilies suddenly sang on this coming morning; if the furniture began to move in procession, as in De Maupassant's tale!"

"I am glad you have come back to that comparison," said Cotgrave, "because I wanted to ask you what it is that corresponds in humanity to these imaginary feats of inanimate things. In a word—what is sin? You have given me, I know, an abstract definition, but I should like a concrete example."

"I told you it was very rare," said Ambrose, who appeared willing to avoid the giving of a direct answer. "The materialism of the age, which has done a good deal to suppress sanctity, has done perhaps more to suppress evil. We find the earth so very comfortable that we have no inclination either for ascents or descents. It would seem as if the scholar who decided to 'specialize' in Tophet, would be reduced to purely antiquarian researches. No palæontologist could show you a live pterodactyl."

"And yet you, I think, have 'specialized,' and I believe that your researches have descended to our modern times."

"You are really interested, I see. Well, I confess, that I have dabbled a little, and if you like I can show you something that bears on the very curious subject we have been discussing."

Ambrose took a candle and went away to a far, dim corner of the room. Cotgrave saw him open a venerable bureau that stood there, and from some secret recess he drew out a parcel, and came back to the window where they had been sitting.

Ambrose undid a wrapping of paper, and produced a green pocket-book.

"You will take care of it?" he said. "Don't leave it lying about. It is one of the choicer pieces in my collection, and I should be very sorry if it were lost."

He fondled the faded binding.

"I knew the girl who wrote this," he said. "When you read it, you will see how it illustrates the talk we have had tonight. There is a sequel, too, but I won't talk of that.

"There was an odd article in one of the reviews some months ago," he began again, with the air of a man who changes the subject. "It was written by a doctor—Dr. Coryn, I think, was the name. He says that a lady, watching her little girl playing at the drawing-room window, suddenly saw the heavy sash give way and fall on the child's fingers. The lady fainted, I think, but at any rate the doctor was summoned, and when he had dressed the child's wounded and maimed fingers he was summoned to the mother. She was groaning with pain, and it was found that three fingers of her hand, corresponding with those that had been injured on the child's hand, were swollen and inflamed, and later, in the doctor's language, purulent sloughing set in."

Ambrose still handled delicately the green volume.

"Well, here it is," he said at last, parting with difficulty, it seemed, from his treasure.

"You will bring it back as soon as you have read it," he said, as they went out into the hall, into the old garden, faint with the odor of white lilies.

There was a broad red band in the east as Cotgrave turned to go, and from the high ground where he stood he saw that awful spectacle of London in a dream.

The Green Book

The morocco binding of the book was faded, and the color had grown faint, but there were no stains nor bruises nor marks of usage. The book looked as if it had been bought "on a visit to London" some seventy or eighty years ago, and had somehow been forgotten and suffered to lie away out of sight. There was an old, delicate, lingering odor about it, such an odor as sometimes haunts an ancient piece of furniture for a century or more. The end-papers, inside the binding, were oddly decorated with colored patterns and faded gold. It looked small, but the paper was fine, and there were many leaves, closely covered with minute, painfully formed characters.

I found this book (the manuscript began) in a drawer in the old bureau that stands on the landing. It was a very rainy day and I could not go out, so in the afternoon I got a candle and rummaged in the bureau. Nearly all the drawers were full of old dresses, but one of the small ones looked empty, and I found this book hidden right at the back. I wanted a book like this, so I took it to write in. It is full of secrets. I have a great many other books of secrets I have written, hidden in a safe place, and I am going to write here many of the old secrets and some new ones; but there are some I shall not put down at all. I must not write down the real names of the days and months which I found out a year ago, nor the way to make the Aklo letters, or the Chian language, or the great beautiful Circles, nor the Mao Games, nor the chief songs. I may write something about all these things but not the way to do them, for peculiar reasons. And I must not say who the Nymphs are, or the Dôls, or Jeelo, or what voolas mean. All these are most secret secrets, and I am glad when I remember what they are, and how many wonderful languages I know, but there are some things that I call the secrets of the secrets of the secrets that I dare not think of unless I am quite alone, and then I shut my eyes, and put my hands over them and whisper the word, and the Alala comes. I only do this at night in my room or in certain woods that I know, but I must not describe them, as they are secret woods. Then there are the Ceremonies, which are all of them important, but some are more delightful than others—there are the White Ceremonies, and the Green Ceremonies, and the Scarlet Ceremonies. The Scarlet Ceremonies are the best, but there is only one place where they can be performed properly, though there is a very nice imitation which I have done in other places. Besides these, I have the dances, and the Comedy, and I have done the Comedy sometimes when the others were looking, and they didn't understand anything about it. I was very little when I first knew about these things.

When I was very small, and mother was alive, I can remember remembering things before that, only it has all got confused. But I remember when I was five or six I heard them talking about me when they thought I was not noticing. They were saying how queer I was a year or two before, and how nurse had called my mother to come and listen to me talking all to myself, and I was saying words that nobody could understand. I was speaking the Xu language, but I only remember a very few of the words, as it was about the little white faces that used to look at me when I was lying in my cradle. They used to talk to me, and I learnt their language and talked to them in it about some great white place where they lived, where the trees and the grass were all white, and there were white hills as high up as the moon, and a cold wind. I have often dreamed of it afterwards, but the faces went away when I was very little. But a wonderful thing happened when I was about five. My nurse was carrying me on her shoulder; there was a field of yellow corn, and we went through it, it was very hot. Then we came to a path through a wood, and a tall man came after us, and went with us till we came to a place where there was a deep pool, and it was very dark and shady. Nurse put me down on the soft moss under a tree, and she said: "She can't get to the pond now." So they left me there, and I sat quite still and watched, and out of the water and out of the wood came two wonderful white people, and they began to play and dance and sing. They were a kind of creamy white like the old ivory figure in the drawing-room; one was a beautiful lady with kind dark eyes, and a grave face, and long black hair, and she smiled such a strange sad smile at the other, who laughed and came to her. They played together, and danced round and round the pool, and they sang a song till I fell asleep. Nurse woke me up when she came back, and she was looking something like the lady had looked, so I told her all about it, and asked her why she looked like that. At first she cried, and then she looked very frightened, and turned quite pale. She put me down on the grass and stared at me, and I could see she was shaking all over. Then she said I

had been dreaming, but I knew I hadn't. Then she made me
promise not to say a word about it to anybody, and if I did I should
be thrown into the black pit. I was not frightened at all, though
nurse was, and I never forgot about it, because when I shut my
eyes and it was quite quiet, and I was all alone, I could see them
again, very faint and far away, but very splendid; and little bits of
the song they sang came into my head, but I couldn't sing it.

I was thirteen, nearly fourteen, when I had a very singular
adventure, so strange that the day on which it happened is always
called the White Day. My mother had been dead for more than a
year, and in the morning I had lessons, but they let me go out for
walks in the afternoon. And this afternoon I walked a new way,
and a little brook led me into a new country, but I tore my frock
getting through some of the difficult places, as the way was through
many bushes, and beneath the low branches of trees, and up thorny
thickets on the hills, and by dark woods full of creeping thorns.
And it was a long, long way. It seemed as if I was going on for ever
and ever, and I had to creep by a place like a tunnel where a brook
must have been, but all the water had dried up, and the floor was
rocky, and the bushes had grown overhead till they met, so that it
was quite dark. And I went on and on through that dark place; it
was a long, long way. And I came to a hill that I never saw before.
I was in a dismal thicket full of black twisted boughs that tore me
as I went through them, and I cried out because I was smarting
all over, and then I found that I was climbing, and I went up and
up a long way, till at last the thicket stopped and I came out crying
just under the top of a big bare place, where there were ugly grey
stones lying all about on the grass, and here and there a little
twisted, stunted tree came out from under a stone, like a snake.
And I went up, right to the top, a long way. I never saw such big
ugly stones before; they came out of the earth some of them, and
some looked as if they had been rolled to where they were, and
they went on and on as far as I could see, a long, long way. I looked
out from them and saw the country, but it was strange. It was
winter time, and there were black terrible woods hanging from

the hills all round; it was like seeing a large room hung with black curtains, and the shape of the trees seemed quite different from any I had ever seen before. I was afraid. Then beyond the woods there were other hills round in a great ring, but I had never seen any of them; it all looked black, and everything had a voor over it. It was all so still and silent, and the sky was heavy and grey and sad, like a wicked voorish dome in Deep Dendo. I went on into the dreadful rocks. There were hundreds and hundreds of them. Some were like horrid-grinning men; I could see their faces as if they would jump at me out of the stone, and catch hold of me, and drag me with them back into the rock, so that I should always be there. And there were other rocks that were like animals, creeping, horrible animals, putting out their tongues, and others were like words that I could not say, and others like dead people lying on the grass. I went on among them, though they frightened me, and my heart was full of wicked songs that they put into it; and I wanted to make faces and twist myself about in the way they did, and I went on and on a long way till at last I liked the rocks, and they didn't frighten me any more. I sang the songs I thought of; songs full of words that must not be spoken or written down. Then I made faces like the faces on the rocks, and I twisted myself about like the twisted ones, and I lay down flat on the ground like the dead ones, and I went up to one that was grinning, and put my arms round him and hugged him. And so I went on and on through the rocks till I came to a round mound in the middle of them. It was higher than a mound, it was nearly as high as our house, and it was like a great basin turned upside down, all smooth and round and green, with one stone, like a post, sticking up at the top. I climbed up the sides, but they were so steep I had to stop or I should have rolled all the way down again, and I should have knocked against the stones at the bottom, and perhaps been killed. But I wanted to get up to the very top of the big round mound, so I lay down flat on my face, and took hold of the grass with my hands and drew myself up, bit by bit, till I was at the top. Then I sat down on the stone in the middle, and looked all round about. I felt I had come such a long, long way, just as if I were a hundred miles from home, or in some other country, or in one of the strange places I had read about in the *Tales of the Genie* and the *Arabian Nights*, or as if I had gone across the sea, far away, for years and I had found another world that nobody had ever seen or heard of before, or as if I had somehow flown through the sky and fallen on one of the stars I had read about where everything is dead and cold and grey, and there is no air, and the wind doesn't blow. I sat on the stone and looked all round and down and round about me. It was just as if I was sitting on a tower in the middle of a great empty town, because I could see nothing all around but the grey rocks on the ground. I couldn't make out their shapes any more, but I could see them on and on for a long way, and I looked at them, and they seemed as if they had been arranged into patterns, and shapes, and figures. I knew they couldn't be, because I had seen a lot of them coming right out of the earth, joined to the deep rocks below, so I looked again, but still I saw nothing but circles, and small circles inside big ones, and pyramids, and domes, and spires, and they seemed all to go round and round the place where I was sitting, and the more I looked, the more I saw great big rings of rocks, getting bigger and bigger, and I stared so long that it felt as if they were all moving and turning, like a great wheel, and I was turning, too, in the middle. I got quite dizzy and queer in the head, and everything began to be hazy and not clear, and I saw little sparks of blue light, and the stones looked as if they were springing and dancing and twisting as they went round and round and round. I was frightened again, and I cried out loud, and jumped up from the stone I was sitting on, and fell down. When I got up I was so glad they all looked still, and I sat down on the top and slid down the mound, and went on again. I danced as I went in the peculiar way the rocks had danced when I got giddy, and I was so glad I could do it quite well, and I danced and danced along, and sang extraordinary songs that came into my head. At last I came to the edge of that great flat hill, and there were no more rocks, and the way went again through a dark thicket in a hollow. It was just as bad as the other one I went through climbing up, but I didn't mind this one, because I was so glad I had seen those singular dances and could imitate them. I went down, creeping through the bushes, and a tall nettle stung me on my leg, and made me burn, but I didn't mind it, and I tingled with the boughs and the thorns, but I only laughed and sang. Then I got out of the thicket into a close valley, a little secret place like a dark passage that nobody ever knows of, because it was so narrow and deep and the woods were so thick round it. There is a steep bank with trees hanging over it, and there the ferns keep green all through the winter, when they are dead and brown upon the hill, and the ferns there have a sweet, rich smell like what oozes out of fir trees. There was a little stream of water running down this valley, so small that I could easily step across it. I drank the water with my hand, and it tasted like bright, yellow wine, and it sparkled and bubbled as it ran down over beautiful red and yellow and green stones, so that it seemed alive and all colors at once. I drank it, and I drank more with my hand, but I couldn't drink enough, so I lay down and bent my head and sucked the water up with my lips. It tasted much better, drinking it that way, and a ripple would come up to my mouth and give me a kiss, and I laughed, and drank again, and pretended there was a nymph, like the one in the old picture at home, who lived in the water and was kissing me. So I bent low down to the water, and put my lips softly to it, and whispered to the nymph that I would come again. I felt sure it could not be common water, I was so glad when I got up and went on; and I danced again and went up and up the valley, under hanging hills. And when I came to the top, the ground rose up in front of me, tall and steep as a wall, and there was nothing but the green wall and the sky. I thought of "for ever and for ever, world without end, Amen;" and I thought I must have really found the end of the world, because it was like the end of everything, as if there could be nothing at all beyond, except the kingdom of Voor, where the light goes when it is put out, and the water goes when the sun takes it away. I began to think of all the long, long way I had journeyed, how I had found a brook and followed it, and followed it on, and gone through bushes and thorny thickets, and dark woods full of creeping thorns. Then I had crept up a tunnel under trees, and climbed a thicket, and seen all the grey rocks, and sat in the middle of them when they turned round, and then I had gone on through the grey rocks and come down the hill through the stinging thicket and up the dark valley, all a long, long way. I wondered how I should get home again, if I could ever find the way, and if my home was there any more, or if it were turned and everybody in it into grey rocks, as in the *Arabian Nights*. So I sat down on the grass and thought what I should do next. I was tired, and my feet were hot with walking, and as I looked about I saw there was a wonderful well just under the high, steep wall of grass. All the ground round it was covered with bright, green, dripping moss; there was every kind of moss there, moss like beautiful little ferns, and like palms and fir trees, and it was all green as jewelry, and drops of water hung on it like diamonds. And in the middle was the great well, deep and shining and beautiful, so clear that it looked as if I could touch the red sand at the bottom, but it was far below. I stood by it and looked in, as if I were looking in a glass. At the bottom of the well, in the middle of it, the red grains of sand were moving and stirring all the time, and I saw how the water bubbled up, but at the top it was quite smooth, and full and brimming. It was a great well, large like a bath, and with the shining, glittering green moss about it, it looked like a great white jewel, with green jewels all round. My feet were so hot and tired that I took off my boots and stockings, and let my feet down into the water, and the water was soft and cold, and when I got up I wasn't tired any more, and I felt I must go on, farther and farther, and see what was on the other side of the wall. I climbed up it very slowly, going sideways all the time, and when I got to the top and looked over, I was in the queerest country I had seen, stranger even than the hill of the grey rocks. It looked as if earth-children had been playing there with their spades, as it was all hills and hollows, and castles and walls made of earth and covered with grass. There were two mounds like big beehives, round and great and solemn, and then hollow basins, and then a steep mounting wall like the ones I saw once by the seaside where the big guns and the soldiers were. I nearly fell into one of the round hollows, it went away from under my feet so suddenly, and I ran fast down the side and stood at the bottom and looked up. It was strange and solemn to look up. There was nothing but the grey, heavy sky and the sides of the hollow; everything else had gone away, and the hollow was the whole world, and I thought that at night it must be full of ghosts and moving shadows and pale things when the moon shone down to the bottom at the dead of the night, and the wind wailed up above. It was so strange and solemn and lonely, like a hollow temple of dead heathen gods. It reminded me of a tale my nurse had told me when I was quite little; it was the same nurse that took me into the wood where I saw the beautiful white people. And I remembered how nurse had told me the story one winter night, when the wind was beating the trees against the wall, and crying and moaning in the nursery chimney. She said there was, somewhere or other, a hollow pit, just like the one I was standing in, everybody was afraid to go into it or near it, it was such a bad place. But once upon a time there was a poor girl who said she would go into the hollow pit, and everybody tried to stop her, but she would go. And she went down into the pit and came back laughing, and said there was nothing there at all, except green grass and red stones, and white stones and yellow flowers. And soon after people saw she had most beautiful emerald earrings, and they asked how she got them, as she and her mother were quite poor. But she laughed, and said her earrings were not made of emeralds at all, but only of green grass. Then, one day, she wore on her breast the reddest ruby that any one had ever seen, and it was as big as a hen's egg, and glowed and sparkled like a hot burning coal of fire. And they asked how she got it, as she and her mother were quite poor. But she laughed, and said it was not a ruby at all, but only a red stone. Then one day she wore round her neck the love-liest necklace that any one had ever seen, much finer than the queen's finest, and it was made of great bright diamonds, hundreds of them, and they shone like all the stars on a night in June. So they asked her how she got it, as she and her mother were quite poor. But she laughed, and said they were not diamonds at all, but only white stones. And one day she went to the Court, and she wore on her head a crown of pure angel-gold, so nurse said, and it shone like the sun, and it was much more splendid than the crown the king was wearing himself, and in her ears she wore the emeralds, and the big ruby was the brooch on her breast, and the great diamond necklace was sparkling on her neck. And the king and queen thought she was some great princess from a long way off, and got down from their thrones and went to meet her, but somebody told the king and queen who she was, and that she was quite poor. So the king asked why she wore a gold crown, and how she got it, as she and her mother were so poor. And she laughed, and said it wasn't a gold crown at all, but only some yellow flowers she had put in her hair. And the king thought it was very strange, and said she should stay at the Court, and they would see what would happen next. And she was so lovely that everybody said that her eyes were greener than the emeralds, that her lips were redder than the ruby, that her skin was whiter than the diamonds, and that her hair was brighter than the golden crown. So the king's son said he would marry her, and the king said he might. And the bishop married them, and there was a great supper, and afterwards the king's son went to his wife's room. But just when he had his hand on the door, he saw a tall, black man, with a dreadful face, standing in front of the door, and a voice said—

> *Venture not upon your life,*
> *This is mine own wedded wife.*

Then the king's son fell down on the ground in a fit. And they came and tried to get into the room, but they couldn't, and they hacked at the door with hatchets, but the wood had turned hard as iron, and at last everybody ran away, they were so frightened at

the screaming and laughing and shrieking and crying that came
out of the room. But next day they went in, and found there was
nothing in the room but thick black smoke, because the black man
had come and taken her away. And on the bed there were two
knots of faded grass and a red stone, and some white stones, and
some faded yellow flowers. I remembered this tale of nurse's while
I was standing at the bottom of the deep hollow; it was so strange
and solitary there, and I felt afraid. I could not see any stones or
flowers, but I was afraid of bringing them away without knowing,
and I thought I would do a charm that came into my head to keep
the black man away. So I stood right in the very middle of the
hollow, and I made sure that I had none of those things on me,
and then I walked round the place, and touched my eyes, and my
lips, and my hair in a peculiar manner, and whispered some queer
words that nurse taught me to keep bad things away. Then I felt
safe and climbed up out of the hollow, and went on through all
those mounds and hollows and walls, till I came to the end, which
was high above all the rest, and I could see that all the different
shapes of the earth were arranged in patterns, something like the
grey rocks, only the pattern was different. It was getting late, and
the air was indistinct, but it looked from where I was standing
something like two great figures of people lying on the grass. And
I went on, and at last I found a certain wood, which is too secret
to be described, and nobody knows of the passage into it, which
I found out in a very curious manner, by seeing some little animal
run into the wood through it. So I went after the animal by a very
narrow dark way, under thorns and bushes, and it was almost dark
when I came to a kind of open place in the middle. And there I
saw the most wonderful sight I have ever seen, but it was only for
a minute, as I ran away directly, and crept out of the wood by the
passage I had come by, and ran and ran as fast as ever I could,
because I was afraid, what I had seen was so wonderful and so
strange and beautiful. But I wanted to get home and think of it,
and I did not know what might not happen if I stayed by the
wood. I was hot all over and trembling, and my heart was beating,

and strange cries that I could not help came from me as I ran from the wood. I was glad that a great white moon came up from over a round hill and showed me the way, so I went back through the mounds and hollows and down the close valley, and up through the thicket over the place of the grey rocks, and so at last I got home again. My father was busy in his study, and the servants had not told about my not coming home, though they were frightened, and wondered what they ought to do, so I told them I had lost my way, but I did not let them find out the real way I had been. I went to bed and lay awake all through the night, thinking of what I had seen. When I came out of the narrow way, and it looked all shining, though the air was dark, it seemed so certain, and all the way home I was quite sure that I had seen it, and I wanted to be alone in my room, and be glad over it all to myself, and shut my eyes and pretend it was there, and do all the things I would have done if I had not been so afraid. But when I shut my eyes the sight would not come, and I began to think about my adventures all over again, and I remembered how dusky and queer it was at the end, and I was afraid it must be all a mistake, because it seemed impossible it could happen. It seemed like one of nurse's tales, which I didn't really believe in, though I was frightened at the bottom of the hollow; and the stories she told me when I was little came back into my head, and I wondered whether it was really there what I thought I had seen, or whether any of her tales could have happened a long time ago. It was so queer; I lay awake there in my room at the back of the house, and the moon was shining on the other side towards the river, so the bright light did not fall upon the wall. And the house was quite still. I had heard my father come upstairs, and just after the clock struck twelve, and after the house was still and empty, as if there was nobody alive in it. And though it was all dark and indistinct in my room, a pale glimmering kind of light shone in through the white blind, and once I got up and looked out, and there was a great black shadow of the house covering the garden, looking like a prison where men are hanged; and then beyond it was all white; and the wood shone white with black gulfs between the trees. It was still and clear, and there were no clouds on the sky. I wanted to think of what I had seen but I couldn't, and I began to think of all the tales that nurse had told me so long ago that I thought I had forgotten, but they all came back, and mixed up with the thickets and the grey rocks and the hollows in the earth and the secret wood, till I hardly knew what was new and what was old, or whether it was not all dreaming. And then I remembered that hot summer afternoon, so long ago, when nurse left me by myself in the shade, and the white people came out of the water and out of the wood, and played, and danced, and sang, and I began to fancy that nurse told me about something like it before I saw them, only I couldn't recollect exactly what she told me. Then I wondered whether she had been the white lady, as I remembered she was just as white and beautiful, and had the same dark eyes and black hair; and sometimes she smiled and looked like the lady had looked, when she was telling me some of her stories, beginning with "Once on a time," or "In the time of the fairies." But I thought she couldn't be the lady, as she seemed to have gone a different way into the wood, and I didn't think the man who came after us could be the other, or I couldn't have seen that wonderful secret in the secret wood. I thought of the moon: but it was afterwards when I was in the middle of the wild land, where the earth was made into the shape of great figures, and it was all walls, and mysterious hollows, and smooth round mounds, that I saw the great white moon come up over a round hill. I was wondering about all these things, till at last I got quite frightened, because I was afraid something had happened to me, and I remembered nurse's tale of the poor girl who went into the hollow pit, and was carried away at last by the black man. I knew I had gone into a hollow pit too, and perhaps it was the same, and I had done something dreadful. So I did the charm over again, and touched my eyes and my lips and my hair in a peculiar manner, and said the old words from the fairy language, so that I might be sure I had not been carried away. I tried again to see the secret wood, and to creep up the passage and see what

I had seen there, but somehow I couldn't, and I kept on thinking of nurse's stories. There was one I remembered about a young man who once upon a time went hunting, and all the day he and his hounds hunted everywhere, and they crossed the rivers and went into all the woods, and went round the marshes, but they couldn't find anything at all, and they hunted all day till the sun sank down and began to set behind the mountain. And the young man was angry because he couldn't find anything, and he was going to turn back, when just as the sun touched the mountain, he saw come out of a brake in front of him a beautiful white stag. And he cheered to his hounds, but they whined and would not follow, and he cheered to his horse, but it shivered and stood stock still, and the young man jumped off the horse and left the hounds and began to follow the white stag all alone. And soon it was quite dark, and the sky was black, without a single star shining in it, and the stag went away into the darkness. And though the man had brought his gun with him he never shot at the stag, because he wanted to catch it, and he was afraid he would lose it in the night. But he never lost it once, though the sky was so black and the air was so dark, and the stag went on and on till the young man didn't know a bit where he was. And they went through enormous woods where the air was full of whispers and a pale, dead light came out from the rotten trunks that were lying on the ground, and just as the man thought he had lost the stag, he would see it all white and shining in front of him, and he would run fast to catch it, but the stag always ran faster, so he did not catch it. And they went through the enormous woods, and they swam across rivers, and they waded through black marshes where the ground bubbled, and the air was full of will-o'-the-wisps, and the stag fled away down into rocky narrow valleys, where the air was like the smell of a vault, and the man went after it. And they went over the great mountains and the man heard the wind come down from the sky, and the stag went on and the man went after. At last the sun rose and the young man found he was in a country that he had never seen before; it was a beautiful valley with a bright stream running through it, and a great, big round hill in the middle. And the stag went down the valley, towards the hill, and it seemed to be getting tired and went slower and slower, and though the man was tired, too, he began to run faster, and he was sure he would catch the stag at last. But just as they got to the bottom of the hill, and the man stretched out his hand to catch the stag, it vanished into the earth, and the man began to cry; he was so sorry that he had lost it after all his long hunting. But as he was crying he saw there was a door in the hill, just in front of him, and he went in, and it was quite dark, but he went on, as he thought he would find the white stag. And all of a sudden it got light, and there was the sky, and the sun shining, and birds singing in the trees, and there was a beautiful fountain. And by the fountain a lovely lady was sitting, who was the queen of the fairies, and she told the man that she had changed herself into a stag to bring him there because she loved him so much. Then she brought out a great gold cup, covered with jewels, from her fairy palace, and she offered him wine in the cup to drink. And he drank, and the more he drank the more he longed to drink, because the wine was enchanted. So he kissed the lovely lady, and she became his wife, and he stayed all that day and all that night in the hill where she lived, and when he woke he found he was lying on the ground, close to where he had seen the stag first, and his horse was there and his hounds were there waiting, and he looked up, and the sun sank behind the mountain. And he went home and lived a long time, but he would never kiss any other lady because he had kissed the queen of the fairies, and he would never drink common wine any more, because he had drunk enchanted wine. And sometimes nurse told me tales that she had heard from her great-grandmother, who was very old, and lived in a cottage on the mountain all alone, and most of these tales were about a hill where people used to meet at night long ago, and they used to play all sorts of strange games and do queer things that nurse told me of, but I couldn't understand, and now, she said, everybody but her great-grandmother had forgotten all about it, and nobody knew where the hill was, not even her great-grandmother. But she told me one very strange story about the hill, and I trembled when I remembered it. She said that people always went there in summer, when it was very hot, and they had to dance a good deal. It would be all dark at first, and there were trees there, which made it much darker, and people would come, one by one, from all directions, by a secret path which nobody else knew, and two persons would keep the gate, and every one as they came up had to give a very curious sign, which nurse showed me as well as she could, but she said she couldn't show me properly. And all kinds of people would come; there would be gentle folks and village folks, and some old people and boys and girls, and quite small children, who sat and watched. And it would all be dark as they came in, except in one corner where some one was burning something that smelt strong and sweet, and made them laugh, and there one would see a glaring of coals, and the smoke mounting up red. So they would all come in, and when the last had come there was no door any more, so that no one else could get in, even if they knew there was anything beyond. And once a gentleman who was a stranger and had ridden a long way, lost his path at night, and his horse took him into the very middle of the wild country, where everything was upside down, and there were dreadful marshes and great stones everywhere, and holes underfoot, and the trees looked like gibbet-posts, because they had great black arms that stretched out across the way. And this strange gentleman was very frightened, and his horse began to shiver all over, and at last it stopped and wouldn't go any farther, and the gentleman got down and tried to lead the horse, but it wouldn't move, and it was all covered with a sweat, like death. So the gentleman went on all alone, going farther and farther into the wild country, till at last he came to a dark place, where he heard shouting and singing and crying, like nothing he had ever heard before. It all sounded quite close to him, but he couldn't get in, and so he began to call, and while he was calling, something came behind him, and in a minute his mouth and arms and legs were all bound up, and he fell into a swoon. And when he came to himself, he was lying by the roadside, just where he had first lost his way, under a blasted oak with a black trunk, and his horse was tied beside him. So he rode on to the town and told the people there what had happened, and some of them were amazed; but others knew. So when once everybody had come, there was no door at all for anybody else to pass in by. And when they were all inside, round in a ring, touching each other, some one began to sing in the darkness, and some one else would make a noise like thunder with a thing they had on purpose, and on still nights people would hear the thundering noise far, far away beyond the wild land, and some of them, who thought they knew what it was, used to make a sign on their breasts when they woke up in their beds at dead of night and heard that terrible deep noise, like thunder on the mountains. And the noise and the singing would go on and on for a long time, and the people who were in a ring swayed a little to and fro; and the song was in an old, old language that nobody knows now, and the tune was queer. Nurse said her great-grandmother had known some one who remembered a little of it, when she was quite a little girl, and nurse tried to sing some of it to me, and it was so strange a tune that I turned all cold and my flesh crept as if I had put my hand on something dead. Sometimes it was a man that sang and sometimes it was a woman, and sometimes the one who sang it did it so well that two or three of the people who were there fell to the ground shrieking and tearing with their hands. The singing went on, and the people in the ring kept swaying to and fro for a long time, and at last the moon would rise over a place they called the Tole Deol, and came up and showed them swinging and swaying from side to side, with the sweet thick smoke curling up from the burning coals, and floating in circles all around them. Then they had their supper. A boy and a girl brought it to them; the boy carried a great cup of wine, and the girl carried a cake of bread, and they passed the bread and the wine round and round, but they tasted quite different from common bread and common wine, and changed everybody that tasted them. Then they all rose up and danced, and secret things were brought out of some hiding place, and they played extraordinary games, and danced round and round and round in the moonlight, and sometimes people would suddenly disappear and never be heard of afterwards, and nobody knew what had happened to them. And they drank more of that curious wine, and they made images and worshipped them, and nurse showed me how the images were made one day when we were out for a walk, and we passed by a place where there was a lot of wet clay. So nurse asked me if I would like to know what those things were like that they made on the hill, and I said yes. Then she asked me if I would promise never to tell a living soul a word about it, and if I did I was to be thrown into the black pit with the dead people, and I said I wouldn't tell anybody, and she said the same thing again and again, and I promised. So she took my wooden spade and dug a big lump of clay and put it in my tin bucket, and told me to say if any one met us that I was going to make pies when I went home. Then we went on a little way till we came to a little brake growing right down into the road, and nurse stopped, and looked up the road and down it, and then peeped through the hedge into the field on the other side, and then she said, "Quick!" and we ran into the brake, and crept in and out among the bushes till we had gone a good way from the road. Then we sat down under a bush, and I wanted so much to know what nurse was going to make with the clay, but before she would begin she made me promise again not to say a word about it, and she went again and peeped through the bushes on every side, though the lane was so small and deep that hardly anybody ever went there. So we sat down, and nurse took the clay out of the bucket, and began to knead it with her hands, and do queer things with it, and turn it about. And she hid it under a big dock-leaf for a minute or two and then she brought it out again, and then she stood up and sat down, and walked round the clay in a peculiar manner, and all the time she was softly singing a sort of rhyme, and her face got very red. Then she sat down again, and took the clay in her hands and began to shape it into a doll, but not like the dolls I have at home, and she made the queerest doll I had ever seen, all out of the wet clay, and hid it under a bush to get dry and hard, and all the time she was making it she was singing these rhymes to herself, and her face got redder and redder. So we left the doll there, hidden away in the bushes where nobody would ever find it. And a few days later we went the same walk, and when we came to that narrow, dark part of the lane where the brake runs down to the bank, nurse made me promise all over again, and she looked about, just as she had done before, and we crept into the bushes till we got to the green place where the little clay man was hidden. I remember it all so well, though I was only eight, and it is eight years ago now as I am writing it down, but the sky was a deep violet blue, and in the middle of the brake where we were sitting there was a great elder tree covered with blossoms, and on the other side there was a clump of meadowsweet, and when I think of that day the smell of the meadowsweet and elder blossom seems to fill the room, and if I shut my eyes I can see the glaring blue sky, with little clouds very white floating across it, and nurse who went away long ago sitting opposite me and looking like the beautiful white lady in the wood. So we sat down and nurse took out the clay doll from the secret place where she had hidden it, and she said we must "pay our respects," and she would show me what to do, and I must watch her all the time. So she did all sorts of queer things with the little clay man, and I noticed she was all streaming with perspiration, though we had walked so slowly, and then she told me to "pay my respects," and I did everything she did because I liked her, and it was such an odd game. And she said that if one loved very much, the clay man was very good, if one did certain things with it, and if one hated very much, it was just as good, only one had to do different things, and we played with it a long time, and pretended all sorts of things. Nurse said her great-grandmother had told her all about these images, but what we did was no harm at all, only a game. But she told me a story about these images that frightened me very much, and that was what I remembered that night when I was lying awake in my room in the pale, empty darkness, thinking of what I had seen and the secret wood. Nurse said there was once a young lady of the high gentry, who lived in a great castle. And she was so beautiful that all the gentlemen wanted to marry her, because she was the loveliest lady that anybody had ever seen, and she was kind to everybody, and everybody thought she was very good. But though she was polite to all the gentlemen who wished to marry her, she put them off, and said she couldn't make up her mind, and she wasn't sure she wanted to marry anybody at all. And her father, who was a very great lord, was angry, though he was so fond of her, and he asked her why she wouldn't choose a bachelor out of all the handsome young men who came to the castle. But she only said she didn't love any of them very much, and she must wait, and if they pestered her, she said she would go and be a nun in a nunnery. So all the gentlemen said they would go away and wait for a year and a day, and when a year and a day were gone, they would come back again and ask her to say which one she would marry. So the day was appointed and they all went away; and the lady had promised that in a year and a day it would be her wedding day with one of them. But the truth was, that she was the queen of the people who danced on the hill on summer nights, and on the proper nights she would lock the door of her room, and she and her maid would steal out of the castle by a secret passage that only they knew of, and go away up to the hill in the wild land. And she knew more of the secret things than any one else, and more than any one knew before or after, because she would not tell anybody the most secret secrets. She knew how to do all the awful things, how to destroy young men, and how to put a curse on people, and other things that I could not understand. And her real name was the Lady Avelin, but the dancing people called her Cassap, which meant somebody very wise, in the old language. And she was whiter than any of them and taller, and her eyes shone in the dark like burning rubies; and she could sing songs that none of the others could sing, and when she sang they all fell down on their faces and worshipped her. And she could do what they called shib-show, which was a very wonderful enchantment. She would tell the great lord, her father, that she wanted to go into the woods to gather flowers, so he let her go, and she and her maid went into the woods where nobody came, and the maid would keep watch. Then the lady would lie down under the trees and begin to sing a particular song, and she stretched out her arms, and from every part of the wood great serpents would come, hissing and gliding in and out among the trees, and shooting out their forked tongues as they crawled up to the lady. And they all came to her, and twisted round her, round her body, and her arms, and her neck, till she was covered with writhing serpents, and there was only her head to be seen. And she whispered to them, and she sang to them, and they writhed round and round, faster and faster, till she told them to go. And they all went away directly, back to their holes, and on the lady's breast there would be a most curious, beautiful stone, shaped something like an egg, and colored dark blue and yellow, and red, and green, marked like a serpent's scales. It was called a glame stone, and with it one could do all sorts of wonderful things, and nurse said her great-grandmother had seen a glame stone with her own eyes, and it was for all the world shiny and scaly like a snake. And the lady could do a lot of other things as well, but she was quite fixed that she would not be married. And there were a great many gentlemen who wanted to marry her, but there were five of them who were chief, and their names were Sir Simon, Sir John, Sir Oliver, Sir Richard, and Sir Rowland. All the others believed she spoke the truth, and that she would choose one of them to be her man when a year and a day was done; it was only Sir Simon, who was very crafty, who thought she was deceiving them all, and he vowed he would watch and try if he could find out anything. And though he was very wise he was very young, and he had a smooth, soft face like a girl's, and he pretended, as the rest did, that he would not come to the castle for a year and a day, and he said he was going away beyond the sea to foreign parts. But he really only went a very little way, and came back dressed like a servant girl, and so he got a place in the castle to wash the dishes. And he waited and watched, and he listened and said nothing, and he hid in dark places, and woke up at night and looked out, and he heard things and he saw things that he thought were very strange. And he was so sly that he told the girl that waited on the lady that he was really a young man, and that he had dressed up as a girl because he loved her so very much and wanted to be in the same house with her, and the girl was so pleased that she told him many things, and he was more than ever certain that the Lady Avelin was deceiving him and the others. And he was so clever, and told the servant so many lies, that one night he managed to hide in the Lady Avelin's room behind the curtains. And he stayed quite still and never moved, and at last the lady came. And she bent down under the bed, and raised up a stone, and there was a hollow place underneath, and out of it she took a waxen image, just like the clay one that I and nurse had made in the brake. And all the time her eyes were burning like rubies. And she took the little wax doll up in her arms and held it to her breast, and she whispered and she murmured, and she took it up and she laid it down again, and she held it high, and she held it low, and she laid it down again. And she said, "Happy is he that begat the bishop, that ordered the clerk, that married the man, that had the wife, that fashioned the hive, that harbored the bee, that gathered the wax that my own true love was made of." And she brought out of an aumbry a great golden bowl, and she brought out of a closet a great jar of wine, and she poured some of the wine into the bowl, and she laid her mannikin very gently in the wine, and washed it in the wine all over. Then she went to a cupboard and took a small round cake and laid it on the image's mouth, and then she bore it softly and covered it up. And Sir Simon, who was watching all the time, though he was terribly frightened, saw the lady bend down and stretch out her arms and whisper and sing, and then Sir Simon saw beside her a handsome young man, who kissed her on the lips. And they drank wine out of the golden bowl together, and they ate the cake together. But when the sun rose there was only the little wax doll,

and the lady hid it again under the bed in the hollow place. So Sir
Simon knew quite well what the lady was, and he waited and he
watched, till the time she had said was nearly over, and in a week
the year and a day would be done. And one night, when he was
watching behind the curtains in her room, he saw her making
more wax dolls. And she made five, and hid them away. And the
next night she took one out, and held it up, and filled the golden
bowl with water, and took the doll by the neck and held it under
the water. Then she said—

> *Sir Dickon, Sir Dickon, your day is done,*
> *You shall be drowned in the water wan.*

And the next day news came to the castle that Sir Richard had
been drowned at the ford. And at night she took another doll
and tied a violet cord round its neck and hung it up on a nail.
Then she said—

> *Sir Rowland, your life has ended its span,*
> *High on a tree I see you hang.*

And the next day news came to the castle that Sir Rowland had
been hanged by robbers in the wood. And at night she took another
doll, and drove her bodkin right into its heart. Then she said—

> *Sir Noll, Sir Noll, so cease your life,*
> *Your heart piercèd with the knife.*

And the next day news came to the castle that Sir Oliver had
fought in a tavern, and a stranger had stabbed him to the heart.
And at night she took another doll, and held it to a fire of charcoal till it was melted. Then she said—

> *Sir John, return, and turn to clay,*
> *In fire of fever you waste away.*

And the next day news came to the castle that Sir John had died in a burning fever. So then Sir Simon went out of the castle and mounted his horse and rode away to the bishop and told him everything. And the bishop sent his men, and they took the Lady Avelin, and everything she had done was found out. So on the day after the year and a day, when she was to have been married, they carried her through the town in her smock, and they tied her to a great stake in the market-place, and burned her alive before the bishop with her wax image hung round her neck. And people said the wax man screamed in the burning of the flames. And I thought of this story again and again as I was lying awake in my bed, and I seemed to see the Lady Avelin in the market-place, with the yellow flames eating up her beautiful white body. And I thought of it so much that I seemed to get into the story myself, and I fancied I was the lady, and that they were coming to take me to be burnt with fire, with all the people in the town looking at me. And I wondered whether she cared, after all the strange things she had done, and whether it hurt very much to be burned at the stake. I tried again and again to forget nurse's stories, and to remember the secret I had seen that afternoon, and what was in the secret wood, but I could only see the dark and a glimmering in the dark, and then it went away, and I only saw myself running, and then a great moon came up white over a dark round hill. Then all the old stories came back again, and the queer rhymes that nurse used to sing to me; and there was one beginning "Halsy cumsy Helen musty," that she used to sing very softly when she wanted me to go to sleep. And I began to sing it to myself inside of my head, and I went to sleep.

The next morning I was very tired and sleepy, and could hardly do my lessons, and I was very glad when they were over and I had had my dinner, as I wanted to go out and be alone. It was a warm day, and I went to a nice turfy hill by the river, and sat down on my mother's old shawl that I had brought with me

on purpose. The sky was grey, like the day before, but there was
a kind of white gleam behind it, and from where I was sitting I
could look down on the town, and it was all still and quiet and
white, like a picture. I remembered that it was on that hill that
nurse taught me to play an old game called "Troy Town," in which
one had to dance, and wind in and out on a pattern in the grass,
and then when one had danced and turned long enough the
other person asks you questions, and you can't help answering
whether you want to or not, and whatever you are told to do
you feel you have to do it. Nurse said there used to be a lot of
games like that that some people knew of, and there was one
by which people could be turned into anything you liked and
an old man her great-grandmother had seen had known a girl
who had been turned into a large snake. And there was another
very ancient game of dancing and winding and turning, by which
you could take a person out of himself and hide him away as
long as you liked, and his body went walking about quite empty,
without any sense in it. But I came to that hill because I wanted
to think of what had happened the day before, and of the secret
of the wood. From the place where I was sitting I could see
beyond the town, into the opening I had found, where a little
brook had led me into an unknown country. And I pretended I
was following the brook over again, and I went all the way in
my mind, and at last I found the wood, and crept into it under
the bushes, and then in the dusk I saw something that made me
feel as if I were filled with fire, as if I wanted to dance and sing
and fly up into the air, because I was changed and wonderful.
But what I saw was not changed at all, and had not grown old,
and I wondered again and again how such things could happen,
and whether nurse's stories were really true, because in the
daytime in the open air everything seemed quite different from
what it was at night, when I was frightened, and thought I was
to be burned alive. I once told my father one of her little tales,
which was about a ghost, and asked him if it was true, and he
told me it was not true at all, and that only common, ignorant

people believed in such rubbish. He was very angry with nurse for telling me the story, and scolded her, and after that I promised her I would never whisper a word of what she told me, and if I did I should be bitten by the great black snake that lived in the pool in the wood. And all alone on the hill I wondered what was true. I had seen something very amazing and very lovely, and I knew a story, and if I had really seen it, and not made it up out of the dark, and the black bough, and the bright shining that was mounting up to the sky from over the great round hill, but had really seen it in truth, then there were all kinds of wonderful and lovely and terrible things to think of, so I longed and trembled, and I burned and got cold. And I looked down on the town, so quiet and still, like a little white picture, and I thought over and over if it could be true. I was a long time before I could make up my mind to anything; there was such a strange fluttering at my heart that seemed to whisper to me all the time that I had not made it up out of my head, and yet it seemed quite impossible, and I knew my father and everybody would say it was dreadful rubbish. I never dreamed of telling him or anybody else a word about it, because I knew it would be of no use, and I should only get laughed at or scolded, so for a long time I was very quiet, and went about thinking and wondering; and at night I used to dream of amazing things, and sometimes I woke up in the early morning and held out my arms with a cry. And I was frightened, too, because there were dangers, and some awful thing would happen to me, unless I took great care, if the story were true. These old tales were always in my head, night and morning, and I went over them and told them to myself over and over again, and went for walks in the places where nurse had told them to me; and when I sat in the nursery by the fire in the evenings I used to fancy nurse was sitting in the other chair, and telling me some wonderful story in a low voice, for fear anybody should be listening. But she used to like best to tell me about things when we were right out in the country, far from the house, because she said she was telling me such secrets, and walls have ears. And if it was something more than ever secret, we had to hide in brakes or woods; and I used to think it was such fun creeping along a hedge, and going very softly, and then we would get behind the bushes or run into the wood all of a sudden, when we were sure that none was watching us; so we knew that we had our secrets quite all to ourselves, and nobody else at all knew anything about them. Now and then, when we had hidden ourselves as I have described, she used to show me all sorts of odd things. One day, I remember, we were in a hazel brake, over-looking the brook, and we were so snug and warm, as though it was April; the sun was quite hot, and the leaves were just coming out. Nurse said she would show me something funny that would make me laugh, and then she showed me, as she said, how one could turn a whole house upside down, without anybody being able to find out, and the pots and pans would jump about, and the china would be broken, and the chairs would tumble over of themselves. I tried it one day in the kitchen, and I found I could do it quite well, and a whole row of plates on the dresser fell off it, and cook's little work-table tilted up and turned right over "before her eyes," as she said, but she was so frightened and turned so white that I didn't do it again, as I liked her. And afterwards, in the hazel copse, when she had shown me how to make things tumble about, she showed me how to make rapping noises, and I learnt how to do that, too. Then she taught me rhymes to say on certain occasions, and peculiar marks to make on other occasions, and other things that her great-grandmother had taught her when she was a little girl herself. And these were all the things I was thinking about in those days after the strange walk when I thought I had seen a great secret, and I wished nurse were there for me to ask her about it, but she had gone away more than two years before, and nobody seemed to know what had become of her, or where she had gone. But I shall always remember those days if I live to be quite old, because all the time I felt so strange, wondering and doubting, and feeling quite sure at one time, and making up my mind, and then I would feel quite sure that such things couldn't happen really, and it began all over again. But I took great care not to do certain things that might be very dangerous. So I waited and wondered for a long time, and though I was not sure at all, I never dared to try to find out. But one day I became sure that all that nurse said was quite true, and I was all alone when I found it out. I trembled all over with joy and terror, and as fast as I could I ran into one of the old brakes where we used to go—it was the one by the lane, where nurse made the little clay man—and I ran into it, and I crept into it; and when I came to the place where the elder was, I covered up my face with my hands and lay down flat on the grass, and I stayed there for two hours without moving, whispering to myself delicious, terrible things, and saying some words over and over again. It was all true and wonderful and splendid, and when I remembered the story I knew and thought of what I had really seen, I got hot and I got cold, and the air seemed full of scent, and flowers, and singing. And first I wanted to make a little clay man, like the one nurse had made so long ago, and I had to invent plans and stratagems, and to look about, and to think of things beforehand, because nobody must dream of anything that I was doing or going to do, and I was too old to carry clay about in a tin bucket. At last I thought of a plan, and I brought the wet clay to the brake, and did everything that nurse had done, only I made a much finer image than the one she had made; and when it was finished I did everything that I could imagine and much more than she did, because it was the likeness of something far better. And a few days later, when I had done my lessons early, I went for the second time by the way of the little brook that had led me into a strange country. And I followed the brook, and went through the bushes, and beneath the low branches of trees, and up thorny thickets on the hill, and by dark woods full of creeping thorns, a long, long way. Then I crept through the dark tunnel where the brook had been and the ground was stony, till at last I came to the thicket that climbed up the hill, and

though the leaves were coming out upon the trees, everything
looked almost as black as it was on the first day that I went
there. And the thicket was just the same, and I went up slowly
till I came out on the big bare hill, and began to walk among
the wonderful rocks. I saw the terrible voor again on everything,
for though the sky was brighter, the ring of wild hills all around
was still dark, and the hanging woods looked dark and dreadful,
and the strange rocks were as grey as ever; and when I looked
down on them from the great mound, sitting on the stone, I saw
all their amazing circles and rounds within rounds, and I had to
sit quite still and watch them as they began to turn about me,
and each stone danced in its place, and they seemed to go round
and round in a great whirl, as if one were in the middle of all
the stars and heard them rushing through the air. So I went
down among the rocks to dance with them and to sing extraordinary songs; and I went down through the other thicket, and
drank from the bright stream in the close and secret valley,
putting my lips down to the bubbling water; and then I went
on till I came to the deep, brimming well among the glittering
moss, and I sat down. I looked before me into the secret darkness
of the valley, and behind me was the great high wall of grass,
and all around me there were the hanging woods that made the
valley such a secret place. I knew there was nobody here at all
besides myself, and that no one could see me. So I took off my
boots and stockings, and let my feet down into the water, saying
the words that I knew. And it was not cold at all, as I expected,
but warm and very pleasant, and when my feet were in it I felt
as if they were in silk, or as if the nymph were kissing them. So
when I had done, I said the other words and made the signs,
and then I dried my feet with a towel I had brought on purpose,
and put on my stockings and boots. Then I climbed up the steep
wall, and went into the place where there are the hollows, and
the two beautiful mounds, and the round ridges of land, and all
the strange shapes. I did not go down into the hollow this time,
but I turned at the end, and made out the figures quite plainly,

as it was lighter, and I had remembered the story I had quite
forgotten before, and in the story the two figures are called Adam
and Eve, and only those who know the story understand what
they mean. So I went on and on till I came to the secret wood
which must not be described, and I crept into it by the way I
had found. And when I had gone about halfway I stopped, and
turned round, and got ready, and I bound the handkerchief tightly
round my eyes, and made quite sure that I could not see at all,
not a twig, nor the end of a leaf, nor the light of the sky, as it
was an old red silk handkerchief with large yellow spots, that
went round twice and covered my eyes, so that I could see
nothing. Then I began to go on, step by step, very slowly. My
heart beat faster and faster, and something rose in my throat that
choked me and made me want to cry out, but I shut my lips,
and went on. Boughs caught in my hair as I went, and great
thorns tore me; but I went on to the end of the path. Then I
stopped, and held out my arms and bowed, and I went round
the first time, feeling with my hands, and there was nothing. I
went round the second time, feeling with my hands, and there
was nothing. Then I went round the third time, feeling with my
hands, and the story was all true, and I wished that the years
were gone by, and that I had not so long a time to wait before
I was happy for ever and ever.

Nurse must have been a prophet like those we read of in the
Bible. Everything that she said began to come true, and since
then other things that she told me of have happened. That was
how I came to know that her stories were true and that I had
not made up the secret myself out of my own head. But there
was another thing that happened that day. I went a second time
to the secret place. It was at the deep brimming well, and when
I was standing on the moss I bent over and looked in, and then
I knew who the white lady was that I had seen come out of the
water in the wood long ago when I was quite little. And I trembled all over, because that told me other things. Then I remembered
how sometime after I had seen the white people in the wood,

nurse asked me more about them, and I told her all over again, and she listened, and said nothing for a long, long time, and at last she said, "You will see her again." So I understood what had happened and what was to happen. And I understood about the nymphs; how I might meet them in all kinds of places, and they would always help me, and I must always look for them, and find them in all sorts of strange shapes and appearances. And without the nymphs I could never have found the secret, and without them none of the other things could happen. Nurse had told me all about them long ago, but she called them by another name, and I did not know what she meant, or what her tales of them were about, only that they were very queer. And there were two kinds, the bright and the dark, and both were very lovely and very wonderful, and some people saw only one kind, and some only the other, but some saw them both. But usually the dark appeared first, and the bright ones came afterwards, and there were extraordinary tales about them. It was a day or two after I had come home from the secret place that I first really knew the nymphs. Nurse had shown me how to call them, and I had tried, but I did not know what she meant, and so I thought it was all nonsense. But I made up my mind I would try again, so I went to the wood where the pool was, where I saw the white people, and I tried again. The dark nymph, Alanna, came, and she turned the pool of water into a pool of fire....

Epilogue

"That's a very queer story," said Cotgrave, handing back the green book to the recluse, Ambrose. "I see the drift of a good deal, but there are many things that I do not grasp at all. On the last page, for example, what does she mean by 'nymphs'?"

"Well, I think there are references throughout the manuscript to certain 'processes' which have been handed down by tradition from age to age. Some of these processes are just beginning to

come within the purview of science, which has arrived at them—
or rather at the steps which lead to them—by quite different
paths. I have interpreted the reference to 'nymphs' as a reference
to one of these processes."

"And you believe that there are such things?"

"Oh, I think so. Yes, I believe I could give you convincing
evidence on that point. I am afraid you have neglected the study
of alchemy? It is a pity, for the symbolism, at all events, is very
beautiful, and moreover if you were acquainted with certain books
on the subject, I could recall to your mind phrases which might
explain a good deal in the manuscript that you have been reading."

"Yes; but I want to know whether you seriously think that
there is any foundation of fact beneath these fancies. Is it not
all a department of poetry; a curious dream with which man has
indulged himself?"

"I can only say that it is no doubt better for the great mass
of people to dismiss it all as a dream. But if you ask my veritable
belief—that goes quite the other way. No; I should not say belief,
but rather knowledge. I may tell you that I have known cases in
which men have stumbled quite by accident on certain of these
'processes,' and have been astonished by wholly unexpected
results. In the cases I am thinking of there could have been no
possibility of 'suggestion' or sub-conscious action of any kind.
One might as well suppose a schoolboy 'suggesting' the existence
of Æschylus to himself, while he plods mechanically through the
declensions.

"But you have noticed the obscurity," Ambrose went on, "and
in this particular case it must have been dictated by instinct, since
the writer never thought that her manuscripts would fall into
other hands. But the practice is universal, and for most excellent
reasons. Powerful and sovereign medicines, which are, of necessity,
virulent poisons also, are kept in a locked cabinet. The child may
find the key by chance, and drink herself dead; but in most cases
the search is educational, and the phials contain precious elixirs
for him who has patiently fashioned the key for himself."

"You do not care to go into details?"

"No, frankly, I do not. No, you must remain unconvinced. But you saw how the manuscript illustrates the talk we had last week?"

"Is this girl still alive?"

"No. I was one of those who found her. I knew the father well; he was a lawyer, and had always left her very much to herself. He thought of nothing but deeds and leases, and the news came to him as an awful surprise. She was missing one morning; I suppose it was about a year after she had written what you have read. The servants were called, and they told things, and put the only natural interpretation on them—a perfectly erroneous one.

"They discovered that green book somewhere in her room, and I found her in the place that she described with so much dread, lying on the ground before the image."

"It was an image?"

"Yes, it was hidden by the thorns and the thick undergrowth that had surrounded it. It was a wild, lonely country; but you know what it was like by her description, though of course you will understand that the colors have been heightened. A child's imagination always makes the heights higher and the depths deeper than they really are; and she had, unfortunately for herself, something more than imagination. One might say, perhaps, that the picture in her mind which she succeeded in a measure in putting into words, was the scene as it would have appeared to an imaginative artist. But it is a strange, desolate land."

"And she was dead?"

"Yes. She had poisoned herself—in time. No; there was not a word to be said against her in the ordinary sense. You may recollect a story I told you the other night about a lady who saw her child's fingers crushed by a window?"

"And what was this statue?"

"Well, it was of Roman workmanship, of a stone that with the centuries had not blackened, but had become white and luminous. The thicket had grown up about it and concealed it, and in the Middle Ages the followers of a very old tradition had known how to use it for their own purposes. In fact it had been incorporated into the monstrous mythology of the Sabbath. You will have noted that those to whom a sight of that shining whiteness had been vouchsafed by chance, or rather, perhaps, by apparent chance, were required to blindfold themselves on their second approach. That is very significant."

"And is it there still?"

"I sent for tools, and we hammered it into dust and fragments.

"The persistence of tradition never surprises me," Ambrose went on after a pause. "I could name many an English parish where such traditions as that girl had listened to in her childhood are still existent in occult but unabated vigor. No, for me, it is the 'story' not the 'sequel,' which is strange and awful, for I have always believed that wonder is of the soul."

THE SHINING PYRAMID

I

THE ARROW-HEAD CHARACTER

"Haunted, you said?"

"Yes, haunted. Don't you remember, when I saw you three years ago, you told me about your place in the west with the ancient woods hanging all about it, and the wild, domed hills, and the ragged land? It has always remained a sort of enchanted picture in my mind as I sit at my desk and hear the traffic rattling in the Street in the midst of whirling London. But when did you come up?"

"The fact is, Dyson, I have only just got out of the train. I drove to the station early this morning and caught the 10.45."

"Well, I am very glad you looked in on me. How have you been getting on since we last met? There is no Mrs. Vaughan, I suppose?"

"No," said Vaughan, "I am still a hermit, like yourself. I have done nothing but loaf about."

Vaughan had lit his pipe and sat in the elbow chair, fidgeting and glancing about him in a somewhat dazed and restless manner. Dyson had wheeled round his chair when his visitor entered and sat with one arm fondly reclining on the desk of his bureau, and touching the litter of manuscript.

"And you are still engaged in the old task?" said Vaughan, pointing to the pile of papers and the teeming pigeon-holes.

"Yes, the vain pursuit of literature, as idle as alchemy, and as entrancing. But you have come to town for some time I suppose; what shall we do tonight?"

"Well, I rather wanted you to try a few days with me down in the west. It would do you a lot of good. I'm sure."

"You are very kind, Vaughan, but London in September is hard to leave. Doré could not have designed anything more wonderful and mystic than Oxford Street as I saw it the other evening; the sunset flaming, the blue haze transmuting the plain street into a road 'far in the spiritual city.'"

"I should like you to come down though. You would enjoy roaming over our hills. Does this racket go on all day and night? It quite bewilders me; I wonder how you can work through it. I am sure you would revel in the great peace of my old home among the woods."

Vaughan lit his pipe again, and looked anxiously at Dyson to see if his inducements had had any effect, but the man of letters shook his head, smiling, and vowed in his heart a firm allegiance to the streets.

"You cannot tempt me," he said.

"Well, you may be right. Perhaps, after all, I was wrong to speak of the peace of the country. There, when a tragedy does occur, it is like a stone thrown into a pond; the circles of disturbance keep on widening, and it seems as if the water would never be still again."

"Have you ever any tragedies where you are?"

"I can hardly say that. But I was a good deal disturbed about a month ago by something that happened; it may or may not have been a tragedy in the usual sense of the word."

"What was the occurrence?"

"Well, the fact is a girl disappeared in a way which seems highly mysterious. Her parents, people of the name of Trevor, are well-to-do farmers, and their eldest daughter Annie was a sort of village beauty; she was really remarkably handsome. One afternoon she thought she would go and see her aunt, a widow who farms her own land, and as the two houses are only about five or six miles apart, she started off, telling her parents she would take the short cut over the hills. She never got to her aunt's, and she never was seen again. That's putting it in a few words."

"What an extraordinary thing! I suppose there are no disused mines, are there, on the hills? I don't think you quite run to anything so formidable as a precipice?"

"No; the path the girl must have taken had no pitfalls of any description; it is just a track over wild, bare hillside, far, even from a byroad. One may walk for miles without meeting a soul, but it is perfectly safe."

"And what do people say about it?"

"Oh, they talk nonsense—among themselves. You have no notion as to how superstitious English cottagers are in out-of-the-way parts like mine. They are as bad as the Irish, every whit, and even more secretive."

"But what do they say?"

"Oh, the poor girl is supposed to have 'gone with the fairies,' or to have been 'taken by the fairies.' Such stuff!" he went on, "one would laugh if it were not for the real tragedy of the case."

Dyson looked somewhat interested.

"Yes," he said, "'fairies' certainly strike a little curiously on the ear in these days. But what do the police say? I presume they do not accept the fairy-tale hypothesis?"

"No; but they seem quite at fault. What I am afraid of is that Annie Trevor must have fallen in with some scoundrels on her way. Castletown is a large seaport, you know, and some of the worst of the foreign sailors occasionally desert their ships and go on the tramp up and down the country. Not many years ago a Spanish sailor named Garcia murdered a whole family for the sake of plunder that was not worth sixpence. They are hardly human, some of these fellows, and I am dreadfully afraid the poor girl must have come to an awful end."

"But no foreign sailor was seen by anyone about the country?"

"No; there is certainly that; and of course country people are quick to notice anyone whose appearance and dress are a little out of the common. Still it seems as if my theory were the only possible explanation."

"There are no data to go upon," said Dyson, thoughtfully. "There was no question of a love affair, or anything of the kind, I suppose?"

"Oh, no, not a hint of such a thing. I am sure if Annie were alive she would have contrived to let her mother know of her safety."

"No doubt, no doubt. Still it is barely possible that she is alive and yet unable to communicate with her friends. But all this must have disturbed you a good deal."

"Yes, it did; I hate a mystery, and especially a mystery which is probably the veil of horror. But frankly, Dyson, I want to make a clean breast of it; I did not come here to tell you all this."

"Of course not," said Dyson, a little surprised at Vaughan's uneasy manner. "You came to have a chat on more cheerful topics."

"No, I did not. What I have been telling you about happened a month ago, but something which seems likely to affect me more personally has taken place within the last few days, and to be quite plain, I came up to town with the idea that you might be able to help me. You recollect that curious case you spoke to me about on our last meeting; something about a spectacle-maker."

"Oh, yes, I remember that. I know I was quite proud of my acumen at the time; even to this day the police have no idea why those peculiar yellow spectacles were wanted. But, Vaughan, you really look quite put out; I hope there is nothing serious?"

"No, I think I have been exaggerating, and I want you to reassure me. But what has happened is very odd."

"And what has happened?"

"I am sure that you will laugh at me, but this is the story. You must know there is a path, a right of way, that goes through my land, and to be precise, close to the wall of the kitchen garden. It is not used by many people; a woodman now and again finds it useful, and five or six children who go to school in the village pass twice a day. Well, a few days ago I was taking a walk about the place before breakfast, and I happened to stop to fill my pipe just by the large doors in the garden wall. The wood, I must tell you, comes to within a few feet of the wall, and the track I spoke of runs right in the shadow of the trees. I thought the shelter from a brisk wind that was blowing rather pleasant, and I stood there smoking with my eyes on the ground. Then something caught my attention. Just under the wall, on the short grass; a number of small flints were arranged in a pattern; something like this": and Mr. Vaughan caught at a pencil and piece of paper, and dotted down a few strokes.

"You see," he went on, "there were, I should think, twelve little stones neatly arranged in lines, and spaced at equal distances, as I have shown it on the paper. They were pointed stones, and the points were very carefully directed one way."

"Yes," said Dyson, without much interest, "no doubt the children you have mentioned had been playing there on their way from school. Children, as you know, are very fond of making such devices with oyster shells or flints or flowers, or with whatever comes in their way."

"So I thought; I just noticed these flints were arranged in a sort of pattern and then went on. But the next morning I was taking the same round, which, as a matter of fact, is habitual with me, and again I saw at the same spot a device in flints. This time it was really a curious pattern; something like the spokes of a wheel, all meeting at a common center, and this center formed by a device which looked like a bowl; all, you understand done in flints."

"You are right," said Dyson, "that seems odd enough. Still it is reasonable that your half-a-dozen school children are responsible for these fantasies in stone."

"Well, I thought I would set the matter at rest. The children pass the gate every evening at half-past five, and I walked by at six, and found the device just as I had left it in the morning. The next day I was up and about at a quarter to seven, and I found the whole thing had been changed. There was a pyramid outlined in flints upon the grass. The children I saw going by an hour and a half later, and they ran past the spot without glancing to right or left. In the evening I watched them going home, and this morning when I got to the gate at six o'clock there was a thing like a half moon waiting for me."

"So then the series runs thus: firstly ordered lines, then, the device of the spokes and the bowl, then the pyramid, and finally, this morning, the half moon. That is the order, isn't it?"

"Yes; that is right. But do you know it has made me feel very uneasy? I suppose it seems absurd, but I can't help thinking that some kind of signaling is going on under my nose, and that sort of thing is disquieting."

"But what have you to dread? You have no enemies?"

"No; but I have some very valuable old plate."

"You are thinking of burglars then?" said Dyson, with an accent of considerable interest, "but you must know your neighbors. Are there any suspicious characters about?"

"Not that I am aware of. But you remember what I told you of the sailors."

"Can you trust your servants?"

"Oh, perfectly. The plate is preserved in a strong room; the butler, an old family servant, alone knows where the key is kept. There is nothing wrong there. Still, everybody is aware that I have a lot of old silver, and all country folks are given to gossip. In that way information may have got abroad in very undesirable quarters."

"Yes, but I confess there seems something a little unsatisfactory in the burglar theory. Who is signaling to whom? I cannot see my way to accepting such an explanation. What put the plate into your head in connection with these flints signs, or whatever one may call them?"

"It was the figure of the Bowl," said Vaughan. "I happen to possess a very large and very valuable Charles II punch-bowl. The chasing is really exquisite, and the thing is worth a lot of money. The sign I described to you was exactly the same shape as my punch-bowl."

"A queer coincidence certainly. But the other figures or devices: you have nothing shaped like a pyramid?"

"Ah, you will think that queerer. As it happens, this punch-bowl of mine, together with a set of rare old ladles, is kept in a mahogany chest of a pyramidal shape. The four sides slope upwards, the narrow towards the top."

"I confess all this interests me a good deal," said Dyson. "Let us go on then. What about the other figures; how about the Army, as we may call the first sign, and the Crescent or Half moon?"

"Ah, there is no reference that I can make out of these two. Still, you see I have some excuse for curiosity at all events. I should be very vexed to lose any of the old plate; nearly all the pieces have been in the family for generations. And I cannot get it out of my head that some scoundrels mean to rob me, and are communicating with one another every night."

"Frankly," said Dyson, "I can make nothing of it; I am as much in the dark as yourself. Your theory seems certainly the only possible explanation, and yet the difficulties are immense."

He leaned back in his chair, and the two men faced each other, frowning, and perplexed by so bizarre a problem.

"By the way," said Dyson, after a long pause, "what is your geological formation down there?"

Mr. Vaughan looked up, a good deal surprised by the question.

"Old red sandstone and limestone, I believe," he said. "We are just beyond the coal measures, you know."

"But surely there are no flints either in the sandstone or the limestone?"

"No, I never see any flints in the fields. I confess that did strike me as a little curious."

"I should think so! It is very important. By the way, what size were the flints used in making these devices?"

"I happen to have brought one with me; I took it this morning."

"From the Half moon?"

"Exactly. Here it is."

He handed over a small flint, tapering to a point, and about three inches in length.

Dyson's face blazed up with excitement as he took the thing from Vaughan.

"Certainly," he said, after a moment's pause, "you have some curious neighbors in your country. I hardly think they can harbour any designs on your punch-bowl. Do you know this is a flint arrowhead of vast antiquity, and not only that, but an arrow-head of a unique kind? I have seen specimens from all parts of the world, but there are features about this thing that are quite peculiar." He laid down his pipe, and took out a book from a drawer.

"We shall just have time to catch the 5.45 to Castletown," he said.

II

THE EYES ON THE WALL

Mr. Dyson drew in a long breath of the air of the hills and felt all the enchantment of the scene about him. It was very early morning, and he stood on the terrace in the front of the house.

Vaughan's ancestor had built on the lower slope of a great hill, in the shelter of a deep and ancient wood that gathered on three sides about the house, and on the fourth side, the south-west, the land fell gently away and sank to the valley, where a brook wound in and out in mystic esses, and the dark and gleaming alders tracked the stream's course to the eye. On the terrace in the sheltered place no wind blew, and far beyond, the trees were still. Only one sound broke in upon the silence, and Dyson heard the noise of the brook singing far below, the song of clear and shining water rippling over the stones, whispering and murmuring as it sank to dark deep pools.

Across the stream, just below the house, rose a grey stone bridge, vaulted and buttressed, a fragment of the Middle Ages, and then beyond the bridge the hills rose again, vast and rounded like bastions, covered here and there with dark woods and thickets of undergrowth, but the heights were all bare of trees, showing only grey turf and patches of bracken, touched here and there with the gold of fading fronds; Dyson looked to the north and south, and still he saw the wall of the hills, and the ancient woods, and the stream drawn in and out between them; all grey and dim with morning mist beneath a grey sky in a hushed and haunted air.

Mr. Vaughan's voice broke in upon the silence.

"I thought you would be too tired to be about so early," he said. "I see you are admiring the view. It is very pretty, isn't it, though I suppose old Meyrick Vaughan didn't think much about the scenery when he built the house. A queer grey, old place, isn't it?"

"Yes, and how it fits into the surroundings; it seems of a piece with the grey hills and the grey bridge below."

"I am afraid I have brought you down on false pretences, Dyson," said Vaughan, as they began to walk up and down the terrace. "I have been to the place, and there is not a sign of anything this morning."

"Ah, indeed. Well, suppose we go round together."

They walked across the lawn and went by a path through the ilex shrubbery to the back of the house. There Vaughan pointed out the track leading down to the valley and up to the heights above the wood, and presently they stood beneath the garden wall, by the door.

"Here, you see, it was," said Vaughan, pointing to a spot on the turf. "I was standing just where you are now that morning I first saw the flints."

"Yes, quite so. That morning it was the Army, as I call it; then the Bowl, then the Pyramid, and, yesterday, the Half moon. What a queer old stone that is," he went on, pointing to a block of limestone rising out of the turf just beneath the wall. "It looks like a sort of dwarf pillar, but I suppose it is natural."

"Oh, yes, I think so. I imagine it was brought here, though, as we stand on the red sandstone. No doubt it was used as a foundation stone for some older building."

"Very likely," Dyson was peering about him attentively, looking from the ground to the wall, and from the wall to the deep wood that hung almost over the garden and made the place dark even in the morning.

"Look here," said Dyson at length, "it is certainly a case of children this time. Look at that." He was bending down and staring at the dull red surface of the mellowed bricks of the wall.

Vaughan came up and looked hard where Dyson's finger was pointing, and could scarcely distinguish a faint mark in deeper red.

"What is it?" he said. "I can make nothing of it."

"Look a little more closely. Don't you see it is an attempt to draw the human eye?"

"Ah, now I see what you mean. My sight is not very sharp. Yes, so it is, it is meant for an eye, no doubt, as you say. I thought the children learnt drawing at school."

"Well, it is an odd eye enough. Do you notice the peculiar almond shape; almost like the eye of a Chinaman?"

Dyson looked meditatively at the work of the undeveloped artist, and scanned the wall again, going down on his knees in the minuteness of his inquisition.

"I should like very much," he said at length, "to know how a child in this out of the way place could have any idea of the shape of the Mongolian eye. You see the average child has a very distinct impression of the subject; he draws a circle, or something like a circle, and put a dot in the center. I don't think any child imagines that the eye is really made like that; it's just a convention of infantile art. But this almond-shaped thing puzzles me extremely. Perhaps it may be derived from a gilt Chinaman on a tea-canister in the grocer's shop. Still that's hardly likely."

"But why are you so sure it was done by a child?"

"Why! Look at the height. These old-fashioned bricks are little more than two inches thick; there are twenty courses from the ground to the sketch if we call it so; that gives a height of three and a half feet. Now, just imagine you are going to draw something on this wall. Exactly; your pencil, if you had one, would touch the wall somewhere on the level with your eyes, that is, more than five feet from the ground. It seems, therefore, a very simple deduction to conclude that this eye on the wall was drawn by a child about ten years old."

"Yes, I had not thought of that. Of course one of the children must have done it."

"I suppose so; and yet as I said, there is something singularly unchildlike about those two lines, and the eyeball itself, you see, is almost an oval. To my mind, the thing has an odd, ancient air; and a touch that is not altogether pleasant. I cannot help fancying that if we could see a whole face from the same hand it would not be altogether agreeable. However, that is nonsense, after all, and we are not getting farther in our investigations. It is odd that the flint series has come to such an abrupt end."

The two men walked away towards the house, and as they went in at the porch there was a break in the grey sky, and a gleam of sunshine on the grey hill before them.

All the day Dyson prowled meditatively about the fields and woods surrounding the house. He was thoroughly and completely puzzled by the trivial circumstances he proposed to elucidate, and now he again took the flint arrow-head from his pocket, turning it over and examining it with deep attention. There was something about the thing that was altogether different from the specimens he had seen at the museums and private collections; the shape was of a distinct type, and around the edge there was a line of little punctured dots, apparently a suggestion of ornament. Who, thought Dyson, could possess such things in so remote a place; and who, possessing the flints, could have put them to the fantastic use of designing meaningless figures under

Vaughan's garden wall? The rank absurdity of the whole affair offended him unutterably; and as one theory after another rose in his mind only to be rejected, he felt strongly tempted to take the next train back to town. He had seen the silver plate which Vaughan treasured, and had inspected the punch-bowl, the gem of the collection, with close attention; and what he saw and his interview with the butler convinced him that a plot to rob the strong box was out of the limits of enquiry. The chest in which the bowl was kept, a heavy piece of mahogany, evidently dating from the beginning of the century, was certainly strongly sugges- tive of a pyramid, and Dyson was at first inclined to the inept manoeuvres of the detective, but a little sober thought convinced him of the impossibility of the burglary hypothesis, and he cast wildly about for something more satisfying. He asked Vaughan if there were any gipsies in the neighborhood, and heard that the Romany had not been seen for years. This dashed him a good deal, as he knew the gipsy habit of leaving queer hieroglyphics on the line of march, and had been much elated when the thought occurred to him. He was facing Vaughan by the old-fash- ioned hearth when he put the question, and leaned back in his chair in disgust at the destruction of his theory.

"It is odd," said Vaughan, "but the gipsies never trouble us here. Now and then the farmers find traces of fires in the wildest part of the hills, but nobody seems to know who the fire-lighters are."

"Surely that looks like gipsies?"

"No, not in such places as those. Tinkers and gipsies and wanderers of all sorts stick to the roads and don't go very far from the farmhouses."

"Well, I can make nothing of it. I saw the children going by this afternoon, and, as you say, they ran straight on. So we shall have no more eyes on the wall at all events."

"No, I must waylay them one of these days and find out who is the artist."

The next morning when Vaughan strolled in his usual course from the lawn to the back of the house he found Dyson already awaiting him by the garden door, and evidently in a state of high excitement, for he beckoned furiously with his hand, and gesticulated violently.

"What is it?" asked Vaughan. "The flints again?"

"No; but look here, look at the wall. There; don't you see it?"

"There's another of those eyes!"

"Exactly. Drawn, you see, at a little distance from the first, almost on the same level, but slightly lower."

"What on earth is one to make of it? It couldn't have been done by the children; it wasn't there last night, and they won't pass for another hour. What can it mean?"

"I think the very devil is at the bottom of all this," said Dyson. "Of course, one cannot resist the conclusion that these infernal almond eyes are to be set down to the same agency as the devices in the arrow-heads; and where that conclusion is to lead us is more than I can tell. For my part, I have to put a strong check on my imagination, or it would run wild."

"Vaughan," he said, as they turned away from the wall, "has it struck you that there is one point—a very curious point—in common between the figures done in flints and the eyes drawn on the wall?"

"What is that?" asked Vaughan, on whose face there had fallen a certain shadow of indefinite dread.

"It is this. We know that the signs of the Army, the Bowl, the Pyramid, and the Half moon must have been done at night. Presumably they were meant to be seen at night. Well, precisely the same reasoning applies to those eyes on the wall."

"I do not quite see your point."

"Oh, surely. The nights are dark just now, and have been very cloudy, I know, since I came down. Moreover, those overhanging trees would throw that wall into deep shadow even on a clear night."

"Well?"

"What struck me was this. What very peculiarly sharp eyesight, they, whoever 'they' are, must have to be able to arrange arrow-heads in intricate order in the blackest shadow of the wood, and then draw the eyes on the wall without a trace of bungling, or a false line."

"I have read of persons confined in dungeons for many years who have been able to see quite well in the dark," said Vaughan.

"Yes," said Dyson, "there was the abbé in Monte Cristo. But it is a singular point."

III

THE SEARCH FOR THE BOWL

"Who was that old man that touched his hat to you just now?" said Dyson, as they came to the bend of the lane near the house.

"Oh, that was old Trevor. He looks very broken, poor old fellow."

"Who is Trevor?"

"Don't you remember? I told you the story that afternoon I came to your rooms—about a girl named Annie Trevor, who disappeared in the most inexplicable manner about five weeks ago. That was her father."

"Yes, yes, I recollect now. To tell the truth I had forgotten all about it. And nothing has been heard of the girl?"

"Nothing whatever. The police are quite at fault."

"I am afraid I did not pay very much attention to the details you gave me. Which way did the girl go?"

"Her path would take her right across those wild hills above the house: the nearest point in the track must be about two miles from here."

"Is it near that little hamlet I saw yesterday?"

"You mean Croesyceiliog, where the children came from? No; it goes more to the north."

"Ah, I have never been that way."

They went into the house, and Dyson shut himself up in his room, sunk deep in doubtful thought, but yet with the shadow of a suspicion growing within him that for a while haunted his brain, all vague and fantastic, refusing to take definite form. He was sitting by the open window and looking out on the valley and saw, as if in a picture, the intricate winding of the brook, the grey bridge, and the vast hills rising beyond; all still and without a breath of wind to stir the mystic hanging woods, and the evening sunshine glowed warm on the bracken, and down below a faint mist, pure white, began to rise from the stream. Dyson sat by the window as the day darkened and the huge bastioned hills loomed vast and vague, and the woods became dim and more shadowy: and the fancy that had seized him no longer appeared altogether impossible. He passed the rest of the evening in a reverie, hardly hearing what Vaughan said; and when he took his candle in the hall, he paused a moment before bidding his friend good-night.

"I want a good rest," he said. "I have got some work to do tomorrow."

"Some writing, you mean?"

"No. I am going to look for the Bowl."

"The Bowl! If you mean my punch-bowl, that is safe in the chest."

"I don't mean the punch-bowl. You may take my word for it that your plate has never been threatened. No; I will not bother you with any suppositions. We shall in all probability have something much stronger than suppositions before long. Good-night, Vaughan."

The next morning Dyson set off after breakfast. He took the path by the garden wall, and noted that there were now eight of the weird almond eyes dimly outlined on the brick.

"Six days more," he said to himself, but as he thought over the theory he had formed, he shrank, in spite of strong conviction, from such a wildly incredible fancy. He struck up through the dense shadows of the wood, and at length came out on the bare hillside, and climbed higher and higher over the slippery turf, keeping well to the north, and following the indications given him by Vaughan. As he went on, he seemed to mount ever higher above the world of human life and customary things; to his right he looked at a fringe of orchard and saw a faint blue smoke rising like a pillar; there was the hamlet from which the children came to school, and there the only sign of life, for the woods embowered and concealed Vaughan's old grey house. As he reached what seemed the summit of the hill, he realized for the first time the desolate loneliness and strangeness of the land; there was nothing but grey sky and grey hill, a high, vast plain that seemed to stretch on for ever and ever, and a faint glimpse of a blue-peaked mountain far away and to the north. At length he came to the path, a slight track scarcely noticeable, and from its position and by what Vaughan had told him he knew that it was the way the lost girl, Annie Trevor, must have taken. He followed the path on the bare hill-top, noticing the great lime-stone rocks that cropped out of the turf, grim and hideous, and of an aspect as forbidding as an idol of the South Seas; and suddenly he halted, astonished, although he had found what he searched for.

Almost without warning the ground shelved suddenly away on all sides, and Dyson looked down into a circular depression, which might well have been a Roman amphitheatre, and the ugly crags of limestone rimmed it round as if with a broken wall. Dyson walked round the hollow, and noted the position of the stones, and then turned on his way home.

"This," he thought to himself, "is more than curious. The Bowl is discovered, but where is the Pyramid?"

"My dear Vaughan," he said, when he got back, "I may tell you that I have found the Bowl, and that is all I shall tell you for the present. We have six days of absolute inaction before us; there is really nothing to be done."

IV

THE SECRET OF THE PYRAMID

"I have just been round the garden," said Vaughan one morning. "I have been counting those infernal eyes, and I find there are fourteen of them. For heaven's sake, Dyson, tell me what the meaning of it all is."

"I should be very sorry to attempt to do so. I may have guessed this or that, but I always make it a principle to keep my guesses to myself. Besides, it is really not worth while anticipating events; you will remember my telling you that we had six days of inaction before us? Well, this is the sixth day, and the last of idleness. Tonight, I propose we take a stroll."

"A stroll! Is that all the action you mean to take?"

"Well, it may show you some very curious things. To be plain, I want you to start with me at nine o'clock this evening for the hills. We may have to be out all night, so you had better wrap up well, and bring some of that brandy."

"Is it a joke?" asked Vaughan, who was bewildered with strange events and strange surmises.

"No, I don't think there is much joke in it. Unless I am much mistaken we shall find a very serious explanation of the puzzle. You will come with me, I am sure?"

"Very good. Which way do you want to go?"

"By the path you told me of; the path Annie Trevor is supposed to have taken."

Vaughan looked white at the mention of the girl's name.

"I did not think you were on that track," he said. "I thought it was the affair of those devices in flint and of the eyes on the wall that you were engaged on. It's no good saying any more, but I will go with you."

At a quarter to nine that evening the two men set out, taking the path through the wood, and up the hill-side. It was a dark and heavy night, the sky was thick with clouds, and the valley full of mist, and all the way they seemed to walk in a world of shadow and gloom, hardly speaking, and afraid to break the haunted silence. They came out at last on the steep hill-side, and instead of the oppression of the wood there was the long, dim sweep of the turf, and higher, the fantastic limestone rocks hinted horror through the darkness, and the wind sighed as it passed across the mountain to the sea, and in its passage beat chill about their hearts. They seemed to walk on and on for hours, and the dim outline of the hill still stretched before them, and the haggard rocks still loomed through the darkness, when suddenly Dyson whispered, drawing his breath quickly, and coming close to his companion:

"Here," he said, "we will lie down. I do not think there is anything yet."

"I know the place," said Vaughan, after a moment. "I have often been by in the daytime. The country people are afraid to come here, I believe; it is supposed to be a fairies' castle, or something of the kind. But why on earth have we come here?"

"Speak a little lower," said Dyson. "It might not do us any good if we are overheard."

"Overheard here! There is not a soul within three miles of us."

"Possibly not; indeed, I should say certainly not. But there might be a body somewhat nearer."

"I don't understand you in the least," said Vaughan, whispering to humor Dyson, "but why have we come here?"

"Well, you see this hollow before us is the Bowl. I think we had better not talk even in whispers."

They lay full length upon the turf; the rock between their faces and the Bowl, and now and again, Dyson, slouching his dark, soft hat over his forehead, put out the glint of an eye, and in a moment drew back, not daring to take a prolonged view. Again he laid an ear to the ground and listened, and the hours went by, and the darkness seemed to blacken, and the faint sigh of the wind was the only sound.

Vaughan grew impatient with this heaviness of silence, this watching for indefinite terror; for to him there was no shape or form of apprehension, and he began to think the whole vigil a dreary farce.

"How much longer is this to last?" he whispered to Dyson, and Dyson who had been holding his breath in the agony of attention put his mouth to Vaughan's ear and said:

"Will you listen?" with pauses between each syllable, and in the voice with which the priest pronounces the awful words.

Vaughan caught the ground with his hands, and stretched forward, wondering what he was to hear. At first there was nothing, and then a low and gentle noise came very softly from the Bowl, a faint sound, almost indescribable, but as if one held the tongue against the roof of the mouth and expelled the breath. He listened eagerly and presently the noise grew louder, and became a strident and horrible hissing as if the pit beneath boiled with fervent heat, and Vaughan, unable to remain in suspense any longer, drew his cap half over his face in imitation of Dyson, and looked down to the hollow below.

It did, in truth, stir and seethe like an infernal caldron. The whole of the sides and bottom tossed and writhed with vague and restless forms that passed to and fro without the sound of feet, and gathered thick here and there and seemed to speak to one another in those tones of horrible sibilance, like the hissing of snakes, that he had heard. It was as if the sweet turf and the cleanly earth had suddenly become quickened with some foul writhing growth. Vaughan could not draw back his face, though he felt Dyson's finger touch him, but he peered into the quaking mass and saw faintly that there were things like faces and human limbs, and yet he felt his inmost soul chill with the sure belief that no fellow soul or human thing stirred in all that tossing and hissing host. He looked aghast, choking back sobs of horror, and at length the loathsome forms gathered thickest about some vague object in the middle of the hollow, and the hissing of their speech grew more venomous, and he saw in the uncertain light the abominable limbs, vague and yet too plainly seen, writhe and intertwine, and he thought he heard, very faint, a low human moan striking through the noise of speech that was not of man. At his heart something seemed to whisper ever "the worm of corruption, the worm that dieth not," and grotesquely the image was pictured to his imagination of a piece of putrid offal stirring through and through with bloated and horrible creeping things. The writhing of the dusky limbs continued, they seemed clustered round the dark form in the middle of the hollow, and the sweat dripped and poured off Vaughan's forehead, and fell cold on his hand beneath his face.

Then, it seemed done in an instant, the loathsome mass melted and fell away to the sides of the Bowl, and for a moment Vaughan saw in the middle of the hollow the tossing of human arms.

But a spark gleamed beneath, a fire kindled, and as the voice of a woman cried out loud in a shrill scream of utter anguish and terror, a great pyramid of flame spired up like a bursting of a pent fountain, and threw a blaze of light upon the whole mountain. In that instant Vaughan saw the myriads beneath; the things made in the form of men but stunted like children hideously deformed, the faces with the almond eyes burning with evil and unspeakable lusts; the ghastly yellow of the mass of naked flesh and then as if by magic the place was empty, while the fire roared and crackled, and the flames shone abroad.

"You have seen the Pyramid," said Dyson in his ear, "the Pyramid of fire."

V

THE LITTLE PEOPLE

"Then you recognize the thing?"

"Certainly. It is a brooch that Annie Trevor used to wear on

Sundays; I remember the pattern. But where did you find it? You don't mean to say that you have discovered the girl?"

"My dear Vaughan, I wonder you have not guessed where I found the brooch. You have not forgotten last night already?"

"Dyson," said the other, speaking very seriously, "I have been turning it over in my mind this morning while you have been out. I have thought about what I saw, or perhaps I should say about what I thought I saw, and the only conclusion I can come to is this, that the thing won't bear recollection. As men live, I have lived soberly and honestly, in the fear of God, all my days, and all I can do is believe that I suffered from some monstrous delusion, from some phantasmagoria of the bewildered senses. You know we went home together in silence, not a word passed between us as to what I fancied I saw; had we not better agree to keep silence on the subject? When I took my walk in the peaceful morning sunshine, I thought all the earth seemed full of praise, and passing by that wall I noticed there were no more signs recorded, and I blotted out those that remained. The mystery is over, and we can live quietly again. I think some poison has been working for the last few weeks; I have trod on the verge of madness, but I am sane now."

Mr. Vaughan had spoken earnestly, and bent forward in his chair and glanced at Dyson with something of entreaty.

"My dear Vaughan," said the other, after a pause, "what's the use of this? It is much too late to take that tone; we have gone too deep. Besides you know as well as I that there is no delusion in the case; I wish there were with all my heart. No, in justice to myself I must tell you the whole story, so far as I know it."

"Very good," said Vaughan with a sigh, "if you must, you must."

"Then," said Dyson, "we will begin with the end if you please. I found this brooch you have just identified in the place we have called the Bowl. There was a heap of grey ashes, as if a fire had been burning, indeed, the embers were still hot, and this brooch was lying on the ground, just outside the range of the flame. It must have dropped accidentally from the dress of the person

who was wearing it. No, don't interrupt me; we can pass now
to the beginning, as we have had the end. Let us go back to that
day you came to see me in my rooms in London. So far as I can
remember, soon after you came in you mentioned, in a somewhat
casual manner, that an unfortunate and mysterious incident had
occurred in your part of the country; a girl named Annie Trevor
had gone to see a relative, and had disappeared. I confess freely
that what you said did not greatly interest me; there are so many
reasons which may make it extremely convenient for a man and
more especially a woman to vanish from the circle of their relations and friends. I suppose, if we were to consult the police,
one would find that in London somebody disappears mysteriously
every other week, and the officers would, no doubt, shrug their
shoulders, and tell you that by the law of averages it could not
be otherwise. So I was very culpably careless to your story, and
besides, here is another reason for my lack of interest; your tale
was inexplicable. You could only suggest a blackguard sailor on
the tramp, but I discarded the explanation immediately.

"For many reasons, but chiefly because the occasional criminal,
the amateur in brutal crime, is always found out, especially if he
selects the country as the scene of his operations. You will
remember the case of that Garcia you mentioned; he strolled into
a railway station the day after the murder, his trousers covered
with blood, and the works of the Dutch clock, his loot, tied in a
neat parcel. So rejecting this, your only suggestion, the whole tale
became, as I say, inexplicable, and, therefore, profoundly uninteresting. Yes, therefore, it is a perfectly valid conclusion. Do you ever
trouble your head about problems which you know to be insoluble? Did you ever bestow much thought on the old puzzle of
Achilles and the tortoise? Of course not, because you knew it was
a hopeless quest, and so when you told me the story of a country
girl who had disappeared I simply placed the whole thing down
in the category of the insoluble, and thought no more about the
matter. I was mistaken, so it has turned out; but if you remember,
you immediately passed on to an affair which interested you more

intensely, because personally, I need not go over the very singular
narrative of the flint signs, at first I thought it all trivial, probably
some children's game, and if not that a hoax of some sort; but
your showing me the arrow-head awoke my acute interest. Here,
I saw, there was something widely removed from the commonplace, and matter of real curiosity; and as soon as I came here I
set to work to find the solution, repeating to myself again and
again the signs you had described. First came the sign we have
agreed to call the Army; a number of serried lines of flints, all
pointing in the same way. Then the lines, like the spokes of a
wheel, all converging towards the figure of a Bowl, then the triangle
or Pyramid, and last of all the Half moon. I confess that I exhausted
conjecture in my efforts to unveil this mystery, and as you will
understand it was a duplex or rather triplex problem. For I had
not merely to ask myself: what do these figures mean? but also,
who can possibly be responsible for the designing of them? And
again, who can possibly possess such valuable things, and knowing
their value thus throw them down by the wayside? This line of
thought led me to suppose that the person or persons in question
did not know the value of unique flint arrow-heads, and yet this
did not lead me far, for a well-educated man might easily be ignorant on such a subject. Then came the complication of the eye
on the wall, and you remember that we could not avoid the
conclusion that in the two cases the same agency was at work.
The peculiar position of these eyes on the wall made me inquire
if there was such a thing as a dwarf anywhere in the neighborhood,
but I found that there was not, and I knew that the children who
pass by every day had nothing to do with the matter. Yet I felt
convinced that whoever drew the eyes must be from three and
a half to four feet high, since, as I pointed out at the time, anyone
who draws on a perpendicular surface chooses by instinct a spot
about level with his face. Then again, there was the question of
the peculiar shape of the eyes; that marked Mongolian character
of which the English countryman could have no conception, and
for a final cause of confusion the obvious fact that the designer

or designers must be able practically to see in the dark. As you remarked, a man who has been confined for many years in an extremely dark cell or dungeon might acquire that power; but since the days of Edmond Dantès, where would such a prison be found in Europe? A sailor, who had been immured for a considerable period in some horrible Chinese oubliette, seemed the individual I was in search of, and though it looked improbable, it was not absolutely impossible that a sailor or, let us say, a man employed on shipboard, should be a dwarf. But how to account for my imaginary sailor being in possession of prehistoric arrowheads? And the possession granted, what was the meaning and object of these mysterious signs of flint, and the almond-shaped eyes? Your theory of a contemplated burglary I saw, nearly from the first, to be quite untenable, and I confess I was utterly at a loss for a working hypothesis. It was a mere accident which put me on the track; we passed poor old Trevor, and your mention of his name and of the disappearance of his daughter, recalled the story which I had forgotten, or which remained unheeded. Here, then, I said to myself, is another problem, uninteresting, it is true, by itself; but what if it prove to be in relation with all these enigmas which torture me? I shut myself in my room, and endeavored to dismiss all prejudice from my mind, and I went over everything de novo, assuming for theory's sake that the disappearance of Annie Trevor had some connection with the flint signs and the eyes on the wall. This assumption did not lead me very far, and I was on the point of giving the whole problem up in despair, when a possible significance of the Bowl struck me. As you know there is a 'Devil's Punch-bowl' in Surrey, and I saw that the symbol might refer to some feature in the country. Putting the two extremes together, I determined to look for the Bowl near the path which the lost girl had taken, and you know how I found it. I interpreted the sign by what I knew, and read the first, the Army, thus "'there is to be a gathering or assembly at the Bowl in a fortnight (that is the Half moon) to see the Pyramid, or to build the Pyramid.'

"The eyes, drawn one by one, day by day, evidently checked off the days, and I knew that there would be fourteen and no more. Thus far the way seemed pretty plain; I would not trouble myself to inquire as to the nature of the assembly, or as to who was to assemble in the loneliest and most dreaded place among these lonely hills. In Ireland or China or the West of America the question would have been easily answered; a muster of the disaffected, the meeting of a secret society; vigilantes summoned to report: the thing would be simplicity itself; but in this quiet corner of England, inhabited by quiet folk, no such suppositions were possible for a moment. But I knew that I should have an opportunity of seeing and watching the assembly, and I did not care to perplex myself with hopeless research; and in place of reasoning a wild fancy entered into judgment: I remembered what people had said about Annie Trevor's disappearance, that she had been 'taken by the fairies.' I tell you, Vaughan, I am a sane man as you are, my brain is not, I trust, mere vacant space to let to any wild improbability, and I tried my best to thrust the fantasy away. And the hint came of the old name of fairies, 'the little people,' and the very probable belief that they represent a tradition of the prehistoric Turanian inhabitants of the country, who were cave dwellers: and then I realized with a shock that I was looking for a being under four feet in height, accustomed to live in darkness, possessing stone instruments, and familiar with the Mongolian cast of features! I say this, Vaughan, that I should be ashamed to hint at such visionary stuff to you, if it were not for that which you saw with your very eyes last night, and I say that I might doubt the evidence of my senses, if they were not confirmed by yours. But you and I cannot look each other in the face and pretend delusion; as you lay on the turf beside me I felt your flesh shrink and quiver, and I saw your eyes in the light of the flame. And so I tell you without any shame what was in my mind last night as we went through the wood and climbed the hill, and lay hidden beneath the rock.

"There was one thing that should have been most evident that puzzled me to the very last. I told you how I read the sign of the Pyramid; the assembly was to see a pyramid, and the true meaning of the symbol escaped me to the last moment. The old derivation from 'up, fire,' though false, should have set me on the track, but it never occurred to me.

"I think I need say very little more. You know we were quite helpless, even if we had foreseen what was to come. Ah, the particular place where these signs were displayed? Yes, that is a curious question. But this house is, so far as I can judge, in a pretty central situation amongst the hills; and possibly, who can say yes or no, that queer, old limestone pillar by your garden wall was a place of meeting before the Celt set foot in Britain. But there is one thing I must add: I don't regret our inability to rescue the wretched girl. You saw the appearance of those things that gathered thick and writhed in the Bowl; you may be sure that what lay bound in the midst of them was no longer fit for earth."

"So?" said Vaughan.

"So she passed in the Pyramid of Fire," said Dyson, "and they passed again to the underworld, to the places beneath the hills."

OUT OF THE EARTH

There was some sort of confused complaint during last August of the ill behavior of the children at certain Welsh watering-places. Such reports and vague rumors are most difficult to trace to their heads and fountains; none has better reason to know that than myself. I need not go over the old ground here, but I am afraid that many people are wishing by this time that they had never heard my name; again, a considerable number of estimable persons are concerning themselves gloomily enough, from my point of view, with my everlasting welfare. They write me letters, some in kindly remonstrance, begging me not to deprive poor, sick-hearted souls of what little comfort they possess amidst their sorrows. Others send me tracts and pink leaflets with allusions to "the daughter of a well-known canon;" others again are violently and anonymously abusive. And then in open print, in fair book form, Mr. Begbie has dealt with me righteously but harshly, as I cannot but think.

Yet, it was all so entirely innocent, nay casual, on my part. A poor linnet of prose, I did but perform my indifferent piping in the Evening News because I wanted to do so, because I felt that the story of "The Bowmen" ought to be told. An inventor of fantasies is a poor creature, heaven knows, when all the world is at war; but I thought that no harm would be done, at any rate, if I bore witness, after the fashion of the fantastic craft, to my belief in the heroic glory of the English host who went back from Mons fighting and triumphing.

And then, somehow or other, it was as if I had touched a button and set in action a terrific, complicated mechanism of rumors that pretended to be sworn truth, of gossip that posed as evidence, of wild tarradiddles that good men most firmly believed. The supposed testimony of that "daughter of a well-known canon" took parish magazines by storm, and equally enjoyed the faith of dissenting divines. The "daughter" denied all knowledge of the matter, but people still quoted her supposed sure word; and the issues were confused with tales, probably true, of painful hallucinations and deliriums of our retreating soldiers, men fatigued and shattered to the very verge of death. It all became worse than the Russian myths, and as in the fable of the Russians, it seemed impossible to follow the streams of delusion to their fountain-head—or heads. Who was it who said that "Miss M. knew two officers who, etc., etc.?" I suppose we shall never know his lying, deluding name.

And so, I dare say, it will be with this strange affair of the troublesome children of the Welsh seaside town, or rather of a group of small towns and villages lying within a certain section or zone, which I am not going to indicate more precisely than I can help, since I love that country, and my recent experience with "The Bowmen" have taught me that no tale is too idle to be believed. And, of course, to begin with, nobody knew how this odd and malicious piece of gossip originated. So far as I know, it was more akin to the Russian myth than to the tale of "The Angels of Mons." That is, rumor preceded print; the thing was talked of here and there and passed from letter to letter long before the papers were aware of its existence. And—here it resembles rather the Mons affair—London and Manchester, Leeds and Birmingham were muttering vague unpleasant things while the little villages concerned basked innocently in the sunshine of an unusual prosperity.

In this last circumstance, as some believe, is to be sought the root of the whole matter. It is well known that certain east coast towns suffered from the dread of air-raids, and that a good many of their usual visitors went westward for the first time. So there is a theory that the east coast was mean enough to circulate reports against the west coast out of pure malice and envy. It may be so; I do not pretend to know. But here is a personal experience, such as it is, which illustrated the way in which the rumor was circulated. I was lunching one day at my Fleet Street tavern—this was early in July—and a friend of mine, a solicitor, of Serjeants' Inn, came in and sat at the same table. We began to talk of holidays and my friend Eddis asked me where I was going. "To the same old place," I said. "Manavon. You know we always go there." "Are you really?" said the lawyer; "I thought that coast had gone off a lot. My wife has a friend who's heard that it's not at all that it was."

I was astonished to hear this, not seeing how a little village like Manavon could have "gone off." I had known it for ten years as having accommodation for about twenty visitors, and I could not believe that rows of lodging houses had sprung up since the August of 1914. Still I put the question to Eddis: "Trippers?" I asked, knowing firstly that trippers hate the solitudes of the country and the sea; secondly, that there are no industrial towns within cheap and easy distance, and thirdly, that the railways were issuing no excursion tickets during the war.

"No, not exactly trippers," the lawyer replied. "But my wife's friend knows a clergyman who says that the beach at Tremaen is not at all pleasant now, and Tremaen's only a few miles from Manavon, isn't it?"

"In what way not pleasant?" I carried on my examination. "Pierrots and shows, and that sort of thing?" I felt that it could not be so, for the solemn rocks of Tremaen would have turned the liveliest Pierrot to stone. He would have frozen into a crag on the beach, and the seagulls would carry away his song and make it a lament by lonely, booming caverns that look on Avalon. Eddis said he had heard nothing about showmen; but he understood that since the war the children of the whole district had gone quite out of hand.

"Bad language, you know," he said, "and all that sort of thing, worse than London slum children. One doesn't want one's wife and children to hear foul talk at any time, much less on their holiday. And they say that Castell Coch is quite impossible; no decent woman would be seen there!"

I said: "Really, that's a great pity," and changed the subject. But I could not make it out at all. I knew Castell Coch well—a little bay bastioned by dunes and red sandstone cliffs, rich with greenery. A stream of cold water runs down there to the sea; there is the ruined Norman Castle, the ancient church and the scattered village; it is altogether a place of peace and quiet and great beauty. The people there, children and grown-ups alike, were not merely decent but courteous folk: if one thanked a child for opening a gate, there would come the inevitable response: "And welcome kindly, sir." I could not make it out at all. I didn't believe the lawyer's tales; for the life of me I could not see what he could be driving at. And, for the avoidance of all unnecessary mystery, I may as well say that my wife and child and myself went down to Manavon last August and had a most delightful holiday. At the time we were certainly conscious of no annoyance or unpleasantness of any kind. Afterwards, I confess, I heard a story that puzzled and still puzzles me, and this story, if it be received, might give its own interpretation to one or two circumstances which seemed in themselves quite insignificant.

But all through July I came upon traces of evil rumors affecting this most gracious corner of the earth. Some of these rumors were repetitions of Eddis's gossip; others amplified his vague story and made it more definite. Of course, no first-hand evidence was available. There never is any first-hand evidence in these cases. But A knew B who had heard from C that her second cousin's little girl had been set upon and beaten by a pack of young Welsh savages. Then people quoted "a doctor in large practice in a well-known town in the Midlands," to the effect that Tremaen was a sink of juvenile depravity. They said that a responsible medical man's evidence was final and convincing; but they didn't bother to find out who the doctor was, or whether there was any doctor at all—or any doctor relevant to the issue. Then the thing began to get into the papers in a sort of oblique, by-the-way sort of manner. People cited the case of these imaginary bad children in support of their educational views. One side said that "these unfortunate little ones" would have been quite well behaved if they had had no education at all; the opposition declared that continuation schools would speedily reform them and make them into admirable citizens. Then the poor Arfonshire children seemed to become involved in quarrels about Welsh disestablishment and in the question of the miners; and all the while they were going about behaving politely and admirably as they always do behave. I knew all the time that it was all nonsense, but I couldn't understand in the least what it meant, or who was pulling the wires of rumor, or their purpose in so pulling. I began to wonder whether the pressure and anxiety and suspense of a terrible war had unhinged the public mind, so that it was ready to believe any fable, to debate the reasons for happenings which had never happened. At last, quite incredible things began to be whispered: visitors' children had not only been beaten, they had been tortured; a little boy had been found impaled on a stake in a lonely field near Manavon; another child had been lured to destruction over the cliffs at Castell Coch. A London paper sent a good man down quietly to Arfon to investigate. He was away for a week, and at the end of that period returned to his office and in his own phrase, "threw the whole story down." There was not a word of truth, he said, in any of these rumors; no vestige of a foundation for the mildest forms of all this gossip. He had never seen such a beautiful country; he had never met pleasanter men, women or children; there was not a single case of anyone having been annoyed or troubled in any sort or fashion.

Yet all the while the story grew, and grew more monstrous and incredible. I was too much occupied in watching the progress of my own mythological monster to pay much attention. The town clerk of Tremaen, to which the legend had at length penetrated, wrote a brief letter to the press indignantly denying that there was the slightest foundation for "the unsavory rumors" which, he understood, were being circulated; and about this time we went down to Manavon and, as I say, enjoyed ourselves extremely. The weather was perfect: blues of paradise in the skies, the seas all a shimmering wonder, olive greens and emeralds, rich purples, glassy sapphires changing by the rocks; far away a haze of magic lights and colors at the meeting of sea and sky. Work and anxiety had harried me; I found nothing better than to rest on the thymy banks by the shore, finding an infinite balm and refreshment in the great sea before me, in the tiny flowers beside me. Or we would rest all the summer afternoon on a "shelf" high on the grey cliffs and watch the tide creaming and surging about the rocks, and listen to it booming in the hollows and caverns below. Afterwards, as I say, there were one or two things that struck cold. But at the time those were nothing. You see a man in an odd white hat pass by and think little or nothing about it. Afterwards, when you hear that a man wearing just such a hat had committed murder in the next street five minutes before, then you find in that hat a certain interest and significance. "Funny children," was the phrase my little boy used; and I began to think they were "funny" indeed.

If there be a key at all to this queer business, I think it is to be found in a talk I had not long ago with a friend of mine named Morgan. He is a Welshman and a dreamer, and some people say he is like a child who has grown up and yet has not grown up like other children of men. Though I did not know it, while I was at Manavon, he was spending his holiday time at Castell Coch. He was a lonely man and he liked lonely places, and when we met in the autumn he told me how, day after day, he would carry his bread and cheese and beer in a basket to a remote headland on that coast known as the Old Camp. Here, far above the waters, are solemn, mighty walls, turf-grown; circumvallations rounded and smooth with the passing of many thousand years. At one end of this most ancient place there is a tumulus, a tower of observation, perhaps, and underneath it slinks the green, deceiving ditch that seems to wind into the heart of the camp, but in reality rushes down to sheer rock and a precipice over the waters.

Here came Morgan daily, as he said, to dream of Avalon, to purge himself from the fuming corruption of the streets.

And so, as he told me, it was with singular horror that one afternoon as he dozed and dreamed and opened his eyes now and again to watch the miracle and magic of the sea, as he listened to the myriad murmurs of the waves, his meditation was broken by a sudden burst of horrible raucous cries—and the cries of children, too, but children of the lowest type. Morgan says that the very tones made him shudder—"They were to the ear what slime is to the touch," and then the words: every foulness, every filthy abomination of speech; blasphemies that struck like blows at the sky, that sank down into the pure, shining depths, defiling them! He was amazed. He peered over the green wall of the fort, and there in the ditch he saw a swarm of noisome children, horrible little stunted creatures with old men's faces, with bloated faces, with little sunken eyes, with leering eyes. It was worse than uncovering a brood of snakes or a nest of worms.

No; he would not describe what they were about. "Read about Belgium," said Morgan, "and think they couldn't have been more than five or six years old." There was no infamy, he said, that they did not perpetrate; they spared no horror of cruelty. "I saw blood running in streams, as they shrieked with laughter, but I could not find the mark of it on the grass afterwards."

Morgan said he watched them and could not utter a word; it was as if a hand held his mouth tight. But at last he found his voice and shrieked at them, and they burst into a yell of obscene laughter and shrieked back at him, and scattered out of sight. He could not trace them; he supposes that they hid in the deep bracken behind the Old Camp.

"Sometimes I can't understand my landlord at Castell Coch," Morgan went on. "He's the village postmaster and has a little farm of his own—a decent, pleasant, ordinary sort of chap. But now and again he will talk oddly. I was telling him about these beastly children and wondering who they could be when he broke into Welsh, something like 'the battle that is for age unto ages; and the People take delight in it.'"

So far Morgan, and it was evident that he did not understand at all. But this strange tale of his brought back an odd circumstance or two that I recollected: a matter of our little boy straying away more than once, and getting lost among the sand dunes and coming back screaming, evidently frightened horribly, and babbling about "funny children." We took no notice; did not trouble, I think, to look whether there were any children wandering about the dunes or not. We were accustomed to his small imaginations.

But after hearing Morgan's story I was interested and I wrote an account of the matter to my friend, old Doctor Duthoit, of Hereford. And he:

"They were only visible, only audible to children and the childlike. Hence the explanation of what puzzled you at first; the rumors, how did they arise? They arose from nursery gossip, from scraps and odds and ends of half-articulate children's talk of horrors that they didn't understand, of words that shamed their nurses and their mothers.

"These little people of the earth rise up and rejoice in these times of ours. For they are glad, as the Welshman said, when they know that men follow their ways."

THE RED HAND

The Problem of the Fish-Hooks

"There can be no doubt whatever," said Mr. Phillipps, "that my theory is the true one; these flints are prehistoric fish-hooks."

"I dare say; but you know that in all probability the things were forged the other day with a door-key."

"Stuff!" said Phillipps; "I have some respect, Dyson, for your literary abilities, but your knowledge of ethnology is insignificant, or rather non-existent. These fish-hooks satisfy every test; they are perfectly genuine."

"Possibly, but as I said just now, you go to work at the wrong end. You neglect the opportunities that confront you and await you, obvious, at every corner; you positively shrink from the chance of encountering primitive man in this whirling and mysterious city, and you pass the weary hours in your agreeable retirement of Red Lion Square fumbling with bits of flint, which are, as I said, in all probability, rank forgeries."

Phillipps took one of the little objects, and held it up in exasperation.

"Look at that ridge," he said. "Did you ever see such a ridge as that on a forgery?"

Dyson merely grunted and lit his pipe and the two sat smoking in rich silence, watching through the open window the children in the square as they flitted to and fro in the twilight of the lamps, as elusive as bats flying on the verge of a dark wood.

"Well," said Phillipps at last, "it is really a long time since you have been round. I suppose you have been working at your old task."

"Yes," said Dyson, "always the chase of the phrase. I shall grow old in the hunt. But it is a great consolation to meditate on the fact that there are not a dozen people in England who know what style means."

"I suppose not; for the matter of that, the study of ethnology is far from popular. And the difficulties! Primitive man stands dim and very far off across the great bridge of years."

"By the way," he went on after a pause, "what was that stuff you were talking just now about shrinking from the chance of encountering primitive man at the corner, or something of the kind? There are certainly people about here whose ideas are very primitive."

"I wish, Phillipps, you would not rationalize my remarks. If, I recollect the phrases correctly, I hinted that you shrank from the chance of encountering primitive man in this whirling and mysterious city, and I meant exactly what I said. Who can limit the age of survival? The troglodyte and the lake-dweller, perhaps representatives of yet darker races, may very probably be lurking in our midst, rubbing shoulders with frock-coated and finely draped humanity, ravening like wolves at heart and boiling with the foul passions of the swamp and the black cave. Now and then as I walk in Holborn or Fleet Street I see a face which I pronounce abhorred, and yet I could not give a reason for the thrill of loathing that stirs within me."

"My dear Dyson, I refuse to enter myself in your literary "trying-on" department. I know that survivals do exist, but all things have a limit, and your speculations are absurd. You must catch me your troglodyte before I will believe in him."

"I agree to that with all my heart," said Dyson, chuckling at the ease with which he had succeeded in "drawing" Phillipps. "Nothing could be better. It's a fine night for a walk," he added taking up his hat.

"What nonsense you are talking, Dyson!" said Phillipps. "However, I have no objection to taking a walk with you: as you say, it is a pleasant night."

"Come along then," said Dyson, grinning, "but remember our bargain."

The two men went out into the square, and threading one of the narrow passages that serve as exits, struck towards the north-east. As they passed along a flaring causeway they could hear at intervals between the clamor of the children and the triumphant *Gloria* played on a piano-organ the long deep hum and roll of the traffic in Holborn, a sound so persistent that it echoed like the turning of everlasting wheels. Dyson looked to the right and left and conned the way, and presently they were passing through a more peaceful quarter, touching on deserted squares and silent streets black as midnight. Phillipps had lost all count of direction, and as by degrees the region of faded respectability gave place to the squalid, and dirty stucco offended the eye of the artistic observer, he merely ventured the remark that he had never seen a neighborhood more unpleasant or more commonplace.

"More mysterious, you mean," said Dyson. "I warn you, Phillipps, we are now hot upon the scent."

They dived yet deeper into the maze of brickwork; some time before they had crossed a noisy thoroughfare running east and west, and now the quarter seemed all amorphous, without character; here a decent house with sufficient garden, here a faded square, and here factories surrounded by high, blank walls, with blind passages and dark corners; but all ill-lighted and unfrequented and heavy with silence.

Presently, as they paced down a forlorn street of two-story houses, Dyson caught sight of a dark and obscure turning.

"I like the look of that," he said; "it seems to me promising." There was a street lamp at the entrance, and another, a mere glimmer, at the further end. Beneath the lamp, on the pavement, an artist had evidently established his academy in the daytime, for the stones were all a blur of crude colors rubbed into each other, and a few broken fragments of chalk lay in a little heap beneath the wall.

"You see people do occasionally pass this way," said Dyson, pointing to the ruins of the screever's work. "I confess I should not have thought it possible. Come, let us explore."

On one side of this byway of communication was a great timber-yard, with vague piles of wood looming shapeless above the enclosing wall; and on the other side of the road a wall still higher seemed to enclose a garden, for there were shadows like trees, and a faint murmur of rustling leaves broke the silence. It was a moonless night, and clouds that had gathered after sunset had blackened, and midway between the feeble lamps the passage lay all dark and formless, and when one stopped and listened, and the sharp echo of reverberant footsteps ceased, there came from far away, as from beyond the hills, a faint roll of the noise of London. Phillipps was bolstering up his courage to declare that he had had enough of the excursion, when a loud cry from Dyson broke in upon his thoughts.

"Stop, stop, for Heaven's sake, or you will tread on it! There! almost under your feet!" Phillipps looked down, and saw a vague shape, dark, and framed in surrounding darkness, dropped strangely on the pavement, and then a white cuff glimmered for a moment as Dyson lit a match, which went out directly.

"It's a drunken man," said Phillipps very coolly.

"It's a murdered man," said Dyson, and he began to call for police with all his might, and soon from the distance running footsteps echoed and grew louder, and cries sounded.

A policeman was the first to come up.

"What's the matter?" he said, as he drew to a stand, panting. "Anything amiss here?" for he had not seen what was on the pavement.

"Look!" said Dyson, speaking out of the gloom. "Look there! My friend and I came down this place three minutes ago, and that is what we found."

The man flashed his light on the dark shape and cried out.

"Why, it's murder," he said; "there's blood all about him, and a puddle of it in the gutter there. He's not dead long, either. Ah! there's the wound! It's in the neck."

Dyson bent over what was lying there. He saw a prosperous gentleman, dressed in smooth, well-cut clothes. The neat whiskers were beginning to grizzle a little; he might have been forty-five an hour before; and a handsome gold watch had half slipped out of his waistcoat pocket. And there in the flesh of the neck, between chin and ear, gaped a great wound, clean cut, but all clotted with drying blood, and the white of the cheeks shone like a lighted lamp above the red.

Dyson turned, and looked curiously about him; the dead man lay across the path with his head inclined towards the wall, and the blood from the wound streamed away across the pavement, and lay a dark puddle, as the policeman had said, in the gutter. Two more policemen had come up, the crowd gathered, humming from all quarters, and the officers had as much as they could do to keep the curious at a distance. The three lanterns were flashing here and there, searching for more evidence, and in the gleam of one of them Dyson caught sight of an object in the road, to which he called the attention of the policeman nearest to him.

"Look, Phillipps," he said, when the man had secured it and held it up. "Look, that should be something in your way!"

It was a dark flinty stone, gleaming like obsidian, and shaped to a broad edge something after the manner of an adze. One end was rough, and easily grasped in the hand, and the whole thing was hardly five inches long. The edge was thick with blood.

"What is that, Phillipps?" said Dyson; and Phillipps looked hard at it.

"It's a primitive flint knife," he said. "It was made about ten thousand years ago. One exactly like this was found near Abury, in Wiltshire, and all the authorities gave it that age."

The policeman stared astonished at such a development of the case; and Phillipps himself was all aghast at his own words. But Mr. Dyson did not notice him. An inspector who had just come up and was listening to the outlines of the case, was holding a lantern to the dead man's head. Dyson, for his part, was staring with a white heat of curiosity at something he saw on the wall, just above where the man was lying; there were a few rude marks done in red chalk.

"This is a black business," said the inspector at length: "does anybody know who it is?"

A man stepped forward from the crowd. "I do, governor," he said, "he's a big doctor, his name's Sir Thomas Vivian; I was in the "orspital abart six months ago, and he used to come round; he was a very kind man."

"Lord," cried the inspector, "this is a bad job indeed. Why, Sir Thomas Vivian goes to the Royal Family. And there's a watch worth a hundred guineas in his pocket, so it isn't robbery."

Dyson and Phillipps gave their cards to the authority, and moved off, pushing with difficulty through the crowd that was still gathering, gathering fast; and the alley that had been lonely and desolate now swarmed with white staring faces and hummed with the buzz of rumor and horror, and rang with the commands of the officers of police. The two men once free from this swarming curiosity stepped out briskly, but for twenty minutes neither spoke a word.

"Phillipps," said Dyson, as they came into a small but cheerful street, clean and brightly lit, "Phillipps, I owe you an apology. I was wrong to have spoken as I did to-night. Such infernal jesting," he went on, with heat, "as if there were no wholesome subjects for a joke. I feel as if I had raised an evil spirit."

"For Heaven's sake say nothing more," said Phillipps, choking down horror with visible effort. "You told the truth to me in my room; the troglodyte, as you said, is still lurking about the earth, and in these very streets around us, slaying for mere lust of blood."

"I will come up for a moment," said Dyson, when they reached Red Lion Square, "I have something to ask you. I think there should be nothing hidden between us at all events."

Phillipps nodded gloomily, and they went up to the room, where everything hovered indistinct in the uncertain glimmer of the light from without.

When the candle was lighted and the two men sat facing each other, Dyson spoke.

"Perhaps," he began, "you did not notice me peering at the wall just above the place where the head lay. The light from the inspector's lantern was shining full on it, and I saw something that looked queer to me, and I examined it closely. I found that some one had drawn in red chalk a rough outline of a hand – a human hand – upon the wall. But it was the curious position of the fingers that struck me; it was like this"; and he took a pencil and a piece of paper and drew rapidly, and then handed what he had done to Phillipps. It was a rough sketch of a hand seen from the back, with the fingers clenched, and the top of the thumb protruded between the first and second fingers, and pointed downwards, as if to something below.

"It was just like that," said Dyson, as he saw Phillipps's face grow still whiter. "The thumb pointed down as if to the body; it seemed almost a live hand in ghastly gesture. And just beneath there was a small mark with the powder of the chalk lying on it – as if someone had commenced a stroke and had broken the chalk in his hand. I saw the bit of chalk lying on the ground. But what do you make of it?"

"It's a horrible old sign," said Phillipps – "one of the most horrible signs connected with the theory of the evil eye. It is used still in Italy, but there can be no doubt that it has been known for ages. It is one of the survivals; you must look for the origin of it in the black swamp whence man first came."

Dyson took up his hat to go.

"I think, jesting apart," said he, "that I kept my promise, and that we were and are hot on the scent, as I said. It seems as if I had really shown you primitive man, or his handiwork at all events."

Incident of the Letter

About a month after the extraordinary and mysterious murder of Sir Thomas Vivian, the well-known and universally respected specialist in heart disease, Mr. Dyson called again on his friend Mr. Phillipps, whom he found, not as usual, sunk deep in painful study, but reclining in his easy-chair in an attitude of relaxation. He welcomed Dyson with cordiality.

"I am very glad you have come," he began; "I was thinking of looking you up. There is no longer the shadow of a doubt about the matter."

"You mean the case of Sir Thomas Vivian?"

"Oh, no, not at all. I was referring to the problem of the fish-hooks. Between ourselves, I was a little too confident when you were here last, but since then other facts have turned up; and only yesterday I had a letter from a distinguished F.R.S. which quite settles the affair. I have been thinking what I should tackle next; and I am inclined to believe that there is a good deal to be done in the way of so-called undecipherable inscriptions."

"Your line of study pleases me," said Dyson, "I think it may prove useful. But in the meantime, there was surely something extremely mysterious about the case of Sir Thomas Vivian."

"Hardly, I think. I allowed myself to be frightened that night; but there can be no doubt that the facts are patient of a comparatively commonplace explanation."

"Really! What is your theory then?"

"Well, I imagine that Vivian must have been mixed up at some period of his life in an adventure of a not very creditable description, and that he was murdered out of revenge by some Italian whom he had wronged."

"Why Italian?"

"Because of the hand, the sign of the *mano in fica*. That gesture is now only used by Italians. So you see that what appeared the most obscure feature in the case turns out to be illuminant."

"Yes, quite so. And the flint knife?"

"That is very simple. The man found the thing in Italy, or possibly stole it from some museum. Follow the line of least resistance, my dear fellow, and you will see there is no need to bring up primitive man from his secular grave beneath the hills."

"There is some justice in what you say," said Dyson. "As I understand you, then, you think that your Italian, having murdered, Vivian, kindly chalked up that hand as a guide to Scotland Yard?"

"Why not? Remember a murderer is always a madman. He may plot and contrive nine-tenths of his scheme with the acuteness and the grasp of a chess-player or a pure mathematician; but somewhere or other his wits leave him and he behaves like a fool. Then you must take into account the insane pride or vanity of the criminal; he likes to leave his mark, as it were, upon his handiwork."

"Yes, it is all very ingenious; but have you read the reports of the inquest?"

"No, not a word. I simply gave my evidence, left the court, and dismissed the subject from my mind."

"Quite so. Then if you don't object I should like to give you an account of the case. I have studied it rather deeply, and I confess it interests me extremely."

"Very good. But I warn you I have done with mystery. We are to deal with facts now."

"Yes, it is fact that I wish to put before you. And this is fact the first. When the police moved Sir Thomas Vivian's body they found an open knife beneath him. It was an ugly-looking thing such as sailors carry, with a blade that the mere opening rendered rigid, and there the blade was all ready, bare and gleaming, but without a trace of blood on it, and the knife was found to be quite new; it had never been used. Now, at the first glance it looks as if your imaginary Italian were just the man to have such a tool. But consider a moment. Would he be likely to buy a new knife expressly to commit murder? And, secondly, if he had such a knife, why didn't he use it, instead of that very odd flint instrument?

"And I want to put this to you. You think the murderer chalked up the hand after the murder as a sort of "melodramatic Italian assassin his mark" touch. Passing over the question as to whether the real criminal ever does such a thing, I would point out that, on the medical evidence, Sir Thomas Vivian hadn't been dead for more than an hour; That would place the stroke at about a quarter to ten, and you know it was perfectly dark when we went out at 9.30. And that passage was singularly gloomy and ill-lighted, and the hand was drawn roughly, it is true, but correctly and without the bungling of strokes and the bad shots that are inevitable when one tries to draw in the dark or with shut eyes. Just try to draw such a simple figure as a square without looking at the paper, and then ask me to conceive that your Italian, with the rope waiting for his neck, could draw the hand on the wall so firmly and truly, in the black shadow of that alley. It is absurd. By consequence, then, the hand was drawn early in the evening, long before any murder was committed; or else – mark this, Phillipps – it was drawn by some one to whom darkness and gloom were familiar and habitual; by some one to whom the common dread of the rope was unknown!

"Again: a curious note was found in Sir Thomas Vivian's pocket. Envelope and paper were of a common make, and the stamp bore the West Central postmark. I will come to the nature of the contents later on, but it is the question of the handwriting that is so remarkable. The address on the outside was neatly written in a small clear hand, but the letter itself might have been written by a Persian who had learnt the English script. It was upright, and the letters were curiously contorted, with an affectation of dashes and backward curves which really reminded me of an Oriental manuscript, though it was all perfectly legible. But – and here comes the poser – on searching the dead man's waistcoat pockets a small memorandum book was found; it was almost filled with pencil jottings. These memoranda related chiefly to matters of a private as distinct from a professional nature; there were appointments to meet friends, notes of theatrical first-nights, the address of a good hotel in Tours, and the title of a new novel – nothing in any way intimate. And the whole of these jottings were written in a hand nearly identical with the writing of the note found in the dead man's coat pocket! There was just enough difference between them to enable the expert to swear that the two were not written by the same person. I will just read you so much of Lady Vivian's evidence as bears on this point of the writing; I have the printed slip with me. Here you see she says: "I was married to my late husband seven years ago; I never saw any letter addressed to him in a hand at all resembling that on the envelope produced, nor have I ever seen writing like that in the letter before me. I never saw my late husband using the memorandum book, but I am sure he did write everything in it; I am certain of that because we stayed last May at the Hotel du Faisan, Rue Royale, Tours, the address of which is given in the book; I remember his getting the novel "A Sentinel" about six weeks ago. Sir Thomas Vivian never liked to miss the first-nights at the theatres. His usual hand was perfectly different from that used in the note-book."

"And now, last of all, we come back to the note itself. Here it is in facsimile. My possession of it is due to the kindness of Inspector Cleeve, who is pleased to be amused at my amateur inquisitiveness. Read it, Phillipps; you tell me you are interested in obscure inscriptions; here is something for you to decipher."

Mr. Phillipps, absorbed in spite of himself in the strange circumstances Dyson had related, took the piece of paper, and scrutinized it closely. The handwriting was indeed bizarre in the extreme, and, as Dyson had noted, not unlike the Persian character in its general effect, but it was perfectly legible.

"Read it aloud," said Dyson, and Phillipps obeyed.

"'Hand did not point in vain. The meaning of the stars is no longer obscure. Strangely enough, the black heaven vanished, or was stolen yesterday, but that does not matter in the least, as I have a celestial globe. Our old orbit remains unchanged; you have not forgotten the number of my sign, or will you appoint some other house? I have been on the other side of the moon, and can bring something to show you.'"

"And what do you make of that?" said Dyson.

"It seems to me mere gibberish," said Phillipps; "you suppose it has a meaning?"

"Oh, surely; it was posted three days before the murder; it was found in the murdered man's pocket; it is written in a fantastic hand which the murdered man himself used for his private memoranda. There must be purpose under all this, and to my mind there is something ugly enough hidden under the circumstances of this case of Sir Thomas Vivian."

"But what theory have you formed?"

"Oh, as to theories, I am still in a very early stage; it is too soon to state conclusions. But I think I have demolished your Italian. I tell you, Phillipps, again the whole thing has an ugly look to my eyes. I cannot do as you do, and fortify myself with cast-iron propositions to the effect that this or that doesn't happen, and never has happened. You note that the first word in the letter is "hand". That seems to me, taken with what we know about the hand on the wall, significant enough, and what you yourself told me of the history and meaning of the symbol, its connection with a world-old belief and faiths of dim far-off years, all this speaks of mischief, for me at all events. No; I stand pretty well to what I said to you half in joke that night before we went out. There are sacraments of evil as well as of good about us, and we live and move to my belief in an unknown world, a place where there are caves and shadows and dwellers in twilight. It is possible that man may sometimes return on the track of evolution, and it is my belief that an awful lore is not yet dead."

"I cannot follow you in all this," said Phillipps; "it seems to interest you strangely. What do you propose to do?"

"My dear, Phillipps," replied Dyson, speaking in a lighter tone, "I am afraid I shall have to go down a little in the world. I have a prospect of visits to the pawnbrokers before me, and the publicans must not be neglected. I must cultivate a taste for four ale; shag tobacco I already love and esteem with all my heart."

Search for the Vanished Heaven

For many days after the discussion with Phillipps, Mr. Dyson was resolute in the line of research he had marked out for himself.

A fervent curiosity and an innate liking for the obscure were great incentives, but especially in this case of Sir Thomas Vivian's death (for Dyson began to boggle a little at the word "murder") there seemed to him an element that was more than curious. The sign of the red hand upon the wall, the tool of flint that had given death, the almost identity between the handwriting of the note and the fantastic script reserved religiously, as it appeared, by the doctor for trifling jottings, all these diverse and variegated threads joined to weave in his mind a strange and shadowy picture, with ghastly shapes dominant and deadly, and yet ill-defined, like the giant figures wavering in an ancient tapestry. He thought he had a clue to the meaning of the note, and in his resolute search for the "black heaven", which had vanished, he beat furiously about the alleys and obscure streets of central London, making himself a familiar figure to the pawn-broker, and a frequent guest at the more squalid pot-houses.

For a long time he was unsuccessful, and he trembled at the thought that the "black heaven" might be hid in the coy retire-ments of Peckham, or lurk perchance in distant Willesden, but finally, improbability, in which he put his trust, came to the rescue. It was a dark and rainy night, with something in the unquiet and stirring gusts that savored of approaching winter, and Dyson, beating up a narrow street not far from the Gray's Inn Road, took shelter in an extremely dirty "public", and called for beer, forgetting for the moment his preoccupations, and only thinking of the sweep of the wind about the tiles and the hissing of the rain through the black and troubled air. At the bar there gathered the usual company: the frowsy women and the men in shiny black, those who appeared to mumble secretly together, others who wrangled in interminable argument, and a few shy drinkers who stood apart, each relishing his dose, and the rank and biting flavor of cheap spirit. Dyson was wondering at the enjoyment of it all, when suddenly there came a sharper accent. The fold-ing-doors swayed open, and a middle-aged woman staggered towards the bar, and clutched the pewter rim as if she stepped

a deck in a roaring gale. Dyson glanced at her attentively as a
pleasing specimen of her class; she was decently dressed in black,
and carried a black bag of somewhat rusty leather, and her
intoxication was apparent and far advanced. As she swayed at
the bar, it was evidently all she could do to stand upright, and
the barman, who had looked at her with disfavour, shook his
head in reply to her thick-voiced demand for a drink. The woman
glared at him, transformed in a moment to a fury, with bloodshot
eyes, and poured forth a torrent of execration, a stream of blasphemies and early English phraseology.

"Get out of this," said the man; "shut up and be off, or I'll
send for the police."

"Police, you —" bawled the woman "I'll—well give you something to fetch the police for!" and with a rapid dive into her bag
she pulled out some object which she hurled furiously at the
barman's head.

The man ducked down, and the missile flew over his head
and smashed a bottle to fragments, while the woman with a peal
of horrible laughter rushed to the door, and they could hear her
steps pattering fast over the wet stones.

The barman looked ruefully about him.

"Not much good going after her," he said, "and I'm afraid what
she's left won't pay for that bottle of whisky." He fumbled amongst
the fragments of broken glass, and drew out something dark, a
kind of square stone it seemed, which he held up.

"Valuable cur'osity," he said, "any gent like to bid?"

The habitues had scarcely turned from their pots and glasses
during these exciting incidents; they gazed a moment, fishily,
when the bottle smashed, and that was all, and the mumble of
the confidential was resumed and the jangle of the quarrelsome,
and the shy and solitary sucked in their lips and relished again
the rank flavor of the spirit.

Dyson looked quickly at what the barman held before him.

"Would you mind letting me see it?" he said; "it's a queer-
looking old thing, isn't it?"

It was a small black tablet, apparently of stone, about four inches long by two and a half broad, and as Dyson took it he felt rather than saw that he touched the secular with his flesh. There was some kind of carving on the surface, and, most conspicuous, a sign that made Dyson's heart leap.

"I don't mind taking it," he said quietly. "Would two shillings be enough?"

"Say half a dollar," said the man, and the bargain was concluded. Dyson drained his pot of beer, finding it delicious, and lit his pipe, and went out deliberately soon after. When he reached his apartment he locked the door, and placed the tablet on his desk, and then fixed himself in his chair, as resolute as an army in its trenches before a beleaguered city. The tablet was full under the light of the shaded candle, and scrutinizing it closely, Dyson saw first the sign of the hand with the thumb protruding between the fingers; it was cut finely and firmly on the dully black surface of the stone, and the thumb pointed downward to what was beneath.

"It is mere ornament," said Dyson to himself, "perhaps symbolical ornament, but surely not an inscription, or the signs of any words ever spoken."

The hand pointed at a series of fantastic figures, spirals and whorls of the finest, most delicate lines, spaced at intervals over the remaining surface of the tablet. The marks were as intricate and seemed almost as much without design as the pattern of a thumb impressed upon a pane of glass.

"Is it some natural marking?" thought Dyson; "there have been queer designs, likenesses of beasts and flowers, in stones with which man's hand had nothing to do"; and he bent over the stone with a magnifier, only to be convinced that no hazard of nature could have delineated these varied labyrinths of line. The whorls were of different sizes; some were less than the twelfth of an inch in diameter, and the largest was a little smaller than a sixpence, and under the glass the regularity and accuracy of the cutting were evident, and in the smaller spirals the lines were graduated at intervals of a hundredth of an inch. The whole thing had a marvellous and fantastic look, and gazing at the mystic whorls beneath the hand, Dyson became subdued with an impression of vast and far-off ages, and of a living being that had touched the stone with enigmas before the hills were formed, when the hard rocks still boiled with fervent heat.

"The 'black heaven' is found again," he said, "but the meaning of the stars is likely to be obscure for everlasting so far as I am concerned."

London stilled without, and a chill breath came into the room as Dyson sat gazing at the tablet shining duskily under the candle-light; and at last as he closed the desk over the ancient stone, all his wonder at the case of Sir Thomas Vivian increased tenfold, and he thought of the well-dressed prosperous gentleman lying dead mystically beneath the sign of the hand, and the insupportable conviction seized him that between the death of this fashionable West End doctor and the weird spirals of the tablet there were most secret and unimaginable links.

For days he sat before his desk gazing at the tablet, unable to resist its lodestone fascination, and yet quite helpless, without even the hope of solving the symbols so secretly inscribed. At last, desperate he called in Mr. Phillipps in consultation, and told in brief the story of finding the stone.

"Dear me!" said Phillipps, "this is extremely curious; you have had a find indeed. Why, it looks to me even more ancient than the Hittite seal. I confess the character, if it is a character, is entirely strange to me. These whorls are really very quaint."

"Yes, but I want to know what they mean. You must remember this tablet is the 'black heaven' of the letter found in Sir Thomas Vivian's pocket; it bears directly on his death."

"Oh, no, that is nonsense! This is, no doubt, an extremely ancient tablet, which has been stolen from some collection. Yes, the hand makes an odd coincidence, but only a coincidence after all."

"My dear Phillipps, you are a living example of the truth of the axiom that extreme skepticism is mere credulity. But can you decipher the inscription?"

"I undertake to decipher anything," said Phillipps. "I do not believe in the insoluble. These characters are curious, but I cannot fancy them to be inscrutable."

"Then take the thing away with you and make what you can of it. It has begun to haunt me; I feel as if I had gazed too long into the eyes of the Sphinx."

Phillipps departed with the tablet in an inner pocket. He had not much doubt of success, for he had evolved thirty-seven rules for the solution of inscriptions. Yet when a week had passed and he called to see Dyson there was no vestige of triumph on his features. He found his friend in a state of extreme irritation, pacing up and down in the room like a man in a passion. He turned with a start as the door opened.

"Well," said Dyson, "you have got it? What is it all about?"

"My dear fellow, I am sorry to say I have completely failed. I have tried every known device in vain. I have even been so officious as to submit it to a friend at the Museum, but he, though a man of prime authority on the subject, tells me he is quite at fault. It must be some wreckage of a vanished race, almost, I think – a fragment of another world than ours. I am not a superstitious man, Dyson, and you know that I have no truck with even the noble delusions, but I confess I yearn to be rid of this small square of blackish stone. Frankly, it has given me an ill week; it seems to me troglodytic and abhorred."

Phillipps drew out the tablet and laid it on the desk before Dyson.

"By the way," he went on, "I was right at all events in one particular; it has formed part of some collection. There is a piece of grimy paper on the back that must have been a label."

"Yes, I noticed that," said Dyson, who had fallen into deepest disappointment; "no doubt the paper is a label. But as I don't much care where the tablet originally came from, and only wish to know what the inscription means, I paid no attention to the paper. The thing is a hopeless riddle, I suppose, and yet it must surely be of the greatest importance."

Phillipps left soon after, and Dyson, still despondent, took the tablet in his hand and carelessly turned it over. The label had so grimed that it seemed merely a dull stain, but as Dyson looked at it idly, and yet attentively, he could see pencil-marks, and he bent over it eagerly, with his glass to his eye. To his annoyance, he found that part of the paper had been torn away, and he could only with difficulty make out odd words and pieces of words. First he read something that looked like "inroad", and then beneath, "stony-hearted step—" and a tear cut off the rest. But in an instant a solution suggested itself, and he chuckled with huge delight.

"Certainly," he said out loud, "this is not only the most charming but the most convenient quarter in all London; here I am, allowing for the accidents of side streets, perched on a tower of observation."

He glanced triumphant out of the window across the street to the gate of the British Museum. Sheltered by the boundary wall of that agreeable institution, a "screever", or artist in chalks, displayed his brilliant impressions on the pavement, soliciting the approval and the coppers of the gay and serious.

"This," said Dyson, "is more than delightful! An artist is provided to my hand."

The Artist of the Pavement

Mr. Phillipps, in spite of all disavowals - in spite of the wall of sense of whose enclosure and limit he was wont to make his boast - yet felt in his heart profoundly curious as to the case of Sir Thomas Vivian. Though he kept a brave face for his friend, his reason could not decently resist the conclusion that Dyson had enunciated, namely, that the whole affair had a look both ugly and mysterious. There was the weapon of a vanished race that had pierced the great arteries; the red hand, the symbol of a hideous faith, that pointed to the slain man; and then the tablet which Dyson declared he had expected to find, and had certainly found, bearing the ancient impress of the hand of malediction, and a legend written beneath in a character compared with which the most antique cuneiform was a thing of yesterday. Besides all this, there were other points that tortured and perplexed. How to account for the bare knife found unstained beneath the body? And the hint that the red hand upon the wall must have been drawn by some one whose life was passed in darkness thrilled him with a suggestion of dim and infinite horror. Hence he was in truth not a little curious as to what was to come, and some ten days after he had returned the tablet he again visited the "mystery-man", as he privately named his friend.

Arrived in the grave and airy chambers in Great Russell Street, he found the moral atmosphere of the place had been transformed. All Dyson's irritation had disappeared, his brow was smoothed with complacency, and he sat at a table by the window gazing out into the street with an expression of grim enjoyment, a pile of books and papers lying unheeded before him.

"My dear Phillipps, I am delighted to see you! Pray excuse my moving. Draw your chair up here to the table, and try this admirable shag tobacco."

"Thank you," said Phillipps, "judging by the flavor of the smoke, I should think it is a little strong. But what on earth is all this? What are you looking at?"

"I am on my watch-tower. I assure you that the time seems short while I contemplate this agreeable street and the classic grace of the Museum portico."

"Your capacity for nonsense is amazing," replied Phillipps, "but have you succeeded in deciphering the tablet? It interests me."

"I have not paid much attention to the tablet recently," said Dyson. "I believe the spiral character may wait."

"Really! And how about the Vivian murder?"

"Ah, you do take an interest in that case? Well, after all, we cannot deny that it was a queer business. But is not 'murder' rather a coarse word? It smacks a little, surely, of the police poster. Perhaps I am a trifle decadent, but I cannot help believing in the splendid word; 'sacrifice,' for example, is surely far finer than 'murder.'"

"I am all in the dark," said Phillipps. "I cannot even imagine by what track you are moving in this labyrinth."

"I think that before very long the whole matter will be a good deal clearer for us both, but I doubt whether you will like hearing the story."

Dyson lit his pipe afresh and leant back, not relaxing, however, in his scrutiny of the street. After a somewhat lengthy pause, he startled Phillipps by a loud breath of relief as he rose from the chair by the window and began to pace the floor.

"It's over for the day," he said, "and, after all, one gets a little tired."

Phillipps looked with inquiry into the street. The evening was darkening, and the pile of the Museum was beginning to loom indistinct before the lighting of the lamps, but the pavements were thronged and busy. The artist in chalks across the way was gathering together his materials, and blurring all the brilliance of his designs, and a little lower down there was the clang of shutters being placed in position. Phillipps could see nothing to justify Mr. Dyson's sudden abandonment of his attitude of surveillance, and grew a little irritated by all these thorny enigmas.

"Do you know, Phillipps," said Dyson, as he strolled at ease up and down the room, "I will tell you how I work. I go upon the theory of improbability. The theory is unknown to you? I will explain. Suppose I stand on the steps of St. Paul's and look out for a blind man lame of the left leg to pass me, it is evidently highly improbable that I shall see such a person by waiting for an hour. If I wait two hours the improbability is diminished, but is still enormous, and a watch of a whole day would give little expectation of success. But suppose I take up the same position day after day, and week after week, don't you perceive that the improbability is lessening constantly – growing smaller day after day. Don't you see that two lines which are not parallel are gradually approaching one another, drawing nearer and nearer to a point of meeting, till at last they do meet, and improbability has vanished altogether. That is how I found the black tablet: I acted on the theory of improbability. It is the only scientific principle I know of which can enable one to pick out an unknown man from amongst five million."

"And you expect to find the interpreter of the black tablet by this method?"

"Certainly."

"And the murderer of Sir Thomas Vivian also?"

"Yes, I expect to lay my hands on the person concerned in the death of Sir Thomas Vivian in exactly the same way."

The rest of the evening after Phillipps had left was devoted by Dyson to sauntering in the streets, and afterwards, when the night grew late, to his literary labors, or the chase of the phrase, as he called it. The next morning the station by the window was again resumed. His meals were brought to him at the table, and he ate with his eyes on the street. With briefest intervals, snatched reluctantly from time to time, he persisted in his survey throughout the day, and only at dusk, when the shutters were put up and the "screever" ruthlessly deleted all his labor of the day, just before the gas-lamps began to star the shadows, did he feel at liberty to quit his post. Day after day this ceaseless glance upon the street continued, till the landlady grew puzzled and aghast at such a profitless pertinacity.

But at last, one evening, when the play of lights and shadows was scarce beginning, and the clear cloudless air left all distinct and shining, there came the moment. A man of middle age, bearded and bowed, with a touch of grey about the ears, was strolling slowly along the northern pavement of Great Russell Street from the eastern end. He looked up at the Museum as he went by, and then glanced involuntarily at the art of the "screever", and at the artist himself, who sat beside his pictures, hat in hand. The man with the beard stood still an instant, swaying slightly to and fro as if in thought, and Dyson saw his fists shut tight, and his back quivering, and the one side of his face in view twitched and grew contorted with the indescribable torment of approaching epilepsy. Dyson drew a soft hat from his pocket, and dashed the door open, taking the stair with a run.

When he reached the street, the person he had seen so agitated had turned about, and, regardless of observation, was racing wildly towards Bloomsbury Square, with his back to his former course. Mr. Dyson went up to the artist of the pavement and gave him some money, observing quietly, "You needn't trouble to draw that thing again."

Then he, too, turned about, and strolled idly down the street in the opposite direction to that taken by the fugitive. So the distance between Dyson and the man with the bowed head grew steadily greater.

Story of the Treasure-house

"There are many reasons why I chose your rooms for the meeting in preference to my own. Chiefly, perhaps because I thought the man would be more at his ease on neutral ground."

"I confess, Dyson," said Phillipps, "that I feel both impatient and uneasy. You know my standpoint: hard matter of fact, materialism if you like, in its crudest form. But there is something about all this affair of Vivian that makes me a little restless. And how did you induce the man to come?"

"He has an exaggerated opinion of my powers. You remember what I said about the doctrine of improbability? When it does work out, it gives results which seem very amazing to a person who is not in the secret. That is eight striking, isn't it? And there goes the bell."

They heard footsteps on the stair, and presently the door opened, and a middle-aged man, with a bowed head, bearded, and with a good deal of grizzling hair about his ears, came into the room. Phillipps glanced at his features, and recognised the lineaments of terror.

"Come in, Mr. Selby," said Dyson. "This is Mr. Phillipps, my intimate friend and our host for this evening. Will you take anything? Then perhaps we had better hear your story – a very singular one, I am sure."

The man spoke in a voice hollow and a little quavering, and a fixed stare that never left his eyes seemed directed to something awful that was to remain before him by day and night for the rest of his life.

"You will, I am sure, excuse preliminaries," he began; "what I have to tell is best told quickly. I will say, then, that I was born in a remote part of the west of England, where the very outlines of the woods and hills, and the winding of the streams in the valleys, are apt to suggest the mystical to any one strongly gifted with imagination. When I was quite a boy there were certain huge and rounded hills, certain depths of hanging wood, and secret valleys bastioned round on every side that filled me with fancies beyond the bourne of rational expression, and as I grew older and began to dip into my father's books, I went by instinct, like the bee, to all that would nourish fantasy. Thus, from a course of obsolete and occult reading, and from listening to certain wild legends in which the older people still secretly believed, I grew firmly convinced of the existence of treasure, the hoard of a race extinct for ages, still hidden beneath the hills, and my every thought was directed to the discovery of the golden heaps that lay, as I fancied within a few feet of the green turf. To one spot, in especial, I was drawn as if by enchantment; it was a tumulus, the domed memorial of some forgotten people, crowning the crest of a vast mountain range; and I have often lingered there on summer evenings, sitting on the great block of limestone at the summit, and looking out far over the yellow sea towards the

Devonshire coast. One day as I dug heedlessly with the ferrule of my stick at the mosses and lichens which grew rank over the stone, my eye was caught by what seemed a pattern beneath the growth of green; there was a curving line, and marks that did not look altogether the work of nature. At first I thought I had bared some rarer fossil, and I took out my knife and scraped away at the moss till a square foot was uncovered. Then I saw two signs which startled me; first, a closed hand, pointing downwards, the thumb protruding between the fingers, and beneath the hand a whorl or spiral, traced with exquisite accuracy in the hard surface of the rock. Here I persuaded myself, was an index to the great secret, but I chilled at the recollection of the fact that some antiquarians had tunneled the tumulus through and through, and had been a good deal surprised at not finding so much as an arrowhead within. Clearly, then, the signs on the limestone had no local significance; and I made up my mind that I must search abroad. By sheer accident I was in a measure successful in my quest. Strolling by a cottage, I saw some children playing by the roadside; one was holding up some object in his hand, and the rest were going through one of the many forms of elaborate pretence which make up a great part of the mystery of a child's life. Something in the object held by the little boy attracted me, and I asked him to let me see it. The plaything of these children consisted of an oblong tablet of black stone; and on it was inscribed the hand pointing downwards, just as I had seen it on the rock, while beneath, spaced over the tablet, were a number of whorls and spirals, cut, as it seemed to me, with the utmost care and nicety. I bought the toy for a couple of shillings; the woman of the house told me it had been lying about for years; she thought her husband had found it one day in the brook which ran in front of the cottage: it was a very hot summer, and the stream was almost dry, and he saw it amongst the stones. That day I tracked the brook to a well of water gushing up cold and clear at the head of a lonely glen in the mountain. That was twenty years ago, and I only succeeded in deciphering the mysterious inscription last August. I must not trouble you with irrelevant details of my life; it is enough for me to say that I was forced, like many another man, to leave my old home and come to London. Of money I had very little, and I was glad to find a cheap room in a squalid street off the Gray's Inn Road. The late Sir Thomas Vivian, then far poorer and more wretched than myself, had a garret in the same house, and before many months we became intimate friends, and I had confided to him the object of my life. I had at first great difficulty in persuading him that I was not giving my days and my nights to an inquiry altogether hopeless and chimerical; but when he was convinced he grew keener than myself, and glowed at the thought of the riches which were to be the prize of some ingenuity and patience. I liked the man intensely, and pitied his case; he had a strong desire to enter the medical profession, but he lacked the means to pay the smallest fees, and indeed he was, not once or twice, but often reduced to the very verge of starvation. I freely and solemnly promised, that under whatever chances, he should share in my heaped fortune when it came, and this promise to one who had always been poor, and yet thirsted for wealth and pleasure in a manner unknown to me, was the strongest incentive. He threw himself into the task with eager interest, and applied a very acute intellect and unwearied patience to the solution of the characters on the tablet. I, like other ingenious young men, was curious in the matter of handwriting, and I had invented or adapted a fantastic script which I used occasionally, and which took Vivian so strongly that he was at the pains to imitate it. It was arranged between us that if we were ever parted, and had occasion to write on the affair that was so close to our hearts, this queer hand of my invention was to be used, and we also contrived a semi-cypher for the same purpose. Meanwhile we exhausted ourselves in efforts to get at the heart of the mystery, and after a couple of years had gone by I could see that Vivian begall to sicken a little of the adventure, and one night he told me with some emotion that he feared both our lives

were being passed away in idle and hopeless endeavor. Not many
months afterwards he was so happy as to receive a considerable
legacy from an aged and distant relative whose very existence
had been almost forgotten by him; and with money at the bank,
he became at once a stranger to me. He had passed his prelim-
inary examination many years before, and forthwith decided to
enter at St. Thomas's Hospital, and he told me that he must look
out for a more convenient lodging. As we said good-bye, I
reminded him of the promise I had given, and solemnly renewed
it; but Vivian laughed with something between pity and contempt
in his voice and expression as he thanked me. I need not dwell
on the long struggle and misery of my existence, now doubly
lonely; I never wearied or despaired of final success, and every
day saw me at work, the tablet before me, and only at dusk would
I go out and take my daily walk along Oxford Street, which
attracted me, I think, by the noise and motion and glitter of
lamps.

"This walk grew with me to a habit; every night, and in all
weathers, I crossed the Gray's Inn Road and struck westward,
sometimes choosing a northern track, by the Euston Road and
Tottenham Court Road, sometimes I went by Holborn, and I
sometimes by way of Great Russell Street. Every night I walked
for an hour to and fro on the northern pavement of Oxford
Street, and the tale of De Quincey and his name for the Street,
'Stony-hearted step mother,' often recurred to my memory. Then
I would return to my grimy den and spend hours more in endless
analysis of the riddle before me.

"The answer came to me one night a few weeks; ago; it flashed
into my brain in a moment, and I read the inscription, and saw
that after all I had not wasted my days. 'The place of the
treasure-house of them that dwell below,' were the first words I
read, and then followed minute indications of the spot in my
own country where the great works of gold were to be kept for
ever. Such a track was to be followed, such a pitfall avoided; here
the way narrowed almost to a fox's hole, and there it broadened,

and so at last the chamber would be reached. I determined to lose no time in verifying my discover—not that I doubted at that great moment, but I would not risk even the smallest chance of disappointing my old friend Vivian, now a rich and prosperous man. I took the train for the West, and one night, with chart in hand, traced out the passage of the hills, and went so far that I saw the gleam of gold before me. I would not go on; I resolved that Vivian must be with me; and I only brought away a strange knife of flint which lay on the path, as confirmation of what I had to tell. I returned to London, and was a good deal vexed to find the stone tablet had disappeared from my rooms. My land-lady, an inveterate drunkard, denied all knowledge of the fact, but I have little doubt she had stolen the thing for the sake of the glass of whisky it might fetch. However, I knew what was written on the tablet by heart, and I had also made an exact facsimile of the characters, so the loss was not severe. Only one thing annoyed me: when I first came into possession of the stone, I had pasted a piece of paper on the back and had written down the date and place of finding, and later on I had scribbled a word or two, a trivial sentiment, the name of my street, and such-like idle pencilings on the paper; and these memories of days that had seemed so hopeless were dear to me: I had thought they would help to remind me in the future of the hours when I had hoped against despair. However, I wrote at once to Sir Thomas Vivian, using the handwriting I have mentioned and also the quasi-cypher. I told him of my success, and after mentioning the loss of the tablet and the fact that I had a copy of the inscription, I reminded him once more of my promise, and asked him either to write or call. He replied that he would see me in a certain obscure passage in Clerkenwell well known to us both in the old days, and at seven o'clock one evening I went to meet him. At the corner of this by-way, as I was walking to and fro, I noticed the blurred pictures of some street artist, and I picked up a piece of chalk he had left behind him, not much thinking what I was doing. I paced up and down the passage, wondering a good deal, as you may imagine, as to what manner of man I was to meet after so many years of parting, and the thoughts of the buried time coming thick upon me, I walked mechanically without raising my eyes from the ground. I was startled out of my reverie by an angry voice and a rough inquiry why I didn't keep to the right side of the pavement, and looking up I found I had confronted a prosperous and important gentleman, who eyed my poor appearance with a look of great dislike and contempt. I knew directly it was my old comrade, and when I recalled myself to him, he apologized with some show of regret, and began to thank me for my kindness, doubtfully, as if he hesitated to commit himself, and, as I could see, with the hint of a suspicion as to my sanity. I would have engaged him at first in reminiscences of our friendship, but I found Sir Thomas viewed those days with a good deal of distaste, and replying politely to my remarks, continually edged in 'business matters,' as he called them. I changed my topics, and told him in greater detail what I have told you. Then I saw his manner suddenly change; as I pulled out the flint knife to prove my journey 'to the other side of the moon,' as we called it in our jargon, there came over him a kind of choking eagerness, his features were somewhat discomposed, and I thought I detected a shuddering horror, a clenched resolution, and the effort to keep quiet succeed one another in a manner that puzzled me. I had occasion to be a little precise in my particulars, and it being still light enough, I remembered the red chalk in my pocket, and drew the hand on the wall. 'Here, you see, is the hand,' I said, as I explained its true meaning, 'note where the thumb issues from between the first and second fingers,' and I would have gone on, and had applied the chalk to the wall to continue my diagram, when he struck my hand down much to my surprise. 'No, no,' he said, 'I do not want all that. And this place is not retired enough; let us walk on, and do you explain everything to me minutely.' I complied readily enough, and he led me away choosing the most unfrequented by-ways, while I drove in the plan of the hidden house word by word. Once or twice as I raised my eyes I caught Vivian looking strangely about him; he seemed to give a quick glint up and down, and glance at the houses; and there was a furtive and anxious air about him that displeased me. 'Let us walk on to the north,' he said at length, 'we shall come to some pleasant lanes where we can discuss these matters, quietly; my night's rest is at your service.' I declined, on the pretext that I could not dispense with my visit to Oxford Street, and went on till he understood every turning and winding and the minutest detail as well as myself. We had returned on our footsteps, and stood again in the dark passage, just where I had drawn the red hand on the wall, for I recognized the vague shape of the trees whose branches hung above us. 'We have come back to our starting-point,' I said; 'I almost think I could put my finger on the wall where I drew the hand. And I am sure you could put your finger on the mystic hand in the hills as well as I. Remember between stream and stone.'

"I was bending down, peering at what I thought must be my drawing, when I heard a sharp hiss of breath, and started up, and saw Vivian with his arm uplifted and a bare blade in his hand, and death threatening in his eyes. In sheer self-defence I caught at the flint weapon in my pocket, and dashed at him in blind fear of my life, and the next instant he lay dead upon the stones.

"I think that is all," Mr. Selby continued after a pause, "and it only remains for me to say to you, Mr. Dyson, that I cannot conceive what means enabled you to run me down."

"I followed many indications," said Dyson, "and I am bound to disclaim all credit for acuteness, as I have made several gross blunders. Your celestial cypher did not, I confess, give me much trouble; I saw at once that terms of astronomy were substituted for common words and phrases. You had lost something black, or something black had been stolen from you; a celestial globe is a copy of the heavens, so I knew you meant you had a copy of what you had lost. Obviously, then, I came to the conclusion that you had lost a black object with characters or symbols written or inscribed on it, since the object in question certainly contained valuable information and all information must be written or pictured. 'Our old orbit remains unchanged;' evidently our old course or arrangement. 'The number of my sign' must mean the number of my house, the allusion being to the signs of the zodiac. I need not say that 'the other side of the moon' can stand for nothing but some place where no one else has been; and 'some other house' is some other place of meeting, the 'house' being the old term 'house of the heavens.' Then my next step was to find the 'black heaven' that had been stolen, and by a process of exhaustion I did so."

"You have got the tablet?"

"Certainly. And on the back of it, on the slip of paper you have mentioned, I read 'inroad,' which puzzled me a good deal, till I thought of Grey's Inn Road; you forgot the second *n*. 'Stony-hearted step—' immediately suggested the phrase of De Quincey you have alluded to; and I made the wild but correct shot, that you were a man who lived in or near the Gray's Inn Road, and had the habit of walking in Oxford Street, for you remember how the opium-eater dwells on his wearying promenades along that thoroughfare. On the theory of improbability, which I have explained to my friend here, I concluded that occasionally, at all events, you would choose the way by Guildford Street, Russell Square, and Great Russell Street, and I knew that if I watched long enough I should see you. But how was I to recognize my man? I noticed the screever opposite my rooms, and got him to draw every day a large hand, in the gesture so familiar to us all, upon the wall behind him. I thought that when the unknown person did pass he would certainly betray some emotion at the sudden vision of the sign, to him the most terrible of symbols. You know the rest. Ah, as to catching you an hour later, that was, I confess, a refinement. From the fact of your having occupied the same rooms for so many years, in a neighborhood moreover where lodgers are migratory to excess, I drew the conclusion that you were a man of fixed habit, and I was sure that after you had got over your fright you would return for the walk down Oxford Street. You did, by way of New Oxford Street, and I was waiting at the corner."

"Your conclusions are admirable," said Mr. Selby. "I may tell you that I had my stroll down Oxford Street the night Sir Thomas Vivian died. And I think that is all I have to say."

"Scarcely," said Dyson. "How about the treasure?"

"I had rather we did not speak of that," said Mr. Selby, with a whitening of the skin about the temples.

"Oh, nonsense, sir, we are not blackmailers. Besides, you know you are in our power."

"Then, as you put it like that, Mr. Dyson, I must tell you I returned to the place. I went on a little farther than before."

The man stopped short; his mouth began to twitch, his lips moved apart, and he drew in quick breaths, sobbing.

"Well, well," said Dyson, "I dare say you have done comfortably."

"Comfortably," Selby went on, constraining himself with an effort, "yes, so comfortably that hell burns hot within me for ever. I only brought one thing away from that awful house within the hills; it was lying just beyond the spot where I found the flint knife."

"Why did you not bring more?"

The whole bodily frame of the wretched man visibly shrank and wasted; his face grew yellow as tallow, and the sweat dropped from his brows. The spectacle was both revolting and terrible, and when the voice came it sounded like the hissing of a snake.

"Because the keepers are still there, and I saw them, and because of this," and he pulled out a small piece of curious gold-work and held it up.

"There," he said, "that is the Pain of the Goat."

Phillipps and Dyson cried out together in horror at the revolting obscenity of the thing.

"Put it away, man; hide it, for Heaven's sake, hide it!"

"I brought that with me; that is all," he said. "You do not wonder that I did not stay long in a place where those who live are a little higher than the beasts, and where what you have seen is surpassed a thousandfold?"

"Take this," said Dyson, "I brought it with me in case it might be useful;" and he drew out the black tablet, and handed it to the shaking, horrible man.

"And now," said Dyson, "will you go out?"

The two friends sat silent a little while, facing one another with restless eyes and lips that quivered.

"I wish to say that I believe him," said Phillipps.

"My dear Phillipps," said Dyson as he threw the windows wide open, "I do not know that, after all, my blunders in this queer case were so very absurd."

THE WHITE POWDER

My name is Leicester; my father, Major-General Wyn Leicester, a distinguished officer of artillery, succumbed five years ago to a complicated liver complaint acquired in the deadly climate of India. A year later my only brother, Francis, came home after an exceptionally brilliant career at the University, and settled down with the resolution of a hermit to master what has been well called the great legend of the law. He was a man who seemed to live in utter indifference to everything that is called pleasure; and though he was handsomer than most men, and could talk as merrily and wittily as if he were a mere vagabond, he avoided society, and shut himself up in a large room at the top of the house to make himself a lawyer. Ten hours a day of hard reading was at first his allotted portion; from the first light in the east to the late afternoon he remained shut up with his books, taking a hasty half-hour's lunch with me as if he grudged the wasting of the moments, and going out for a short walk when it began to grow dusk. I thought that such relentless application must be injurious, and tried to cajole him from the crabbed textbooks, but his ardor seemed to grow rather than diminish, and his daily tale of hours increased. I spoke to him seriously, suggesting some occasional relaxation, if it were but an idle afternoon with a harmless novel; but he laughed, and said that he read about feudal tenures when he felt in need of amusement, and scoffed at the notions of theatres, or a month's fresh air. I confessed that he looked well, and seemed not to suffer from his labors, but I knew that such unnatural toil would take revenge at last, and I was not mistaken. A look of anxiety began to lurk about his eyes, and he seemed languid, and at last he avowed that he was no longer in perfect health; he was troubled, he said, with a sensation of dizziness, and awoke now and then of nights from fearful dreams, terrified and cold with icy sweats. "I am taking care of myself," he said, "so you must not trouble; I passed the whole of yesterday afternoon in idleness, leaning back in that comfortable chair you gave me, and scribbling nonsense on a sheet of paper. No, no; I will not overdo my work; I shall be well enough in a week or two, depend upon it."

Yet in spite of his assurances I could see that he grew no better, but rather worse; he would enter the drawing-room with a face all miserably wrinkled and despondent, and endeavor to look gaily when my eyes fell on him, and I thought such symptoms of evil omen, and was frightened sometimes at the nervous irritation of his movements, and at glances which I could not decipher. Much against his will, I prevailed on him to have medical advice, and with an ill grace he called in our old doctor.

Dr. Haberden cheered me after examination of his patient.

"There is nothing really much amiss," he said to me. "No doubt he reads too hard and eats hastily, and then goes back again to his books in too great a hurry, and the natural sequence is some digestive trouble and a little mischief in the nervous system. But I think—I do indeed, Miss Leicester—that we shall be able to set this all right. I have written him a prescription which ought to do great things. So you have no cause for anxiety."

My brother insisted on having the prescription made up by a chemist in the neighborhood. It was an odd, old-fashioned shop, devoid of the studied coquetry and calculated glitter that make so gay a show on the counters and shelves of the modern apothecary; but Francis liked the old chemist, and believed in the scrupulous purity of his drugs. The medicine was sent in due course, and I saw that my brother took it regularly after lunch and dinner. It was an innocent-looking white powder, of which a little was dissolved in a glass of cold water; I stirred it in, and it seemed to disappear, leaving the water clear and colorless. At first Francis seemed to benefit greatly; the weariness vanished from his face, and he became more cheerful than he had ever been since the time when he left school; he talked gaily of reforming himself, and avowed to me that he had wasted his time.

"I have given too many hours to law," he said, laughing; "I think you have saved me in the nick of time. Come, I shall be Lord Chancellor yet, but I must not forget life. You and I will have a holiday together before long; we will go to Paris and enjoy ourselves, and keep away from the Bibliothèque Nationale."

I confessed myself delighted with the prospect.

"When shall we go?" I said. "I can start the day after to-morrow if you like."

"Ah! that is perhaps a little too soon; after all, I do not know London yet, and I suppose a man ought to give the pleasures of his own country the first choice. But we will go off together in a week or two, so try and furbish up your French. I only know law French myself, and I am afraid that wouldn't do."

We were just finishing dinner, and he quaffed off his medicine with a parade of carousal as if it had been wine from some choicest bin.

"Has it any particular taste?" I said.

"No; I should not know I was not drinking water," and he got up from his chair and began to pace up and down the room as if he were undecided as to what he should do next.

"Shall we have coffee in the drawing-room?" I said; "or would you like to smoke?"

"No, I think I will take a turn; it seems a pleasant evening. Look at the afterglow; why, it is as if a great city were burning in flames, and down there between the dark houses it is raining blood fast. Yes, I will go out; I may be in soon, but I shall take my key; so good-night, dear, if I don't see you again."

The door slammed behind him, and I saw him walk lightly down the street, swinging his malacca cane, and I felt grateful to Dr. Haberden for such an improvement.

I believe my brother came home very late that night, but he was in a merry mood the next morning.

"I walked on without thinking where I was going," he said, "enjoying the freshness of the air, and livened by the crowds as I reached more frequented quarters. And then I met an old college

friend, Orford, in the press of the pavement, and then—well, we
enjoyed ourselves, I have felt what it is to be young and a man;
I find I have blood in my veins, as other men have. I made an
appointment with Orford for to-night; there will be a little party
of us at the restaurant. Yes; I shall enjoy myself for a week or
two, and hear the chimes at midnight, and then we will go for
our little trip together."

Such was the transmutation of my brother's character that in
a few days he became a lover of pleasure, a careless and merry
idler of western pavements, a hunter out of snug restaurants,
and a fine critic of fantastic dancing; he grew fat before my eyes,
and said no more of Paris, for he had clearly found his paradise
in London. I rejoiced, and yet wondered a little; for there was, I
thought, something in his gaiety that indefinitely displeased me,
though I could not have defined my feeling. But by degrees there
came a change; he returned still in the cold hours of the morning,
but I heard no more about his pleasures, and one morning as
we sat at breakfast together I looked suddenly into his eyes and
saw a stranger before me.

"Oh, Francis!" I cried. "Oh, Francis, Francis, what have you
done?" and rending sobs cut the words short. I went weeping
out of the room; for though I knew nothing, yet I knew all, and
by some odd play of thought I remembered the evening when
he first went abroad, and the picture of the sunset sky glowed
before me; the clouds like a city in burning flames, and the rain
of blood. Yet I did battle with such thoughts, resolving that
perhaps, after all, no great harm had been done, and in the
evening at dinner I resolved to press him to fix a day for our
holiday in Paris. We had talked easily enough, and my brother
had just taken his medicine, which he continued all the while.
I was about to begin my topic when the words forming in my
mind vanished, and I wondered for a second what icy and intolerable weight oppressed my heart and suffocated me as with
the unutterable horror of the coffin-lid nailed down on the living.

We had dined without candles; the room had slowly grown

from twilight to gloom, and the walls and corners were indistinct in the shadow. But from where I sat I looked out into the street; and as I thought of what I would say to Francis, the sky began to flush and shine, as it had done on a well-remembered evening, and in the gap between two dark masses that were houses an awful pageantry of flame appeared – lurid whorls of writhed cloud, and utter depths burning, grey masses like the fume blown from a smoking city, and an evil glory blazing far above shot with tongues of more ardent fire, and below as if there were a deep pool of blood. I looked down to where my brother sat facing me, and the words were shaped on my lips, when I saw his hand resting on the table. Between the thumb and forefinger of the closed hand there was a mark, a small patch about the size of a sixpence, and somewhat of the color of a bad bruise. Yet, by some sense I cannot define, I knew that what I saw was no bruise at all; oh! if human flesh could burn with flame, and if flame could be black as pitch, such was that before me. Without thought or fashioning of words grey horror shaped within me at the sight, and in an inner cell it was known to be a brand. For the moment the stained sky became dark as midnight, and when the light returned to me I was alone in the silent room, and soon after I heard my brother go out.

Late as it was, I put on my hat and went to Dr. Haberden, and in his great consulting room, ill lighted by a candle which the doctor brought in with him, with stammering lips, and a voice that would break in spite of my resolve, I told him all, from the day on which my brother began to take the medicine down to the dreadful thing I had seen scarcely half an hour before.

When I had done, the doctor looked at me for a minute with an expression of great pity on his face.

"My dear Miss Leicester," he said, "you have evidently been anxious about your brother; you have been worrying over him, I am sure. Come, now, is it not so?"

"I have certainly been anxious," I said. "For the last week or two I have not felt at ease."

"Quite so; you know, of course, what a queer thing the brain is?"

"I understand what you mean; but I was not deceived. I saw what I have told you with my own eyes."

"Yes, yes of course. But your eyes had been staring at that very curious sunset we had tonight. That is the only explanation. You will see it in the proper light to-morrow, I am sure. But, remember, I am always ready to give any help that is in my power; do not scruple to come to me, or to send for me if you are in any distress."

I went away but little comforted, all confusion and terror and sorrow, not knowing where to turn. When my brother and I met the next day, I looked quickly at him, and noticed, with a sickening at heart, that the right hand, the hand on which I had clearly seen the patch as of a black fire, was wrapped up with a handkerchief.

"What is the matter with your hand, Francis?" I said in a steady voice.

"Nothing of consequence. I cut a finger last night, and it bled rather awkwardly. So I did it up roughly to the best of my ability."

"I will do it neatly for you, if you like."

"No, thank you, dear; this will answer very well. Suppose we have breakfast; I am quite hungry."

We sat down and I watched him. He scarcely ate or drank at all, but tossed his meat to the dog when he thought my eyes were turned away; there was a look in his eyes that I had never yet seen, and the thought flashed across my mind that it was a look that was scarcely human. I was firmly convinced that awful and incredible as was the thing I had seen the night before, yet it was no illusion, no glamor of bewildered sense, and in the course of the evening I went again to the doctor's house.

He shook his head with an air puzzled and incredulous, and seemed to reflect for a few minutes.

"And you say he still keeps up the medicine? But why? As I understand, all the symptoms he complained of have disappeared long ago; why should he go on taking the stuff when he is quite well? And by the by, where did he get it made up? At Sayce's? I never send any one there; the old man is getting careless. Suppose you come with me to the chemist's; I should like to have some talk with him."

We walked together to the shop; old Sayce knew Dr. Haberden, and was quite ready to give any information.

"You have been sending that in to Mr. Leicester for some weeks, I think, on my prescription," said the doctor, giving the old man a penciled scrap of paper.

The chemist put on his great spectacles with trembling uncertainty, and held up the paper with a shaking hand. "Oh, yes," he said, "I have very little of it left; it is rather an uncommon drug, and I have had it in stock some time. I must get in some more, if Mr. Leicester goes on with it."

"Kindly let me have a look at the stuff," said Haberden, and the chemist gave him a glass bottle. He took out the stopper and smelt the contents, and looked strangely at the old man.

"Where did you get this?" he said, "and what is it? For one thing, Mr. Sayce, it is not what I prescribed. Yes, yes, I see the label is right enough, but I tell you this is not the drug."

"I have had it a long time," said the old man in feeble terror; "I got it from Burbage's in the usual way. It is not prescribed often, and I have had it on the shelf for some years. You see there is very little left."

"You had better give it to me," said Haberden. "I am afraid something wrong has happened."

We went out of the shop in silence, the doctor carrying the bottle neatly wrapped in paper under his arm.

"Dr. Haberden," I said, when we had walked a little way—"Dr. Haberden."

"Yes," he said, looking at me gloomily enough.

"I should like you to tell me what my brother has been taking twice a day for the last month or so."

"Frankly, Miss Leicester, I don't know. We will speak of this when we get to my house."

We walked on quickly without another word till we reached Dr. Haberden's. He asked me to sit down, and began pacing up and down the room, his face clouded over, as I could see, with no common fears.

"Well," he said at length, "this is all very strange; it is only natural that you should feel alarmed, and I must confess that my mind is far from easy. We will put aside, if you please, what you told me last night and this morning, but the fact remains that for the last few weeks Mr. Leicester has been impregnating his system with a drug which is completely unknown to me. I tell you, it is not what I ordered; and what the stuff in the bottle really is remains to be seen."

He undid the wrapper, and cautiously tilted a few grains of the white powder on to a piece of paper, and peered curiously at it.

"Yes," he said, "it is like the sulphate of quinine, as you say; it is flaky. But smell it."

He held the bottle to me, and I bent over it. It was a strange, sickly smell, vaporous and overpowering, like some strong anaesthetic.

"I shall have it analyzed," said Haberden; "I have a friend who has devoted his whole life to chemistry as a science. Then we shall have something to go upon. No, no; say no more about that other matter; I cannot listen to that; and take my advice and think no more about it yourself."

That evening my brother did not go out as usual after dinner.

"I have had my fling," he said with a queer laugh, "and I must go back to my old ways. A little law will be quite a relaxation after so sharp a dose of pleasure," and he grinned to himself, and soon after went up to his room. His hand was still all bandaged.

Dr. Haberden called a few days later.

"I have no special news to give you," he said. "Chambers is out of town, so I know no more about that stuff than you do. But I should like to see Mr. Leicester, if he is in."

"He is in his room," I said; "I will tell him you are here."

"No, no, I will go up to him; we will have a little quiet talk together. I dare say that we have made a good deal of fuss about a very little; for, after all, whatever the powder may be, it seems to have done him good."

The doctor went upstairs, and standing in the hall I heard his knock, and the opening and shutting of the door; and then I waited in the silent house for an hour, and the stillness grew more and more intense as the hands of the clock crept round. Then there sounded from above the noise of a door shut sharply, and the doctor was coming down the stairs. His footsteps crossed the hall, and there was a pause at the door; I drew a long, sick breath with difficulty, and saw my face white in a little mirror, and he came in and stood at the door. There was an unutterable horror shining in his eyes; he steadied himself by holding the back of a chair with one hand, his lower lip trembled like a horse's, and he gulped and stammered unintelligible sounds before he spoke.

"I have seen that man," he began in a dry whisper. "I have been sitting in his presence for the last hour. My God! And I am alive and in my senses! I, who have dealt with death all my life, and have dabbled with the melting ruins of the earthly tabernacle. But not this, oh! not this," and he covered his face with his hands as if to shut out the sight of something before him.

"Do not send for me again, Miss Leicester," he said with more composure. "I can do nothing in this house. Good-bye."

As I watched him totter down the steps; and along the pavement towards his house, it seemed to me that he had aged by ten years since the morning.

My brother remained in his room. He called out to me in a voice I hardly recognized that he was very busy, and would like his meals brought to his door and left there, and I gave the order to the servants. From that day it seemed as if the arbitrary conception we call time had been annihilated for me; I lived in an ever-present sense of horror, going through the routine of the house mechanically, and only speaking a few necessary words

to the servants. Now and then I went out and paced the streets
for an hour or two and came home again; but whether I were
without or within, my spirit delayed before the closed door of
the upper room, and, shuddering, waited for it to open. I have
said that I scarcely reckoned time; but I suppose it must have
been a fortnight after Dr. Haberden's visit that I came home from
my stroll a little refreshed and lightened. The air was sweet and
pleasant, and the hazy form of green leaves, floating cloud-like
in the square, and the smell of blossoms, had charmed my senses,
and I felt happier and walked more briskly. As I delayed a moment
at the verge of the pavement, waiting for a van to pass by before
crossing over to the house, I happened to look up at the windows,
and instantly there was the rush and swirl of deep cold waters
in my ears, my heart leapt up and fell down, down as into a
deep hollow, and I was amazed with a dread and terror without
form or shape. I stretched out a hand blindly through the folds
of thick darkness, from the black and shadowy valley, and held
myself from falling, while the stones beneath my feet rocked and
swayed and tilted, and the sense of solid things seemed to sink
away from under me. I had glanced up at the window of my
brother's study, and at that moment the blind was drawn aside,
and something that had life stared out into the world. Nay, I
cannot say I saw a face or any human likeness; a living thing,
two eyes of burning flame glared at me, and they were in the
midst of something as formless as my fear, the symbol and presence of all evil and all hideous corruption. I stood shuddering
and quaking as with the grip of ague, sick with unspeakable
agonies of fear and loathing, and for five minutes I could not
summon force or motion to my limbs. When I was within the
door, I ran up the stairs to my brother's room and knocked.

"Francis, Francis," I cried, "for Heaven's sake, answer me. What
is the horrible thing in your room? Cast it out, Francis; cast it
from you."

I heard a noise as of feet shuffling slowly and awkwardly, and
a choking, gurgling sound, as if some one was struggling to find

utterance, and then the noise of a voice, broken and stifled, and words that I could scarcely understand.

"There is nothing here," the voice said. "Pray do not disturb me. I am not very well to-day."

I turned away, horrified, and yet helpless. I could do nothing, and I wondered why Francis had lied to me, for I had seen the appearance beyond the glass too plainly to be deceived, though it was but the sight of a moment. And I sat still, conscious that there had been something else, something I had seen in the first flash of terror, before those burning eyes had looked at me.

Suddenly I remembered; as I lifted my face the blind was being drawn back, and I had had an instant's glance of the thing that was moving it, and in my recollection I knew that a hideous image was engraved forever on my brain. It was not a hand; there were no fingers that held the blind, but a black stump pushed it aside, the mouldering outline and the clumsy movement as of a beast's paw had glowed into my senses before the darkling waves of terror had overwhelmed me as I went down quick into the pit. My mind was aghast at the thought of this, and of the awful presence that dwelt with my brother in his room; I went to his door and cried to him again, but no answer came. That night one of the servants came up to me and told me in a whisper that for three days food had been regularly placed at the door and left untouched; the maid had knocked but had received no answer; she had heard the noise of shuffling feet that I had noticed. Day after day went by, and still my brother's meals were brought to his door and left untouched; and though I knocked and called again and again, I could get no answer. The servants began to talk to me; it appeared they were as alarmed as I; the cook said that when my brother first shut himself up in his room she used to hear him come out at night and go about the house; and once, she said, the hall door had opened and closed again, but for several nights she had heard no sound.

The climax came at last; it was in the dusk of the evening, and I was sitting in the darkening dreary room when a terrible shriek jarred and rang harshly out of the silence, and I heard a frightened scurry of feet dashing down the stairs. I waited, and the servant-maid staggered into the room and faced me, white and trembling.

"Oh, Miss Helen!" she whispered; "oh! for the Lord's sake, Miss Helen, what has happened? Look at my hand, miss; look at that hand!" I drew her to the window, and saw there was a black wet stain upon her hand.

"I do not understand you," I said. "Will you explain to me?"

"I was doing your room just now," she began. "I was turning down the bed-clothes, and all of a sudden there was something fell upon my hand, wet, and I looked up, and the ceiling was black and dripping on me."

I looked hard at her and bit my lip.

"Come with me," I said. "Bring your candle with you."

The room I slept in was beneath my brother's, and as I went in I felt I was trembling. I looked up at the ceiling, and saw a patch, all black and wet, and a dew of black drops upon it, and a pool of horrible liquor soaking into the white bed-clothes.

I ran upstairs and knocked loudly.

"Oh, Francis, Francis, my dear brother," I cried, "what has happened to you?"

And I listened. There was a sound of choking, and a noise like water bubbling and regurgitating, but nothing else, and I called louder, but no answer came.

In spite of what Dr. Haberden had said, I went to him; with tears streaming down my cheeks I told him all that had happened, and he listened to me with a face set hard and grim.

"For your father's sake," he said at last, "I will go with you, though I can do nothing."

We went out together; the streets were dark and silent, and heavy with heat and a drought of many weeks. I saw the doctor's face white under the gas-lamps, and when we reached the house his hand was shaking.

We did not hesitate, but went upstairs directly. I held the lamp, and he called out in a loud, determined voice—"Mr.

Leicester, do you hear me? I insist on seeing you. Answer me at once."

There was no answer, but we both heard that choking noise I have mentioned.

"Mr. Leicester, I am waiting for you. Open the door this instant, or I shall break it down." And he called a third time in a voice that rang and echoed from the walls—"Mr. Leicester! For the last time I order you to open the door."

"Ah!" he said, after a pause of heavy silence, "we are wasting time here. Will you be so kind as to get me a poker, or something of the kind?"

I ran into a little room at the back where odd articles were kept, and found a heavy adze-like tool that I thought might serve the doctor's purpose.

"Very good," he said, "that will do, I dare say. I give you notice, Mr. Leicester," he cried loudly at the keyhole, "that I am now about to break into your room."

Then I heard the wrench of the adze, and the woodwork split and cracked under it; with a loud crash the door suddenly burst open, and for a moment we started back aghast at a fearful screaming cry, no human voice, but as the roar of a monster, that burst forth inarticulate and struck at us out of the darkness.

"Hold the lamp," said the doctor, and we went in and glanced quickly round the room.

"There it is," said Dr. Haberden, drawing a quick breath; "look, in that corner."

I looked, and a pang of horror seized my heart as with a white-hot iron. There upon the floor was a dark and putrid mass, seething with corruption and hideous rottenness, neither liquid nor solid, but melting and changing before our eyes, and bubbling with unctuous oily bubbles like boiling pitch. And out of the midst of it shone two burning points like eyes, and I saw a writhing and stirring as of limbs, and something moved and lifted up what might have been an arm. The doctor took a step forward, raised the iron bar and struck at the burning points; he drove in the weapon, and struck again and again in the fury of loathing.

A week or two later, when I had recovered to some extent from the terrible shock, Dr. Haberden came to see me.

"I have sold my practice," he began, "and tomorrow I am sailing on a long voyage. I do not know whether I shall ever return to England; in all probability I shall buy a little land in California, and settle there for the remainder of my life. I have brought you this packet, which you may open and read when you feel able to do so. It contains the report of Dr. Chambers on what I submitted to him. Good-bye, Miss Leicester, good-bye."

When he was gone I opened the envelope; I could not wait, and proceeded to read the papers within. Here is the manuscript, and if you will allow me, I will read you the astounding story it contains.

"My dear Haberden," the letter began, "I have delayed inexcusably in answering your questions as to the white substance you sent me. To tell you the truth, I have hesitated for some time as to what course I should adopt, for there is a bigotry and orthodox standard in physical science as in theology, and I knew that if I told you the truth I should offend rooted prejudices which I once held dear myself. However, I have determined to be plain with you, and first I must enter into a short personal explanation.

"You have known me, Haberden, for many years as a scientific man; you and I have often talked of our profession together, and discussed the hopeless gulf that opens before the feet of those who think to attain the truth by any means whatsoever except the beaten way of experiment and observation in the sphere of material things. I remember the scorn with which you have spoken to me of men of science who have dabbled a little in the unseen, and have timidly hinted that perhaps the senses are not, after all, the eternal, impenetrable bounds of all knowledge, the everlasting walls beyond which no human being has ever passed. We have laughed together heartily, and I think justly, at the 'occult' follies of the day, disguised under various names – the mesmerisms, spiritualisms, materializations, theosophies, all the rabble rout of imposture, with their machinery of poor tricks and feeble conjuring, the true back-parlor of shabby London streets. Yet, in spite of what I have said, I must confess to you that I am no materialist, taking the word of course in its usual signification. It is now many years since I have convinced myself— convinced myself, a skeptic, remember—that the old ironbound theory is utterly and entirely false. Perhaps this confession will not wound you so sharply as it would have done twenty years ago; for I think you cannot have failed to notice that for some time hypotheses have been advanced by men of pure science which are nothing less than transcendental, and I suspect that most modern chemists and biologists of repute would not hesitate to subscribe the dictum of the old Schoolman, *Omnia exeunt in mysterium*, which means, I take it, that every branch of human knowledge if traced up to its source and final principles vanishes into mystery. I need not trouble you now with a detailed account of the painful steps which led me to my conclusions; a few simple experiments suggested a doubt as to my then standpoint, and a train of thought that rose from circumstances comparatively trifling brought me far; my old conception of the universe has been swept away, and I stand in a world that seems as strange and awful to me as the endless waves of the ocean seen for the first time, shining, from a peak in Darien. Now I know that the walls of sense that seemed so impenetrable, that seemed to loom up above the heavens and to be founded below the depths, and to shut us in for evermore, are no such everlasting impassable barriers as we fancied, but thinnest and most airy veils that melt away before the seeker, and dissolve as the early mist of the morning about the brooks. I know that you never adopted the extreme materialistic position; you did not go about trying to prove a universal negative, for your logical sense withheld you from that crowning absurdity; but I am sure that you will find all that I am saying strange and repellent to your habits of thought. Yet, Haberden, what I tell you is the truth, nay, to adopt our common language, the sole and scientific truth, verified by experience; and the universe is verily more splendid and more awful than we used to dream. The whole universe, my friend, is a tremendous sacrament; a mystic, ineffable force and energy, veiled by an outward form of matter; and man, and the sun and the other stars, and the flower of the grass, and the crystal in the test-tube, are each and every one as spiritual, as material, and subject to an inner working.

"You will perhaps wonder, Haberden, whence all this tends; but I think a little thought will make it clear. You will understand that from such a standpoint the whole view of things is changed, and what we thought incredible and absurd may be possible enough. In short, we must look at legend and belief with other eyes, and be prepared to accept tales that had become mere fables. Indeed this is no such great demand. After all, modern science will concede as much, in a hypocritical manner; you must not, it is true, believe in witchcraft, but you may credit hypnotism; ghosts are out of date, but there is a good deal to be said for the theory of telepathy. Give superstition a Greek name, and believe in it, should almost be a proverb.

"So much for my personal explanation. You sent me, Haberden, a phial, stoppered and sealed, containing a small quantity of flaky white powder, obtained from a chemist who has been dispensing it to one of your patients. I am not surprised to hear that this powder refused to yield any results to your analysis. It is a substance which was known to a few many hundred years ago, but which I never expected to have submitted to me from the shop of a modern apothecary.

"There seems no reason to doubt the truth of the man's tale; he no doubt got, as he says, the rather uncommon salt you prescribed from the wholesale chemist's, and it has probably remained on his shelf for twenty years, or perhaps longer. Here what we call chance and coincidence begin to work; during all these years the salt in the bottle was exposed to certain recurring variations of temperature, variations probably ranging from 40° to 80°. And, as it happens, such changes, recurring year after year at irregular intervals, and with varying degrees of intensity and duration, have constituted a process, and a process so complicated and so delicate, that I question whether modern scientific apparatus directed with the utmost precision could produce the same result.

"The white powder you sent me is something very different from the drug you prescribed; it is the powder from which the wine of the Sabbath, the *Vinum Sabbati*, was prepared. No doubt you have read of the Witches' Sabbath, and have laughed at the tales which terrified our ancestors; the black cats, and the broomsticks, and dooms pronounced against some old woman's cow.

"Since I have known the truth I have often reflected that it is on the whole a happy thing that such burlesque as this is believed, for it serves to conceal much that it is better should not be known generally. However, if you care to read the appendix to Payne Knight's monograph, you will find that the true Sabbath was something very different, though the writer has very nicely refrained from printing all he knew. The secrets of the true Sabbath were the secrets of remote times surviving into the Middle Ages, secrets of an evil science which existed long before Aryan man entered Europe. Men and women, seduced from their homes on specious pretences, were met by beings well qualified to assume, as they did assume, the part of devils, and taken by their guides to some desolate and lonely place, known to the initiate by long tradition, and unknown to all else. Perhaps it was a cave in some bare and wind-swept hill, perhaps some inmost recess of a great forest, and there the Sabbath was held. There, in the blackest hour of night, the Vinum Sabbati was prepared, and this evil gruel was poured forth and offered to the neophytes, and they partook of an infernal sacrament; *sumentes calicem principis inferorum*, as an old author well expresses it. And suddenly, each one that had drunk found himself attended by a companion, a share of glamor and unearthly allurement, beckoning him apart, to share in joys more exquisite, more piercing than the thrill of any dream, to the consummation of the marriage of the Sabbath.

"It is hard to write of such things as these, and chiefly because that shape that allured with loveliness was no hallucination, but, awful as it is to express, the man himself. By the power of that Sabbath wine, a few grains of white powder thrown into a glass of water, the house of life was riven asunder and the human trinity dissolved, and the worm which never dies, that which lies sleeping within us all, was made tangible and an external thing, and clothed with a garment of flesh. And then, in the hour of midnight, the primal fall was repeated and re-presented, and the awful thing veiled in the mythos of the *Tree in the Garden* was done anew. Such was the *nuptiæ Sabbati*.

"I prefer to say no more; you, Haberden, know as well as I do that the most trivial laws of life are not to be broken with impunity; and for so terrible an act as this, in which the very inmost place of the temple was broken open and defiled, a terrible vengeance followed. What began with corruption ended also with corruption."

Underneath is the following in Dr. Haberden's writing:

> "The whole of the above is unfortunately strictly and entirely true. Your brother confessed all to me on that morning when I saw him in his room. My attention was first attracted to the bandaged hand, and I forced him to show it to me. What I saw made me, a medical man of many years' standing, grow sick with loathing, and the story I was forced to listen to was infinitely more frightful than I could have believed possible. It has tempted me to doubt the Eternal Goodness which can permit nature to offer such hideous possibilities; and if you had not with your own eyes seen the end, I should have said to you— disbelieve it all. I have not, I think, many more weeks to live, but you are young, and may forget all this.
>
> JOSEPH HABERDEN, M.D.

In the course of two or three months I heard that Dr. Haberden had died at sea shortly after the ship left England.